LOOK BOTH WAYS

Also by Alison Cherry

TEEN

Red

For Real

—

MIDDLE GRADE

The Classy Crooks Club

LOOK BOTH WAYS

Alison Cherry

DELACORTE PRESS

Text copyright © 2016 by Alison Cherry
Jacket photographs © 2016 by Jovana Rikalo/Stocksy

randomhouseteens.com
Educators and librarians, for a variety of teaching tools,
visit us at RHTeachersLibrarians.com

Library of Congress Cataloging-in-Publication Data
Cherry, Alison.
Look both ways / Alison Cherry. — First edition.
pages cm
Summary: "The story of a girl who apprentices at a summer theater festival hoping
she's finally found a place to belong only to learn that neither talent nor love is as
straightforward as she thinks"—Provided by publisher.
ISBN 978-0-553-51186-4 (hc) — ISBN 978-0-553-51188-8 (ebook)
[1. Theater—Fiction. 2. Acting—Fiction. 3. Love—Fiction. 4. Apprentices—Fiction.]
I. Title.
PZ7.C41987Lo 2016 [Fic]—dc23
2015010919

The text of this book is set in 11.5-point Celeste.
Interior design by Heather Kelly

Printed in the United States of America
10 9 8 7 6 5 4 3 2 1
First Edition

For Marianna, Evie, and Rachel,
my fellow warriors for art

1

It's weird how you can feel nostalgic for something that hasn't actually happened yet.

My last Family Night of the summer is about to start. Our guests will arrive any second, and Dad is in the kitchen putting the finishing touches on my favorite dinner. The apartment smells like curry and chocolate and warmth, and I should be in a penny-bright mood, buoyed by the big band music on the stereo and the prospect of seeing all my favorite people. But it's hard to focus on the sweetness of now when I'm already anticipating the bitter tang of later, when I'll have to hug my family goodbye and try to squeeze enough love out of them to last nine weeks. Part of me wishes I could hit pause, wrap this moment around me like a quilt, and live inside it forever.

But then I'd never make it to the Allerdale Playhouse, and if I don't go, how can I come back better?

When our buzzer rings for the first time, I dash out of

my bedroom and press the intercom button that unlocks the lobby door. I'm sure it'll be Uncle Harrison; he always arrives first, bearing a bag of weird produce from the fruit stand near his office. But when I open the door, ready to unburden myself of all my pre-nostalgic feelings, I'm surprised to see an unfamiliar girl. It's not unusual for strangers to show up at Family Night—when you're raised by theater people, "family" is a stretchy, nebulous word that can encompass practically anyone. But since tonight is doubling as my goodbye party, I'm not expecting someone new.

The girl's a little older than me and almost model-beautiful, but her teeth are a tiny bit too big for her mouth, which keeps her from looking generic. Several layers of lace-edged tank tops peek out from under her filmy blue romper, and there's an ostentatious feather clip in her hair. She's obviously surprised to see me, too, but she rallies and holds out her hand, palm down like she thinks I might kiss it.

"Hi, I'm Skye," she says. "Is Lana here?"

She's projecting from her diaphragm in this way that's totally unnecessary for a face-to-face conversation, so she must be one of my mom's voice students. Mom takes on a new college senior almost every year, but it kind of seems like the same person over and over, bright and shellacked and trying too hard.

I try to force my face into a friendly, welcoming mask as I shake her hand. "I'm Brooklyn," I say. "Come on in. My mom should be out in a second."

"Lana's your *mom*?" Skye's voice goes breathy, and her eyes widen to show her entire pale gray-green irises. She's probably the kind of person who refers to that color as "seafoam." "Oh my God, what is that *like*? Is it *so amazing*?"

My mom's students ask me this constantly, like I've had a bunch of mothers to compare and contrast. "She does a pretty good job," I tell Skye. "I'm housebroken and everything."

Before she can answer, my mother comes sweeping down the hall, and I step aside so she can gather her latest protégé into her arms. "Lovely Skye," she says in her warm-honey voice. "I'm so delighted you could make it."

"I'm *delighted* to be here," Skye says from inside the voluminous folds of my mom's dress. The word sounds wrong in her mouth, but I can see her resolving to use it more often. She pulls back and thrusts a sweating bottle of wine into my mom's hands. "Thank you for inviting me into your home."

"It's a pleasure to have you. I see you've met my daughter?"

"Yes. It's such an honor to meet your family."

My mom has always told me to visualize what I want out of life so the universe will know what to give me. I take a moment to picture Skye being swept up in a *Wizard of Oz*–style tornado and being deposited gently in Los Angeles.

"Come in and say hello to my husband," my mom says, and we follow her into the living room. There's a lot to take in—the teetering piles of books stacked on the floor; the mismatched Oriental rugs; the enormous black-and-white photograph of my naked, pregnant mother. My dad's Drama Desk Award and my mom's Tony share mantel space with a framed cross-stitch of David Bowie's face. Skye turns in a slow circle, her eyes huge and her mouth half-open, and then she drops her purse onto the armchair closest to the

3

piano. It's prime real estate; she obviously knows what happens after dinner.

The buzzer rings again, and it really is Uncle Harrison this time, wearing his standard madras shorts and button-down shirt. He hands me a bag of dragon fruits I won't have time to eat before I leave and pulls me into his arms, squeezing so hard that my feet leave the ground. I can barely breathe, but it feels safe and familiar.

"How's my summer-stock girl?" he asks.

"Nervous. But excited? But really nervous."

"You're going to blow them away, Brookie. Allerdale doesn't take just anyone." He says the word "Allerdale" the way everyone else does, with the same sort of reverence usually reserved for Nobel laureates and Olympic gold medalists.

"I know," I say. I still have no idea how I managed to land a spot in such a renowned apprentice company. It's not like my audition was *bad* or anything—I sang part of "Much More" from *The Fantasticks* and did one of Ophelia's monologues from *Hamlet,* and they both went fine. None of the directors seemed very excited, though; they watched with stony, expressionless faces, and nobody even wrote anything down. When I was done, I thought for sure the artistic director, Marcus Spooner, would say something about how he's known my mom forever, but he didn't even bother to thank me before he told me to send in the next person. Two months later, I still have to remind myself that they wouldn't have let me in if they hadn't liked what they saw.

"What a wonderful opportunity for you, kiddo," Uncle

Harrison says. "Family Night won't be the same without you, though."

"It's only nine weeks. You won't even know I'm gone." I drop my voice. "Plus, there's someone in the living room who's dying to take my place."

"Oh no. Another one?"

The buzzer goes off again, and Uncle Harrison opens the door for Marisol and Christa, opera singers who used to study with my mom. Marisol is hugely pregnant, and after we kiss them hello, Christa steers her toward the couch and props her up with pillows. "She's been on her feet all day," she announces. "Nobody let her move again, or she'll be up the entire night bitching about her ankles."

Marisol swats at her. "I will not. My ankles are willowy and delicate. They are, right? I can't actually see them."

"Like slender little reeds," I say, and she reaches out and affectionately pats my butt.

Skye introduces herself, her eyes pinned to Marisol's monstrous belly like it's a candy-filled piñata. "When are you due?" she asks.

"Not soon enough. If you can believe it, I've got another six weeks of this hell."

"She's having twins," Christa says.

"Twins!" I swear Skye's eyes would glow in the dark like a raccoon's if someone switched off the lights. "Boys or girls?"

"One of each," Christa says. "She wants to name the boy Pierre. *Pierre.* Please tell her he's gonna get his ass kicked on the playground."

"But I could dress him in tiny sailor suits!" Marisol says. "It would be *adorable*."

"Your giant farm baby is not going to fit into tiny sailor suits."

Skye's eyes bounce back and forth between the women like she's watching a tennis match. "Is your husband a farmer?"

Marisol laughs. "No, honey. Pierre's daddy is a canister of sperm."

"Strapping Ohio farm-boy sperm," Christa adds. She sweeps her dreadlocks up into a ponytail. "I need wine. What can I get you, baby?"

"Sparkling water, please," Marisol says.

The buzzer rings again, and when I open the door, Jermaine, Desi, and their daughters spill into the apartment in an explosion of noise. Twyla, who's eighteen months, reaches out to me from Jermaine's arms, and four-year-old Sutton wraps both arms around my leg. "Did you know I have two daddies at the *same time*?" she demands.

I stroke her shiny hair and try not to laugh at her belligerent tone. "I did know that. What are you wearing? You look so fancy."

Sutton spins around to show off her red-and-gold satin pajamas with a dragon embroidered on the back. "It's for Chinese New Year. Did you know I'm Chinese?"

"Yes. I remember when Daddy and Papa went to China to get you." I turn to Desi. "Isn't Chinese New Year in, like, January?"

He shrugs. "Whatever. It's good to see her embracing her cultural identity."

Jermaine kisses both my cheeks. "How are you, poodle? Ready for your big summer?"

"So ready," I tell him. Maybe if I say it enough times, it'll start being true.

"What're the main stage shows this year?"

"*A Midsummer Night's Dream, Catch Me If You Can, Hedda Gabler, Dreamgirls, Bye Bye Birdie,* and *Macbeth.*"

Desi nods. "Good season."

"You don't know what-all you're in yet, right?" asks Jermaine.

"They post the cast lists after the first company meeting, so I'll know by this time tomorrow." I've spent entire nights lying awake, imagining myself effortlessly playing Rosie in *Birdie* or Hermia in *Midsummer,* but I know there's no way that's going to happen. "I'd really be happy with anything," I say. "Being in rehearsals and watching those directors work is going to be amazing no matter what."

"That's exactly the right attitude," Desi says. "I played Spear-Carrier Number Four in *Richard III* my first time there, and it was still one of the best summers of my life."

Desi and Jermaine shout hello to my dad in the kitchen as we head inside, and Sutton marches up to Skye with her tiny fists on her hips. "Did you know I'm *adopted*?" she challenges.

Skye's eyes go all soft and gooey. "Aren't you precious," she croons.

"I'm not precious. I'm *Chinese.*"

Jermaine leans over to kiss Marisol's mouth, then her belly. "How're you feeling, sweet girl?"

"Like a giant bacon-wrapped scallop trying to balance on

a tiny, unsupportive toothpick," she says. "Ooh, are there any bacon-wrapped scallops? I have the strongest craving all of a sudden."

Mom comes in with overfull wineglasses for Desi and Jermaine and a half glass for me. "Where's your girlfriend tonight, Harrison?" she asks. "What's this one's name? Candy? Cinnamon?"

"Her name is Cassandra, and she's working late."

"What does your girlfriend do?" Skye asks.

My mom snorts. "Yes, Harrison, remind us all what Cassandra does."

"She's a financial analyst," he says, the way most people might say "She's a call girl." He takes a very large gulp of wine as my mom breaks into riotous laughter.

"Oh man, that never gets less funny. My mainstream little brother. Before we know it, you're going to start ditching us for Monday Night Football." She's obviously teasing, but the word "mainstream" is a pretty serious insult around here, and my uncle flinches. This is exactly why I tried to keep my last boyfriend away from my parents; Jason loved things like laser tag and video games and the Super Bowl. He had never been inside a Broadway theater until I dragged him to see the *Les Miz* revival for our two-month anniversary. He fell asleep fifteen minutes in.

"I'll make sure the next person I date is a burlesque dancer, okay, Lana?" Uncle Harrison says. "Because my love life is a hundred percent your business."

"I'm just trying to make sure you end up with someone who suits you! Financial analysts aren't like us."

"Simon, how're we doing on dinner?" Uncle Harrison shouts toward the other room.

"Almost ready," my dad calls back. "Are we waiting on anyone?"

"No, this is it for tonight." My mom beams at me. "A nice intimate gathering in honor of our girl." There are eleven people in the apartment, but this is what counts as intimate for the Shepard clan.

"What are we celebrating?" Skye asks.

When Uncle Harrison explains that I'm leaving for Allerdale tomorrow, Skye looks genuinely interested in me for the first time. "Oh, that's great, Brooklyn! I was there the last two summers. Are you in the non-equity company?"

"Maybe next year. I'm an apprentice this time."

"Oh," Skye says, her voice falling just short of supportive. "Well, everyone has to start somewhere, I guess."

I'm grateful when my dad distracts everyone by carrying in giant serving platters of mango chicken and coconut rice. "Thanks for cooking," I say to him as we get on line to serve ourselves. "It smells delicious."

Dad wraps an arm around my shoulders, and his salt-and-pepper beard hooks on to my hair like Velcro when he kisses the side of my head. He's wearing a frilly pink apron, and even after cooking curry all afternoon, he smells like wintergreen Life Savers. "I have to feed you while I can," he says. "Summerstock kids survive on ramen and ice cream."

"Dad, I have a meal plan."

My dad looks skeptical that anyone else can nourish me properly. He has always been a man of few words—Mom has

9

such a big personality that he's had to retreat a few steps into himself to make room for her—but food is how he says he loves us. Mom can barely heat up canned soup without setting something on fire, but she tells everyone she lets Dad do all the cooking because we don't believe in heteronormative gender roles.

When everyone is settled with heaping plates balanced on their laps, my mom raises her glass. "I'd like to propose a toast to my beautiful daughter, who's headed off on her very first summer theater adventure," she says. "She deserves the best of the best. May Allerdale teach her as much as it taught the rest of us." Her eyes are bright and kind and focused right on me, and it makes me feel warm all the way through. It's not easy to impress her, and even though I know how much she loves me, times like these are few and far between.

"We're so proud of you, Brookie," Uncle Harrison adds, and my dad chimes in with a "Hear, hear."

"And while she's at Allerdale," my mom continues, "may she meet a nice boy or girl to date. Or one of each. Or more than one of each!"

I roll my eyes. "You know I'd be totally happy with one boy."

"You don't *know* that if you haven't tried—" she starts, but I cut her off.

"Let's just eat, okay?"

To my relief, the conversation turns away from my love life and toward everyone's favorite Allerdale memories. My family tells me which ice cream place is better, which coffee shop I should avoid, and—because my mother is who she is—

which nooks and crannies of the theaters are best for illicit sex. (She was horrified when she offered to have her doctor prescribe me birth control pills last month and I told her I was a virgin.) Mom raves about how brilliant Marcus Spooner is, and Desi reminisces about Pandemonium, the legendary party that happens midfestival. Skye tells us about her friend who was so exhausted, she fell asleep in the catwalks while running a follow-spot, and Jermaine screams with laughter and says the same thing happened to him.

"Third rotation?" guesses Skye.

"Exactly!"

She nods in sympathy, and I feel a stab of annoyance. This girl has known us all of thirty minutes, but she already has a mysterious, exclusive shorthand with my family, and I'm the one on the outside. I suddenly wish it were nine weeks from now, when I'll be back on this couch with firsthand experience of what "third rotation" is like. I almost want to have *been* to Allerdale more than I want to actually *go*.

When everyone's finished with their food, my mom claps once like she always does when we're about to transition into the performance part of the evening, and my stomach does a Pavlovian nervous twist. "Do you want to start us off tonight, Brookie?" she asks.

Being asked to perform first is an honor, and if I were the right kind of Shepard, I'd jump at the chance. But instead I say, "Why don't we let our newest guest start? I'm happy to play for her." I put my empty plate on the coffee table and slide onto the piano bench, where I always take refuge during Family Nights. Since eighth grade, when I realized I didn't have my parents' superstar performance genes, I've become a master of dodging the spotlight, and acting as accompanist is a way I can participate without anyone scrutinizing me. Late in the evening, when everyone's drunker and more forgiving, I always agree to sing an easy duet with someone. It gets me off the hook until the following week, and it hides the fact that my voice doesn't stand on its own.

Strategizing like this is exhausting, but tonight is the last time I'll ever have to do it. Things will be totally different once Allerdale has worked its magic on me and shaped me into the performer I'm supposed to be. It'll be such a relief to finally feel joy when I sing, like the rest of my family does. I can't wait to slough off this sticky web of anxiety and shame that forces me to hide behind the piano.

I wonder if my mom will insist I get up and sing, but her eyes slide right off me and onto Skye. I almost wish she'd put up a fight. "Would you like to go first?" she asks.

Skye's eyes go all wide and innocent, like she's surprised to be singled out, but she's on her feet almost before my mom finishes asking. "Oh, um, okay." She turns to me. "Do you know 'Out Tonight' from *Rent*?"

Of course she'd pick that—it's a big, flashy, cliché number with lots of impressive high notes. I want to glance up and exchange a Look-with-a-capital-*L* with Uncle Harrison, but I already know he's on the same page as me. "Sure," I say. "I'm ready whenever you are."

She nods, and I launch into the opening bars from memory; I've played this song enough times that I don't need the music. Skye knows everyone's watching her, sizing her up, but she bites her lower lip, closes her eyes, and moves to the music like she's alone in her bedroom. It seems impossible that I could ever be that un–self-conscious. Sutton gets up and dances along, and Twyla giggles as Desi bounces her to the beat.

The minute Skye starts to sing, I see why my mom took her on as a student. Her voice is flawless, warm and playful and caramel-rich. She doesn't even seem like she's trying, but every note is spot-on, even the really high ones. Like me, she has obviously listened to the original cast recording countless times—she mimics everything Daphne Rubin-Vega did when she played Mimi, including all the ad-libs. It doesn't seem like there's much of anything for my mom to teach her, aside from how to make the music her own. She seems like she's having such a good time, like she never wants the song to end, and I envy that passion so much that it hurts.

When Skye finishes, everyone claps and cheers, and she grins and does a stupid little curtsy. "Girl, you are freaking *amazing*," Desi tells her. "Where has that voice been all my life?"

"Thank you," Skye says. She looks incredibly pleased with herself, and I try not to hate her, but I can't help it. I take note of exactly how I feel right now so I can pull the memory out this summer whenever my motivation flags. *That* is what I have to become at Allerdale.

The night progresses like it usually does. Jermaine sings "Being Alive" from *Company,* Marisol does "I'd Be Surprisingly Good for You" from *Evita,* and my mom does "Last Midnight" from *Into the Woods.* It's obvious how much they all love the music, how happy they are to be sharing it with us—even my staid, quiet father seems delighted as he belts out "Stars" from *Les Miz.* By the time an hour and a half has passed, everyone's starting to get tipsy and loud and a little bit silly, and when Uncle Harrison asks me to sing with him, it finally seems safe to agree.

"Should we do the *Phantom* parody we were working on the other day?" he asks.

I'm about to say yes, relieved that I'm getting off this easily; when you perform something funny that nobody's ever heard before, everyone concentrates on the lyrics instead of the person who's singing them. But before I can answer, my mom rolls her eyes. "Harrison, I know you like horrible puns, but that doesn't mean you have to fill my daughter's head with trash."

"There's nothing *trashy* about parodies. They're—" Uncle Harrison begins, but I cut him off.

"It's okay," I say. "We'll sing something else." Even if the classics are more nerve-racking for me, it's my last night with my mom, and I don't want to antagonize her. I can suck it up one more time if it means she'll be proud of me as she sends me off to Allerdale.

Uncle Harrison and I decide on "Big Spender" from *Sweet Charity,* and Mom rewards me with a smile as she pours herself more wine. I've always liked the song, but the entire time we're performing, I'm just waiting for it to be over, praying I can get through it without making a fool of myself. I don't slip up in any obvious ways, but my rendition is mediocre at best, and by the time we're finished, my heart is beating wildly and my palms are damp. I catch a smug smile on Skye's face as she applauds for us, and I feel my cheeks going hot. I don't open my mouth again.

Uncle Harrison takes over as accompanist after a while, and my family keeps singing until Twyla's asleep in my dad's lap and Sutton's conked out facedown on the rug. Around midnight, we all crowd around the piano for our final ensemble number; our neighbors are understanding up to a point, but when we go too late, they start whacking their ceiling with a broom handle. My uncle pats the bench, and I sit down beside him, hip to hip. As he plays the opening chords to another song from *Rent,* he shoots me a smile that says he'll miss having me next to him.

I look around at my family, their eyes bright, their arms twined around each other, and I vow that by the end of the summer, I'll be the passionate, seasoned theater professional I'm supposed to be. I will push through my nervousness and uncertainty until I'm the kind of girl who can't wait to nestle into the crook of the piano like it's her boyfriend's arm and let her voice fly free. The brilliant Allerdale directors will break me down and build me back up into a totally new person, and by the time they send me back home, I'm going to *belong* here.

"No day but today," everyone around me sings in perfect four-part harmony.

Not for me, I think. *Today is just the beginning for me.*

2

My first few minutes in the professional theater world feel a lot like the first day of high school. The Adirondack Trailways bus drops me off a couple of blocks from the Allerdale Playhouse, and when I reach the wide green lawns of the theater's grounds, I find them swarming with strangers. As I try to wheel my suitcase up the path to the company management office, I have to keep ducking and dodging as shrieking girls and flailing guys fling themselves at each other. Some of them embrace so enthusiastically that they collapse on the ground and roll around like puppies. I have a brief fantasy that that'll be me next summer, reuniting with all the friends I'm about to make.

I finally find company management, where five or six people are waiting on line. Everyone seems tall and shiny and glamorous, even in their cutoffs and flip-flops, and I'm a little afraid to make eye contact with anybody as I shuffle toward the registration table. The company manager is wearing a polo shirt with the Allerdale logo, and a name tag that says "Barb." Her boobs are so enormous, it's almost like she has a shelf attached to her front.

"Hi," I say when I reach the front of the line. "Brooklyn Shepard, apprentice company." I make an effort to say it confidently, like I totally deserve to be here.

Barb searches her clipboard for my name, and I half expect she's going to say this is all a joke and send me home on the next bus. But instead she makes a couple of check marks, riffles through the stack of manila envelopes, and slaps one into my palm a little harder than necessary. "You're in Ramsey Hall. Room number, swipe card, and key are in here. Don't lose them."

"Don't worry, I won't," I say. "I'm very organized."

"Company meeting tonight at seven. Cast lists'll be posted at eight. Map, company rules, season calendar, and orientation packet are in your envelope. Read them carefully. It's nobody's fault but yours if you don't show up where you're supposed to be. *Next!*"

"Thanks for your help," I say, but Barb doesn't even respond; she's clearly waiting for me to move along. I scoot out of the way as fast as I can, trying not to whack anyone with my huge duffel bag as I push out the door.

I've been to Allerdale a bunch of times to see shows my parents have worked on, but I've never been inside the dorms, and it takes me a while to find Ramsey Hall. As I walk, I catch myself staring at the trees and rolling hills in the distance with the same bug-eyed wonder as the Times Square tourists who drive me crazy at home. I'm only three hours upstate of the city, and it's not like we don't have plants in Manhattan. But New York City parks are more like urban spaces auditioning for the role of nature. It's almost disconcerting to see the real thing.

There's no air-conditioning in the dorm, and by the time I lug all my stuff up two flights of stairs, I'm disheveled and sticky. The hall is filled with people chattering and laughing and shaking hands, and I know I should make an effort to meet some of them, but everything's starting to feel a little overwhelming. I've always had trouble connecting to the other theater kids at school, who are ridiculously competitive and gossip about each other constantly. I can fake it well enough that they consider me part of the group, but I'm not sure I can handle *living* with people like that for nine whole weeks. Maybe coming here was a mistake.

Put on your game face, I order myself. *Allerdale is exactly what you need.* I vow that after I put down my stuff and rest for a minute, I'll come back out here with a big, bright smile and make some friends.

My room is near the end of the hall, and I unlock the door and drag my luggage behind me as I back inside. It's not till I hear a surprised "Oh!" that I realize there's already someone in the room. The first thing I notice about the other girl is her long blond hair, which almost brushes the floor as she leans over to dig through her suitcase. The second thing I notice is that she isn't wearing a shirt.

I spin around so my back is to her. "Oh my God, sorry, I'm so sorry," I blurt out. "I thought this was 309."

"It is," she says. "I'm Zoe. You must be my roommate?"

I had no idea I was getting a roommate, but I'm obviously in the right place, or my key wouldn't have worked. "Oh. Yeah. I guess I am. I'm Brooklyn. I'm really sorry about barging in on you. I should've knocked."

"It's okay. You can turn around."

Zoe's holding a red tank top now, but she comes over and holds out her hand to me before she bothers to put it on. Her hand feels cool even in the heat, and I'm impressed by how purposefully she moves in her shorts and pink bra. I'm pretty sure I never look that comfortable, even when I'm fully dressed. I shake her hand, careful to keep my eyes on her heart-shaped face. There's a smattering of freckles across her cheeks, and her eyes are big and blue with a ring of golden brown around the pupils. My mom calls those "sunflower eyes." Zoe is way prettier than I am, but I try not to care.

"It's really nice to meet you," she says. She lets go of my hand and pulls on her shirt, and I feel a little less awkward once she's dressed. "I put my stuff over there, but if you'd rather have the left side, we can switch."

"No, this is fine. It's good to meet you, too." I plunk my duffel bag down on the bare mattress, which has a green stain near the end, like someone was eating a lime Popsicle as a midnight snack. "Are you in the apprentice company, too?" I ask.

"Yup, it's my first year here. I'm so excited."

"Me too." As I start unpacking my sheets, I realize I forgot to bring my pillow, and an intense pang of sadness washes over me as I picture it sitting next to the front door of my apartment. "Crap," I say. "Do you think there's anywhere in town that sells pillows?"

Zoe laughs. "Have you been into town yet? There's, like, a bar and three restaurants and a bakery, and that's pretty much it. You can have one of mine, though."

"Thanks," I say, and she tosses me a pillow that smells faintly of grapefruit. "I'll find one of my own soon so you can have it back."

"Don't worry about it. I think there's a Target, like, thirty minutes away, but that seems like a long way to go for one pillow."

"I don't know how I'd get there, anyway," I say. "I don't have a car. I don't even know how to *drive* a car."

I have no idea why I said that to a total stranger, but Zoe's face lights up. "Are you from New York City?"

"Yeah."

"Please tell me you live in Brooklyn."

This question usually annoys me, but somehow it's different with Zoe; she looks like she'd be genuinely, unironically delighted if I were Brooklyn from Brooklyn. "My parents used to live there, but we live in Manhattan now," I say. "I think they named me that because they felt bad about abandoning their bohemian roots or whatever."

"Man, I wish I'd grown up there. I'm from Colorado, and I feel like a total hick. I've only seen, like, four shows *on* Broadway. But I'm moving to the city in the fall, so I'll make up for it then. You have to tell me all the good places to eat and stuff on the Upper West Side, okay?"

"Totally. I actually live up there, too. Are you going to Columbia?"

"Juilliard," she says. I've heard a lot of people say that word, and it usually comes out sounding stuck-up, but Zoe manages to strike exactly the right balance of excitement and matter-of-factness. She's not bragging about her talent, but she's not apologizing for it, either. My heart sinks; she seems really nice, but I doubt she'll stick around and be my friend once she realizes how vastly different our talent levels are.

"Wow," I say, trying not to let my disappointment show. "Congratulations."

"Thanks." Zoe twists her hair up into a complicated knot, and when she turns around to search her dresser for a ponytail holder, I notice that the entire top of her back is inked with delicate twisting branches and tiny pink blossoms.

"I love your tattoo," I say. "What kind of flowers are those?"

"Thanks! They're cherry blossoms. In Japan, they symbolize that life is beautiful but short, so you should take advantage of every day." She gives me a sheepish smile. "I know it's kind of cheesy. Mostly I just like how they look."

"No, that's cool. Did it hurt?"

"Yeah, it totally sucked—it felt like being stung by a million bees. And I had to go back three different times so they could do the shading."

"Wow," I say. She must be pretty badass to withstand that much pain for something beautiful. It makes total sense that she'd be a good actor.

"So, you go to Columbia?" Zoe asks.

"Oh, no. I've actually got one more year of high school. I'll probably apply there and to Juilliard, but they're both long shots." Just thinking about spending four years under that kind of pressure makes my stomach turn over, but I push the thought away. By the time I'm done with Allerdale, I'll be able to handle it.

Zoe shrugs. "You never know. That's what I thought, too. Hey, are you hungry? I think the dining hall opened a couple of minutes ago. If we want to grab something before the company meeting, we should go soon." I love the way she says "we," like she automatically wants to eat dinner with me. Maybe it'll be easier to connect with people here than I thought.

The dining hall is packed when we arrive. Half the people seem to be sitting on each other's laps, touching each other's hair, and kissing each other's cheeks, and it kind of reminds me of the way my family acts. As I pass a table full of girls, one of them squeals, "OH EM GEE, we have the same shoes!" and the other replies, "OH EM GEE, besties!"

Zoe and I get in line for food behind a tall black girl with a poofy cloud of a ponytail and a tiny girl with a blond pixie cut. When we hear them mention Ramsey, we introduce ourselves, and it turns out their room is two doors down from ours. The blonde introduces herself as Livvy, and the other girl says her name is Jessa. When she shakes my hand, she squeezes so hard, it hurts.

Zoe and I each grab two slices of pizza and a side salad. I was kind of afraid nobody here would eat, but it seems like she's as hungry as I am. When we head into the fray to find an empty table, Livvy and Jessa trail along behind us, and I realize Zoe's the alpha dog here. I stay close to her, hoping some of her coolness will rub off.

The second we sit down, Zoe crams an enormous bite of pizza crust into her mouth, and I almost laugh—she seems like the kind of person who would eat in small, ladylike bites. "I'm *so* hungry," she mumbles around the food. "Denver to New York is four hours, and I got to the airport too late to grab a sandwich."

Jessa stares at her. "Girl, didn't anyone ever show you how to eat pizza? You're supposed to start with the *end*."

"But that's the best part. I like to save it for last." Zoe shrugs. "My boyfriend always makes fun of me for it, too."

"Do you eat pie that way?" I ask at the same time that Livvy says, "What's your boyfriend's name?"

"His name's Carlos. And of course I eat pie like this. Who wants to eat pie crust last?"

"That is *messed up*," Jessa says, but she's smiling.

"So, what shows are you guys hoping for?" asks Livvy, stabbing at her salad. She has so many croutons piled on top that I can barely see the lettuce.

Jessa rolls her eyes. "I think it's pretty clear where *my* black ass is going to end up."

"Allerdale's actually pretty good about color-blind casting," Zoe says. "When my sister was here, they did—"

"Are you seriously trying to tell me there's gonna be *color-blind casting* for *Dreamgirls*? Because that is *not* gonna happen."

"All right, fair enough," Zoe says.

"I'll take anything as long as I don't have to play someone's little brother," Livvy says. "I'm so sick of getting cast as a ten-year-old boy. Maybe I should get a boob job. How do you guys think I would look with a D-cup?"

"You'd look like someone's little brother in drag," Jessa says.

"Oliver Twisted," I offer. Zoe snort-laughs into her Diet Coke, and Livvy throws a crouton at me. I love that I barely know these girls and we're already comfortable enough to tease each other. They don't seem catty and competitive like the girls at home—maybe they're confident enough about their talent that they don't need to cut each other down all the time. I know I'm getting ahead of myself, but part of me can't help wondering whether Zoe and Jessa and Livvy will be my old friends when I'm my parents' age. In the charged atmosphere of this dining hall, it seems possible.

"How high can you guys belt?" Jessa asks, reminding me that this is still a competition.

"I can hit an E," Livvy says.

"Damn. I can only hit a D on a really good day. What about you guys?"

"I'm not much of a belter," Zoe says.

"She's being modest," I tell Jessa. "She's going to Juilliard in the fall."

Jessa's eyes get big. "Holy shit, are you serious? And here I was thinking I was cool 'cause I got into Carnegie Mellon."

"Oh, shut up. Carnegie Mellon's got a fantastic program," Zoe says, and Jessa puffs up with pride.

"I'm going to Syracuse," Livvy offers. It reminds me of how cats stick their heads right under your hand to demand petting, and Zoe indulges her by making an impressed face. Livvy smiles and turns to me. "What about you, Brooklyn?"

"I've got one more year of high school," I answer, and I wonder how many times I'm going to have to say that. Maybe I should write it in Sharpie on my shirt.

Livvy looks confused. "Wait, are you not eighteen?"

"Not till November."

"Girl, you must be *amazing*," Jessa says. "I tried to get in here last year, and all I got was a form letter telling me to apply again when I was old enough."

I give her a modest shrug, but I hadn't realized until this moment that there is an age restriction on the apprentice company. How did I miss that on the application? I'm only a few months under the limit, so it's possible the administration decided to let it slide. But it's also possible I'm here because my mom called in a favor with the artistic director. What if I didn't earn my spot in the company at all? I start to feel a little dizzy.

Knock it off, I tell myself. *It doesn't matter why you're here. You'll get the same training either way. It's not like anyone's going to know.* I take a few deep breaths and try to pull myself together before anyone notices I'm acting weird.

Zoe takes another bite from the wrong end of her pizza. "Have you guys heard any rumors about who's teaching our master classes?" she asks.

"Marcus always teaches one," Livvy says.

Jessa wiggles her fingers. "Oooh, the high-and-mighty festival director comes down off his pedestal."

"I can't wait," I say. "I hear he's the absolute best." Everyone in the theater world knows how great Marcus Spooner is, but it still makes me feel like I'm on the inside to be able to say it with authority.

"I heard Susan Margolis might come do a voice class with us," Jessa says.

"Isn't she supposed to be a little weird?" Livvy asks. "I heard she carries around a bunch of plastic dinosaurs in her bag, like, *all the time.* She calls them her muses."

Zoe shrugs. "I mean, let's be honest, who in this business *isn't* a little weird?"

"I'd rather have someone like Lana Blake Shepard," Livvy says. "She did a workshop at my high school once, and it was unreal."

I'm in the middle of a sip of water, and I inhale it and start coughing like crazy. Zoe whacks me on the back, but she's totally focused on Livvy. "You've *met* Lana Blake Shepard? That woman is my *idol.* Did you talk to her at all? Like, one-on-one?"

"A little. She's a total genius. And she told me I had 'serious potential.' Can you believe that? I thought I was going to die."

"Do you live in the city? I heard she visits high schools there all the time."

Livvy sighs. "I wish. I'm from north Jersey. But it's really close to the city."

"I listen to Lana's cast recording of *Sunset Boulevard* constantly," Zoe says. "It's perfect. She totally deserved that Tony."

It would be so easy for me to say, *Hey, guys, guess what? Lana's actually my mom.* Even though I can't hit a high E, I'd become an instant celebrity at this table. I could tell them all kinds of insider information—how my mom sings "I'm Gonna Wash That Man Right Outa My Hair" every single time she takes a shower, or how she once kissed the UPS guy on the mouth when he delivered an exciting package. But if I do, it's possible my new friends will put the pieces together and realize I might not have earned my spot in the company. It's probably better to wait and tell them later, after the cast lists are up and I've proven I belong here.

Zoe turns to me. "I read an interview that said Lana lives on the Upper West Side. Has she ever done a workshop at your school?"

"No," I say. It's technically true. Of course, I started listening in on my mom's workshops before I could read, but that's not what Zoe asked.

"She probably lives right near you," she says. "Oh my God, Brooklyn, what if she's secretly been living *in your building* all this time? How amazing would that be?"

I think about my mom's high, screaming laugh, the vocal warm-ups she does every morning, the way my whole family belts show tunes late into the night on Mondays. The idea of my mother living anywhere *secretly* is pretty ridiculous.

I laugh like this whole conversation is just a big joke. "Nah," I say. "If Lana Blake Shepard were my neighbor, I'm pretty sure I would know."

3

Legrand Auditorium is one of those gorgeous, old-fashioned theaters with dusty red-velvet seats and gold acanthus leaves climbing up the proscenium. There's a giant crystal chandelier hanging from the ceiling, surrounded by paintings of naked cherubs and muses in flowing robes. Even though the work lights are on and there's nothing on the stage but a scuffed podium and a bunch of A-frame ladders, the space still feels as magical as it did when I was five and saw it for the first time.

I catch Zoe looking at me, and I realize I must have a goofy smile on my face. But instead of making fun of me, she slips her arm through mine and cranes her neck back to look at the ceiling. "It's beautiful, isn't it?" she says.

"I love this theater so much," I say. "My parents brought me here to see *The Secret Garden* when I was little, and my mom says I took one look at that chandelier and announced that I wanted to be an actor. I thought it meant I'd get to live here."

"You must've been so cute," Zoe says. "Come on. Let's find somewhere to sit."

The theater's not as loud as the dining hall, but the anticipation is palpable. Everyone knows Marcus Spooner is coming, followed by cast lists in one short hour. Zoe, Jessa, Livvy, and I are settling into row F when a spotlight comes up on the empty podium, and Company Manager Barb starts making her way toward it. Everyone cheers, and I wonder if she's actually a nicer person than she seemed at registration. Maybe she has a cult following at the festival. I clap for her, just in case.

"Hi, everyone," she says with a totally genuine smile. "Welcome to the Allerdale Playhouse. I'd like to extend a very special welcome to our brand-new company members; we're so pleased to have you with us. Are you ready to make our forty-seventh season our best yet?"

Everyone around us cheers. I hesitate for a second, not sure if my new friends are as caught up in the excitement as I am. But then Zoe and Jessa let out shrieks on either side of me, so I do it, too. I'm a *company member*. Nobody can take this away from me.

"Where's my non-equity company?" calls Barb, and a few rows of people to our left raise their arms in the air and scream. Equity is the actors' union; the non-equity people are all here working toward eligibility so they can take jobs in higher-profile shows.

"Where's my equity company?" Scattered grown-ups around the auditorium whoop and shout; the equity actors are the only ones who already know what roles they're playing, and they stay only long enough to rehearse and perform in their own shows. The equity actors who are in *Hedda Gabler, Dreamgirls, Bye Bye Birdie,* and *Macbeth* don't even get here for a few more weeks. It's nice to see that the adults are as enthusiastic as we are, though.

"Where's my apprentice company?" Barb asks, and my new friends and I cheer for all we're worth. About twenty other people do the same, and I look around the theater and try to see who I'll be spending my time with.

"Where are my tech and design interns?" calls Barb.

Someone whoops so loudly right behind me that I nearly jump out of my chair. I spin around to see a guy with dark curly hair and such long legs that they're folded up against the back of my seat, his knees almost level with his chin. When he's done screaming, he smiles self-consciously at me and mouths, *Sorry.* He looks friendly, and I kind of want to introduce myself, but I don't want to miss a thing that's happening onstage, so I smile back and turn around.

Barb speeds through a bunch of logistical stuff—emergency phone numbers, where the nurse's office is, how to check the electronic call board to see where we're supposed to meet for rehearsals each day. When she's done, she says, "Now I'd like to turn the podium over to our managing director, Mr. Bob Sussman. Let's give him a hand."

Everyone claps as Bob bounds onto the stage, waving to us with both hands. He's a wiry little man with a trim beard, and he's wearing a gray suit with navy sneakers. When he reaches

Barb, he gives her a hug, which she clearly doesn't expect or want, and then he takes his place at the microphone.

"Good evening, warriors for art!" he shouts, and the microphone squeals with feedback. "I'm so thrilled to welcome you to another summer of creativity and collaboration. Working at Allerdale is such a unique experience. No matter what your role is, I promise that you will never forget your time here." A warm, exquisite feeling of being part of something blooms in my chest like a big orange flower. Coming here was the right decision. There's no way Allerdale could fail to make me fall head over heels in love with performing.

"I'm so looking forward to getting to know you and soaking up your creative genius," Bob says, "but for now, I'm sure everyone's eager to move on to the main event. So without further ado, let me introduce our incomparable festival director and my dear friend, *Mr. Marcus Spooner!*"

The auditorium erupts in screams so loud and frenetic, it reminds me of the videos I've seen of middle school girls at One Direction concerts. As Marcus enters from stage left and crosses to the podium, I half expect someone to whip off her bra and throw it at his feet. He keeps his eyes straight forward and his face blank, like there's a one-way mirror between him and us. He's wearing a blue button-down over a T-shirt that appears to bear the image of his own face. I turn to Zoe, eager to share this observation, but then Marcus opens his mouth, and everyone shuts up all at once.

"Every story that can be told has already been told!" he booms into the sudden silence. "That sounds discouraging, doesn't it? To hear me tell you there's nothing fresh, nothing original, nothing *new* in this whole crazy, goddamn world?"

He pauses and stares us down, waiting long enough for the silence to become intensely uncomfortable. Two seats away, Livvy fidgets in her chair, and it makes a tiny squeaking sound that echoes through the otherwise silent theater. She freezes in place, one leg half crossed.

"It is *not* discouraging," Marcus finally says. "Why? Because we don't need *new* stories to tell *spectacular* stories. This summer, we will say all the things that have already been said, but we will say them *better.* Each of us—each of *you*—has a unique perspective that has never been seen before. And because we are more evolved than previous generations, our perspectives are *better* than anything that has come before us. We are the pinnacle of human thought, and it is our responsibility to show everyone how we see the world. If you don't strive to tell your story as carefully, as masterfully as you can, you are robbing the world of your voice, and *that is unacceptable.*

"This summer will be difficult. You will work harder than you have ever worked in your entire miserable lives. You will work until your flesh hangs from your bones in gruesome, bloody strips. If you are not willing to work that hard, there is no point in you being here at all. If any of you feels that hard, unrelenting labor is beyond the scope of your ability, you should leave right now. *Leave!* If you aren't one of us, no one will be sad to see you go!"

Marcus points to the door. We all surreptitiously glance around, but of course nobody gets up, because we all belong here. I sneak a look at Zoe, and her face is upturned and radiant, like Marcus's words are snowflakes falling on her cheeks.

"Good," Marcus says. "Everyone here is prepared to work. Luckily for you, it won't feel like work. It will feel like *transcendence*. Some people say that true theater, true art, comes from the outside and fills us up. They credit their inspiration to the muses, or to God. That is *idiocy*. It's not *God* who creates theater! God is *dead*! And that is why we must *transcend*, why we must lay the world bare with our voices and our gestures and our sheer, raw power! The world needs gods, so we must *become* gods! We must allow ourselves to be nothing short of spectacular, because to do so is to *spit in the face of the world*! We are Titans, and we *shall not be conquered*!"

And then, with no warning at all, Marcus turns and strides off the stage. There's no *thank you*, no *goodbye*, no *I look forward to working with you*. The auditorium is dead silent for a full count of ten, like everyone is waiting for him to jump back out and keep going. But then Barb reappears, and we all exhale in unison. By the time people realize it's okay to clap, Marcus is long gone. We give him a standing ovation anyway.

Zoe slumps against me like her strings have been cut. "He's *unbelievable*, isn't he?"

I'm not totally convinced everything Marcus said made sense, but I don't really care, either. I feel like my brain is emitting sparks, and there's a slight tingling sensation in the tips of my fingers. *This* is what true inspiration must feel like. "Totally unreal," I say.

When Barb reaches the podium again, she bows dramatically, acknowledging our thunderous applause, and everyone laughs and sits down. "All right, kids," she says. "Cast lists are up in the usual place. Try not to trample—"

I don't even hear the rest of her sentence; the entire company leaps back up, shouting and pushing and bottlenecking as they try to get out the door. My instinct is to wait until the path is clearer, but Jessa grabs my wrist and pulls me forward. I reach back for Zoe's hand as I stumble into the aisle, and her fingers close around mine.

Going through the auditorium doors is like being squeezed through a funnel, and then we're outside in the cool evening air. People stream across the lawn and down the hill in the direction of the box office, so we sprint after them. Jessa lets go of me so she can run faster, but Zoe keeps a firm grip on my hand, and I time my steps to hers.

"Are you nervous?" I ask.

"A little, I guess. Are you?"

"Sort of," I say, trying not to show that my heart is actually going about five times its normal speed. "I really hope I get something good, you know? Something with lines. I mean, obviously I'll take anything, and I don't expect much, but . . ."

I realize I'm babbling, and I break off as the box office comes into view. It's a freestanding, hexagonal kiosk with glass walls, and there's a cast list posted on each side. People swarm around it, shrieking with joy and dismay and hugging each other; it's like the gravitational force of the kiosk has pulled all the emotions in the world into a ten-foot radius. A girl with a black ponytail dashes past us in the direction of the dorms, tears streaming down her face.

"Wow," Zoe says. "This is intense. Are you ready?"

I don't want to seem like a wimp, so I say, "Ready."

"Let's make a pact not to cry, okay?"

"We're not going to cry," I say. "We're at *Allerdale*."

I try to stay near Zoe when we get to the box office, but we're immediately separated by the jostling crowd. I run my eyes down the first cast list I see, which is for *Dreamgirls*. Jessa's name is listed under "Ensemble," and I wonder if she's excited or pissed. My name isn't on this list, so I move to the right and scan the one for *Macbeth*. It's not there, either, though I check the list of spear-carriers, guards, and servants several times to be sure. *Hedda Gabler*'s next—my dad took me to see it last year, and I thought it was kind of boring. Fortunately, my name's nowhere to be found.

I wipe my sweaty palms on my shorts as I scan the list for *Catch Me If You Can*. Nothing. *A Midsummer Night's Dream* is next, and the number of names printed on the paper sends a wash of relief through me. There are at least twenty fairies, probably mostly apprentices, and I feel certain I'm going to be one of them. I find Livvy's and Zoe's names, and I send the universe an image of the three of us huddled together backstage, wearing gauzy costumes. It's so close I can taste it.

Except my name isn't on the list.

This can mean only one thing—my audition was good enough to land me a part in *Bye Bye Birdie*. My mom is going to *flip out* when I tell her. With a sense of delicious anticipation, I move toward the sixth side of the kiosk. A cheer starts building in my throat, ready to burst out as soon as I see my name. I feel like one of those aerosol cans that say, "Warning: contents under pressure."

The first thing I see when I round the corner is Zoe, her hands clapped over her mouth as she stares up at the list. People keep bumping into her, but she doesn't even seem to notice. "Hey," I say as I squeeze in next to her. "I saw your name on the *Midsummer* list! Are you in *Birdie,* too?" My backstage fantasies come rushing back, only this time Zoe and I are in bright fifties-style clothes and pigtails. *This is the right visualization,* I think to the universe as loudly as I can. *Scratch that other one, okay?*

My roommate doesn't say anything. Her face is filled to the brim with emotion, but I can't tell *which* emotion. "Zoe?" I say. "Are you okay?"

"I got Kim," she says in a small voice.

"What?" Kim is one of the lead roles; it must be unheard of for an apprentice to get something that big. "Seriously? Zoe, that's *amazing!*" I throw my arms around her, and she hugs me back, her happy tears hot on my cheek. She's totally breaking our no-crying pact. "Am I in *Birdie,* too?"

"I didn't see, I was too distracted. Holy shit, I'm Kim. *Kim.* On the *main stage.*"

"I'm so happy for you," I say, but I'm already pulling away and scanning the list for my own name. The first time through barely registers—I'm so nervous, I can't even see straight—so I make myself start over and look again carefully. There's Zoe's name, third from the top. I laugh a little when I see that Livvy has been cast as Kim's little brother. And then I'm at the bottom of the list again, and I still haven't seen my name.

36

"Are you in it with me?" Zoe asks.

"No," I say, and the word comes out oddly detached and calm.

"Aw, man, that sucks," Zoe says. "What did you get?"

"I, um. I can't actually find my name anywhere."

A crinkle of confusion appears between Zoe's eyebrows. "You must've missed it," she says. "Come on. Let's look again. I'll go with you."

We circle the kiosk in the other direction this time, but when we end up back at *Dreamgirls* and I see Zoe's face, I know I wasn't wrong. "Is it possible not to get cast at all?" I ask, and my voice shakes in a way that makes me sound very young.

"I don't think so. They wouldn't put you in the company if they didn't have a part for you, right?"

Maybe they would if I'm here as a favor to my mom, but I obviously can't say that to Zoe. "Do you think there's been a mistake?" I ask. "Should I find Barb?"

"I don't know. Did you check the list of side projects? Maybe you're in a bunch of those."

I completely forgot about the side projects, which are run by directing interns and performed in the smaller, experimental theaters after the main stage shows are over each night. I don't even know which shows they're doing. "Where are the lists?" I ask.

Zoe points to a freestanding notice board off to the side. "Come on."

There are six sheets of paper on the board, and I start scouring them. I've gotten through three without finding my name, when Zoe calls, "Brooklyn, over here."

I look where she's pointing, my heart in my throat. Maybe it's a really good show after all, even if it's not on the main stage. *Please,* I ask the universe, without any specific instructions, and then I look at the list.

Señor Hidalgo's Circus of Wonders, it reads.

What the hell is *that*? It sounds like an animated television show for preschoolers. There are six other names on the list besides mine, but there's no corresponding list of roles.

Zoe has a weird look on her face. "Your last name is Shepard?" she asks.

"Yeah," I say, but I can't deal with the implications of that right now. "Do you know what this show is?"

"No. It's probably new—playwrights workshop stuff here all the time. That's kind of exciting, right? You might be the very first one in this part."

I don't point out that there aren't even any parts listed. Across the bottom of the page, it says, "Please report to the Slice for an introductory meeting at 9:00 PM on Friday."

"What's the Slice?" I ask.

"It's one of the experimental spaces," Zoe says. "It's called that because it's shaped like a triangle, like a slice of pizza. My sister did a show there when she was an apprentice." It's embarrassing how much more Zoe knows about Allerdale than me, considering I'm the one who's been here before.

"What am I supposed to do until Friday? That's three entire days from now."

"You're probably on one of the tech crews first rotation. The assignments are on the other side of this board. Maybe we'll have a rotation together!" I can tell Zoe feels bad for me, even though she's trying hard to sound positive. Her kindness nearly makes my eyes well up, but I forbid myself to cry. I have to learn to deal with rejection or I'm never going to be a real actor.

The crew call sheets are surrounded by people rolling their eyes and groaning, but I push my way through like I'm trying to get on the L train at rush hour. This time it's not hard to find my name—it's all over the board. I'm doing tech for *all three* rotations, never in the same department as Zoe. Tomorrow I'm supposed to report for lighting crew at Legrand at eight-thirty in the morning. I'm also on run crew for *Midsummer,* which means I'll have to show up at every single performance and creep around in the dark like a cockroach while my new friends frolic around the stage in their fairy wings.

I have a sudden urge to sit down on the ground with my arms over my head and let the crowd swirl around me like a river around a rock. I'm *so* glad I didn't tell anyone who my mom is, or I'd be even more embarrassed right now. *What* am I going to tell my family? And how is Allerdale supposed to teach me to love performing if I'm barely allowed to perform?

Zoe puts a hand on my back, and as I look at her, I think, *Well, it was nice while it lasted.* This is clearly where things end between us. Tomorrow, she'll start learning her solos, and I'll start learning . . . how to use a wrench or something, I guess. Honestly, I have no idea what the lighting crew even does.

"Hey," Zoe says, and I'm sure she's going to say, "I'm sorry for how things turned out," or even "It was nice meeting you." But instead she says, "I'm going to call my boyfriend for a second, but then do you want to walk into town and get ice cream?"

I stare at her. There are joyful groups of actors all over the lawn, singing snippets of songs from their new shows and passing flasks around. *Those* are her people, not me. "Don't you want to celebrate?" I ask.

Zoe looks puzzled. "I *am* celebrating," she says. "Do you want to come with me?"

I'm in no mood to act cheerful, but that's not really the point. Zoe is telling me it doesn't matter to her that I wasn't cast; she's offering me her friendship anyway. If I say I don't want any ice cream and go back to our room to sulk, there's no guarantee she'll reach out again.

"Of course I want to come," I say.

"Perfect," Zoe says. And before I know it, her arm is linked through mine, and we're walking away from the horrible, disappointing cast lists and toward the glorious sunset.

4

I'm headed over to Legrand Auditorium the next morning, clutching the biggest available cup of watery dining hall coffee, when my phone rings. My mom's picture pops up on the screen, one I took of her wearing three pairs of sunglasses at a flea market, and I'm surprised that she's up this early. I really don't want to talk to her right now, but I ignored her texts last night, and I know she'll keep calling until I answer.

I hit talk. "Hey, Mom."

"I got you!" She sounds genuinely delighted. "How *are* you, Brookie? Do you love it there? How did casting go last night? Tell me *everything*."

"This place is pretty incredible," I say. "I've only got a minute to talk, though. I'm headed to the theater."

"Your very first rehearsal!" she squeals. "Which show is it for? I'm so excited for you."

"This is just a crew call. My rehearsals aren't starting for a while, so I'm doing lighting and run crew first rotation."

"Well, everyone has to pay her dues," my mom says. "Tell me what you're in, sweetheart! I'm dying from the suspense!"

I steel myself for the sympathy in her voice when I tell her I'm not cast in anything. But when I open my mouth, what comes out is, "I'm in the ensemble of *Bye Bye Birdie.*"

My mom gasps. "Oh, Brookie, that's *wonderful!* *Birdie* means you'll get coaching in singing and dancing *and* acting! The full Allerdale experience. Are you thrilled?"

I can't believe I just flat-out lied to my mother. What am I going to do when she comes up to see the show and I'm not in it? I guess I could fake an injury or the flu at the last minute. *Birdie* is the last show of the season, so I have some time to figure it out.

"Yeah, totally," I say. "It's exactly what I wanted."

"When is it running?"

"The last two weeks. I'm in a side project, too, but I don't know anything about that yet."

"Ugh, I remember those side projects." I can hear my mom's eye-roll even over the phone. "They're so silly. I was in one that was a series of monologues about going to the post office. Don't spend too much of your energy on that; you have bigger things to worry about."

I definitely do, but not the way she means. "Hey, Mom?" I say.

"Yes, sweetheart?"

I'm about to ask her if she pulled any strings with Marcus to get me into the festival; maybe it would be easier to know so I can make peace with it and move on. But I can't make myself ask the question. If I don't hear her say it, I can keep believing there's a chance it's not true.

"I miss you guys," I say instead. "How's everything at home?"

"Oh, everything's fine. We all miss you like crazy, though."

Talking to her is making me really homesick, so I say, "I've gotta go, Mom. I'm at the theater. I'll call you soon, okay?"

"I love you, sweetie," she says. "Dad and Uncle Harrison send love, too."

"Love you back," I say. I swallow down all my *I wish I hadn't come*s and *I don't belong here*s and *I want to go home*s, and I hang up the phone.

When I arrive at Legrand, about ten other people are grouped around the loading dock. Nobody's really talking to each other, and at first I think it's because it's too early in the morning for getting-to-know-you chatter. But then a girl extends her cigarette pack to the guy next to her, and when he takes one without even thanking her, like it's a routine, it occurs to me that the crew probably arrived at the festival before we did. The silence between them feels like the kind that can exist only between people who already know each other. I take a fortifying sip of my coffee and approach them.

The actor moves into enemy territory, I hear in a nature-documentary voice inside my head. *Note the way her eyes dart from side to side. Her fight-or-flight response is working overtime.*

There are only two other girls, and I approach the one with the cigarettes, whose stick-straight ponytail is so light

43

blond, it looks almost white. I give her a big, friendly smile and say, "Hi!"

The girl's almost invisible eyebrows scrunch together as she takes in my lip gloss and white tank top and shorts printed with stars. Everyone else is dressed in jeans, dark T-shirts, and sneakers, and they all have tons of stuff hanging from their belts—wrenches, rolls of black tape, paint pens, heavy-duty gloves, tiny flashlights. Where did they get all that stuff? Am *I* supposed to have that stuff? *The actor and the techie have markedly different plumage,* says the nature-documentary voice.

"The rehearsal rooms are over in Haydu Hall," the girl says between drags.

"I . . . um, I know," I say. "I think I'm supposed to be here, though. Is this the lighting crew?"

"Yeah. Who are you?"

The guy next to her flicks his cigarette onto the asphalt and grinds it out with the toe of his boot. "We get actors today, remember?" he says.

"Oh, *right.*" The girl stubs out her cigarette, too. "You guys are only supposed to be here in the afternoons, though. Don't you have rehearsal or something?"

"My show's not rehearsing yet," I say, hoping they won't ask which one I'm in. Fortunately, nobody seems interested. "I'm Brooklyn, by the way."

"Courtney," the girl says. She doesn't extend her hand.

Nobody else introduces themselves, so I say, "Did you guys get here yesterday, too?"

"About a week ago. We had to load everything in."

A tall, lanky guy arrives at the loading dock and slides a box of doughnuts onto the concrete next to Courtney. "Morning, all," he says. He's wearing those thick leather wristbands with a bunch of studs, the kind Marisol and Christa refer to as "douchebands."

"Dude, doughnuts *already*?" one of the other guys says.

"You don't waste time, do you?" says Courtney as she flips the box open.

The guy smirks. "Fresh meat," he says. "Why wait?"

This makes absolutely no sense, but the guy sitting next to Courtney laughs and says, "Respect." I make a mental note to pick up some doughnuts for everyone later this week. I could use some respect.

"Speaking of fresh meat . . ." Douchebands turns to me. "Who's this?"

"Brooklyn," I say.

"Pretty." I can't tell whether he means my name or me, but either way, I'm creeped out.

"Yo," the guy next to Courtney says. "Gimme another cigarette?"

Before she can dig out her pack, a woman with dark curly hair and a clipboard comes around the corner. I assume she's the boss, from the way everyone starts gathering their stuff. "Listen up," she says when she gets close. "We're going to start hanging the rep plot today. Grab a piece of the plot, check in when you're done, and I'll give you another. Remember to pull out your shutters and label your circuits, okay?" She looks up. "Who brought doughnuts?"

Douchebands smiles and gives her a little salute.

45

"Of course," she says. She plunks a folder down onto the concrete and takes a doughnut with pink frosting. "Get to work."

Everyone descends on the folder and extracts little slips of paper while I stand off to the side. Finally, the boss notices me and asks, "Can I help you?"

"Um, I'm one of the acting apprentices?" I say. "I guess I'm assigned to lighting this rotation. I'm Brooklyn."

"I'm Dana Solomon. You can call me Solomon. Grab a piece of the plot from the folder, and let me know if you have questions, okay?"

I don't know what a plot is, but I pull out a slip of paper, hoping there'll be instructions on it or something. But all I see is a bunch of symbols, boxes and circles and slashes and shapes that look like little milk bottles. I can only tell which is the top because of the heading, which says "MID-GAL R" in block letters.

"Um," I say. "I'm really sorry, but I don't know what any of this means."

"You ever seen a light plot before?"

"Not really, no."

"No tech requirement for actors at your school, huh?"

"I'm still in high school," I say. I can practically see Solomon suppressing an eye-roll, but it's not *my* fault I don't know how to do this. I didn't come to Allerdale to do lighting.

"Do you have tools?"

"No," I say. "I'm sorry. I didn't know I was going to be—"

"Zach!" Solomon yells, and the guy who was bumming cigarettes turns around. "Brooklyn's with you today. Get her a wrench, okay?"

Zach doesn't even try to hide his exasperation. "Fine," he says. "Come on."

He leads me into a small, cluttered room he calls the "LX office," tells me to leave my bag on the ratty couch, and hands me a wrench. "Tie that off," he says. "There are tie line spools all over the place." I have no idea what any of those words mean, but I don't want to look like an idiot, so I nod. Zach seems to be carrying his wrench in his back pocket, so that's where I stick mine. I'm not wearing a belt, and my shorts immediately start to fall down on one side.

"Which piece of the plot do you have?" he asks.

"Um . . ." I look at the piece of paper clutched in my hand, now slightly damp from my nervous sweat. "Mid-gal R?"

"Mid-gallery, stage right. Okay, we'll do that first." Zach leads me onto the stage and points to a metal balcony about twenty-five feet in the air. "You're not afraid of heights, are you?"

"No," I say. Finally, a question I have the right answer to.

"Good." He looks at the paper for a minute. "Okay, we need three Source Four thirty-sixes, three twenty-sixes, and a nineteen. Let's go." I trot along behind him, hoping this is going to start making sense soon.

Source Fours turn out to be big black lights with clamps attached to the tops. We cart them up a narrow, winding, metal staircase; Zach carries four at a time, but I'm barely able to manage two. The floor of the mid-gallery is a metal grid, and I can see what's happening on the stage below my feet. It's a little disconcerting, and I feel a tiny wave of vertigo, but I don't say anything.

I watch Zach hang one of the lights, and it looks pretty easy—slip the clamp over the bar, attach this thin piece of metal he calls a safety cable, tighten the bolt with the wrench. "That doesn't look too hard," I tell him cheerfully.

He looks at me like, *How did I get stuck with this moron?* "It's not," he says. "Put a twenty-six there and a thirty-six here, okay?"

"Sure." I heft one of the lights up onto the bar. "So, where are you from?"

"Chapel Hill," Zach says.

I dig my wrench out of my pocket. "I've never been. Do you go to UNC? I've heard it's really—"

And that's when the wrench slips out of my hand and falls through the grid in the floor.

"Heads!" Zach bellows at the top of his lungs, and everyone on the ground ducks and takes a step back. The wrench smacks the stage floor with an enormous bang about five feet from Courtney, who looks up and shouts, "What the fuck, dude!"

"I'm *so* sorry!" I yell back.

Courtney shakes her head. I'm too high up to clearly hear what she says, but I'm pretty sure it's something like, "Figures."

Zach wheels on me. "What the hell was *that*? I told you to tie your wrench off!"

"I'm so sorry," I repeat. It seems like those are the only words I'm going to get to say today. "I didn't know what that meant."

"Jesus. If you don't know what something means, you *ask*! She could've ended up with a fractured skull! I know you're

48

used to flouncing around and listening to people clap for you, but what we do up here isn't a game. Do you understand?"

"Yes," I say, and I'm suddenly afraid I'm going to burst into tears.

Zach pulls a knife out of his belt and flips it open, and for a second I have this crazy thought that he's going to stab me and get rid of me once and for all. But instead he storms over to a spool of thin black rope, cuts off a piece, and hands it to me. "This is tie line," he says, like he's speaking to someone who might not understand English. "Tie one end to your wrench and the other end to your belt loop. Don't *ever* let that happen again."

"I won't," I choke out.

"Good. While you're downstairs getting the wrench, go down to the storage room—it's the staircase next to the office—and get me two ten-foot jumpers, two feds, and a sidearm, okay?"

For a second I think he's messing with me, throwing around words that don't even mean anything to make fun of all the jargon and tell me he knows how I feel. I smile at him gratefully, but then he says, "Okay?" again, and I realize those were actual instructions.

"Um. Two ten-foot jumpers, two feds? And . . ."

"A sidearm," he says.

I know he told me to ask for clarification if I don't understand something, but everything in storage will probably be labeled, so I should be able to figure this one out on my own. "Okay," I say, and I head downstairs.

The air in the basement is dank and clammy and smells

vaguely chemical, and one of the fluorescent lights is making an annoying buzzing sound. But at least nobody down here is yelling at me, so I hang out by the bottom of the stairs for a minute and take some deep breaths while I tie my wrench tightly to my belt loop. Finally, when I'm feeling a little calmer, I head down the hall until I find a door with a piece of tape across it that reads "LIGHTING STORAGE."

The room is packed floor-to-ceiling with crates of equipment, and absolutely *nothing* is labeled. The only objects I recognize are some normal lightbulbs like the kind we have at home and a bunch of disassembled Source Fours. I don't see anything that resembles jumper cables, which I'm pretty sure is what Zach asked for. What am I even *doing* here? I should be doing vocal warm-ups with Zoe and Livvy and Jessa in a rehearsal room right now.

There's nobody else down here, so I grit my teeth and make one of those frustrated screamy noises. It feels good to let some of my aggression out, so I do it again, louder this time, and plant a good, solid kick on a box of metal clamps. It hurts me a lot more than it hurts the box, and that makes me even angrier. I swear and massage my throbbing toes through my sneaker.

"Um, everything okay in there?"

I whirl around, and there in the doorway is the tall guy who was sitting behind me at the company meeting last night. He's got a can of paint in one hand and a cordless drill in the other.

"I, um," I stammer. "Yeah. Sorry. I didn't know anyone else was down here."

The guy nods at the box. "Those C-clamps getting fresh with you?"

I can't tell if he's flirting with me or not, but he's much cuter than I realized from my brief glimpse yesterday, so I force a smile, and I'm gratified when he smiles back. "I'm pretty sure I showed them who's boss," I say.

"Glad to hear that. Seriously, though, do you need help with something?"

I don't want to look stupid in front of this guy, but there's no way I'm going to find the equipment I need on my own. "Actually, yeah. I need two ten-foot jumper cables, or something? And two feds, and a . . . sidecar?"

The guy puts down his stuff and picks up a foot-long bar with a clamp attached to the end. "This is a side*arm*. A sidecar is a drink."

"I think I'd rather have a sidecar, then."

The guy laughs. "Rough morning?"

"I've been on the lighting crew for all of fifteen minutes, and I almost killed someone already."

"By accident or on purpose?"

This time my smile is real. "By accident."

"Cool. You don't look like a murderer, but it never hurts to check."

"I mean, if I *were* a murderer, it's not like I'd tell you."

"Damn. Good point. Maybe I'd better hang on to this." He clutches the sidearm and strides over to a shelf full of thick black cables. "Jumpers are extension cables; that's these guys. They're color-coded by length, and these ones with the yellow tape on the ends are the ten-footers. And this"—he holds up a small device with different kinds of plugs on each end—"is a fed. That's short for 'female Edison to male stage-pin adapter.' Cool?"

"Thank you so much," I say. "Nobody upstairs explains anything to me."

"You'll get it," he says. "I'm Russell, by the way." He puts down the sidearm and holds out his hand. It's so enormous that when I take it, I'm reminded of that scene in *Beauty and the Beast* where Belle's dainty little hand is engulfed by the beast's giant paw. It makes me feel tiny and delicate.

"Brooklyn," I say. "Nice to meet you."

"Wait, are we already at the 'where are you from' part of the conversation? I'm from Needham, Massachusetts, but I go to NYU."

"No, sorry. Brooklyn's my name. I live in Manhattan."

"Well, that's . . . unnecessarily complicated," Russell says, but he smiles. I'm pretty sure he *is* into me, which is kind of awesome. Having someone to flirt with this summer would improve things a lot. I wonder how long I can draw out this conversation before Zach gets pissed and comes looking for me.

"Hey," Russell says, like he's just remembered something really important. "Did you know that there are more than eighty-five thousand Elvis impersonators in the world?"

I blink at him, certain I've heard him wrong. "I . . . What?"

"You could have a city the size of Duluth, Minnesota, made entirely of Elvises," he says. "How great is that?"

I didn't even realize what a big knot I had in the center of my chest until I burst out laughing and feel it start to dissolve. "Why do you even know that?"

"I collect weird facts."

"And what made you think of that *now*?"

He shrugs. "I don't know. I thought you might be interested. Was I wrong?"

"No, I definitely feel like a more well-rounded person now that I know that," I say. I gesture to his drill. "So, you do . . . set stuff?"

"Yup. We're building today, but I mostly do scenic design. I get to assist Olivier von Drasek on *Midsummer* and *Dreamgirls*. Have you seen him around?"

"I'm not sure. Maybe. What does he look like?"

"Here." Russell pulls his phone out of his pocket, taps it a few times, and holds it out to me. Smiling up from the screen is a guy a little younger than my dad with a roguish, dimpled smile, an artfully scruffy beard, and a dashing swoop of silver hair. He's wearing a perfectly fitted suit and a purple tie, and he looks like he'd be more at home walking red carpets than designing sets.

"Pretty sure I haven't seen him," I say. As I hand the phone back, I notice the picture's not up in the Internet browser; Russell has it saved in his phone. That's a little bizarre.

"The man's a complete *genius;* his work is so freaking stunning, I can't even deal. I applied to Allerdale the second I heard he was going to be here. I don't even believe I get to spend six weeks with him. Being near him is, like, *inspirational,* you know? I wish I could staple myself to him and soak up his amazingness every second of the day." He gazes down at the photo. "And look at his *hair.* How does he even get it to *do* that?"

Russell's face has taken on a whole new quality, like someone has plugged him into one of those jumper cables and lit him up from the inside, and the picture on his phone starts to make sense. I guess he wasn't flirting with me after all. Well, that totally sucks.

"That's really cool," I say. I hope he doesn't hear the disappointment in my voice.

"If I impress him here, I'm hoping he'll let me assist him on shows in the city this fall. Can you even imagine? I would *die* to get inside that man's studio." The way he says it, it kind of seems like the last word of that sentence should be "pants."

Russell hands me the sidearm and picks up his own stuff. "Sorry, I'm rambling. I should probably get back up to the scene shop. But it was really nice to meet you."

I've only known him five minutes, but I'm already really disappointed to see him go. Even if he's not going to flirt with me, he's still the first person who's been nice to me since last night. All the other acting apprentices feel far away right now, and the lighting people clearly aren't interested in letting me be one of them. Russell feels like the kind of friend I'm going to be allowed to have here.

"Nice to meet you, too," I say. "Thanks so much for the help. See you around?"

"See you, Brooklyn from Manhattan," he says. "Don't worry. You're going to be fine."

He gives me such a reassuring smile that I almost feel ready to go back upstairs and face Zach. Almost.

5

I wake up the next morning when a balled-up pair of socks bounces off my head.

I squint against the light coming through the windows and try to move, but my body won't cooperate. Every single muscle in my arms and legs and back aches like crazy from hauling lights up and down stairs yesterday, and I find a raised bruise under my hair from when I banged my head into a pipe. There is absolutely no way I can make it through nine weeks of Allerdale if I'm going to feel like *this* every morning.

"Brooklyn!" Another pair of socks hits my shoulder; Zoe's obviously not going to leave me alone to wallow. I force myself to roll over.

"Stop," I groan. "Sleeping."

"You have to get up! We have a master class with Marcus this morning!"

I'm suddenly very, very awake. "What? Already? We just got here!"

"I *know*! Oh my God, what should I wear?"

I throw the covers off and stumble over to Zoe's desk, where the electronic call board is up on her laptop screen. Sure enough, the apprentice company is supposed to meet in front of Haydu Hall in an hour. The *whole* apprentice company, not "the apprentice company minus Brooklyn Shepard." Somehow I assumed I no longer had any apprentice privileges since I wasn't cast, but that's not true at all. I still have a chance to make a good impression on Marcus, the person who matters most. According to my mom, he can work miracles; maybe he'll make all the misaligned pieces click inside me and today will be the day I transform from a hesitant amateur into a real actor.

Zoe and I spend way too long getting ready—we want to look pretty enough to be memorable, but casual enough that it doesn't look like we put in a ton of effort. There's no time for coffee by the time we're done, but I have so much nervous adrenaline running through my blood that I don't even need it. We meet up with Livvy and Jessa in the hall, and as we head over to Haydu, the modern steel-and-glass theater where all the musicals are performed, we try to guess what Marcus will teach us. As we pass Legrand, I worry for a minute that someone will see me and report me for skipping lighting crew, but logically I know that's not going to happen. Today I'm not an expendable manual laborer. Today I'm a performer.

About half the apprentices are already gathered in front of Haydu, and everyone looks as apprehensive as I feel. The moment we arrive, the group subtly rearranges itself to center around Zoe, and I realize I'm not the only one who feels her magnetic pull. She seems to know everyone already, though I'm not sure how that's possible. I make an effort to stay right next to her; the closest moon is the one that shines brightest.

Two of the boys come over to hug her, and she introduces them to me as Kenji and Todd. Todd's totally my type—he looks a little like Russell, actually—and I shoot him the flirtiest smile I can muster at nine in the morning. He smiles back, but two seconds later he reaches for Kenji's hand. Of *course*.

"These guys are in *Midsummer* with me," Zoe says, leaning an arm on Todd's shoulder like he's a piece of furniture. "They're also the cutest couple on the face of the earth, in case you haven't noticed."

"There's no way we're cuter than Sean and Dmitri," Kenji says, and they all laugh, including Livvy. I figure that must be a reference to something that happened at *Midsummer* rehearsal, and I hate that after only one day, they've already formed inside jokes without me. Nobody bothers to fill me in.

"So, which show are you in?" Todd asks.

"I'm just in one of the side projects," I say. "We haven't started rehearsals yet."

Kenji looks confused. "But . . . you're an apprentice, right? I thought everyone got cast in *something* on the main stage."

I can feel my face turning pink, but I shrug and try to look like it doesn't bother me. "I guess my audition wasn't as good as I thought?"

"I'm sure it was fine," Kenji says, but he doesn't look sure. He looks like he feels really sorry for me.

"You weren't cast at *all*?" Livvy asks. "Man, I'm sorry. I guess I should stop complaining that I have to play a little boy again."

"So, what, you're spending the whole summer doing *tech*?" asks a redheaded girl who wasn't even part of our conversation, and I wonder how many other people are listening in. I guess it doesn't really matter. Everyone's going to find out eventually anyway.

"Well, I still have my side project," I say. "But, yeah, I am doing a lot of tech."

"Wow. That's *awful*," says the redhead. She moves a little farther away from me, like my lack of talent might be contagious.

Before I can answer, Marcus bursts through the doors of Haydu with a big canvas bag over his shoulder, and everyone falls silent and backs up to clear a path for him. He doesn't even glance at us, and when he hits the bottom of the steps, he keeps going, heading around to the back of the building like we're not even here. We look at each other, unsure of what to do, but nobody moves until he barks, "Are you coming or not?"

We scramble into a duckling-like row behind him, and I wonder if we've already failed our first test. Jessa strides along in front of me, her giant puffball ponytail bobbing up and down. She looks a lot more confident than I feel, but maybe that's because she's so tall. I concentrate on holding my head as high as I can.

Marcus stops on a stretch of flat lawn surrounded by weeping willow trees. "Sit," he orders, like we're dogs, and everyone does. I expect him to lay out what we're going to do for the next couple of hours, but instead, he launches right in like we're already in the middle of a conversation. "Acting is not about *pretending* to be another person. Any actor who tells you that deserves to be blacklisted from every stage in America. Acting is an embodiment of *real life.* When you act, you are not recreating. You are *creating.*"

I'm not totally sure I agree with that. If the actors are supposed to create the play, what's the playwright's job? When we do text analysis and stuff, isn't the whole point that it helps us understand our characters and embody them instead of drawing from our real lives? I glance around to see how everyone else is reacting and see that most people are nodding, including Zoe.

"I had a student once," Marcus continues. "She was rehearsing Lady Macbeth's raven speech late one night in her room. *'Come, you spirits that tend on mortal thoughts, unsex me here, and fill me from the crown to the toe top-full of direst cruelty!'*" The Shakespearean language rolls off Marcus's tongue like it's as familiar to him as a nursery rhyme. "As she said Lady Macbeth's lines, she noticed the dagger-shaped letter opener on her desk. She grabbed it, feeling the surge of power that the blade in her hand put behind her words. She wasn't herself any longer. She *was* Lady Macbeth. She gestured wildly with the knife, heedless of where her blade might fall. She didn't even realize what she was doing until she had already plunged the knife deep into her own leg."

Everyone gasps, and Livvy wraps her arms around her skinny thighs like she's trying to protect them. I wait for Marcus to say something about how dangerous it is to *completely* lose ourselves, even as we *appear* to come apart in front of our audience. But instead he says, "*That* is dedication to craft. That is what I want to see from each and every one of you. If you are not prepared to stab yourself in the leg for art, you will never truly be an actor."

"Um," says a lanky apprentice with hipster glasses. "Was she okay?"

Marcus nods. "Yes, after three hours of surgery. She has a scar that will last forever. I envy her that. Every time she looks at it, she will be reminded what true transcendence feels like. Most of us have scars only on the inside." His eyes sweep around the semicircle. "I need a volunteer."

Under normal circumstances, I would never put myself out there without knowing what I was getting into. Just the thought of standing up in front of the whole apprentice company makes my stomach twist unpleasantly, much worse than it ever does at Family Night. But this is really, really important; half the company already knows I wasn't cast in anything, and I need to prove to them that I belong here. Even if I fail completely, maybe they'll respect the courage it took to get up first, especially after that story about the virtues of being injured. And if I do a really good job, it's possible Marcus will even find a tiny role for me on the main stage.

I put my hand in the air.

Marcus zeroes in on me. His gaze makes me feel like I'm under the superbright light they shine into your mouth at the dentist. "Name?" he asks.

"Brooklyn." My last name is on the tip of my tongue;

maybe Marcus would go easier on me if he knew I was Lana's kid. But it's more critical now than ever that none of the other apprentices find out who my mom is.

"Stand over there," Marcus says, gesturing to a stretch of grass in front of the trees.

I go where he's pointing and face the group, chin up and shoulders back so nobody can tell how thoroughly freaked out I am. "A great actor never loses focus, no matter what is going on around him," Marcus says. "Why is this?"

The redheaded girl who sneered at me earlier raises her hand. "Because you're becoming another person, not playing a part," she says. "Nothing can make you stop being you, no matter what happens."

"Exactly," Marcus thunders, and the girl flinches, even though he's agreeing with her. "Name?"

"Pandora," she says. I catch Zoe's eye, and she raises her eyebrow like, *Seriously?*

"I've never heard it put better," Marcus says, and the girl preens and blushes. "*Nothing can make you stop being you*— not a missing prop or a coughing audience member or a siren going off down the block. Do you understand?" We all nod. "It is time to see if Brooklyn has what it takes to be a real actor." Marcus turns to me. "What was your audition monologue?"

"Ophelia. *'O, what a noble mind is here o'erthrown.'*"

"You will do your monologue now," he tells me. "You will become Ophelia. Your surroundings, your colleagues, and I will cease to exist for you. You will not stop, no matter what happens. Do I make myself clear?"

"Yes, sir," I say.

He moves to stand next to his bag. "Whenever you're ready, then."

I close my eyes and try to let the willows, the summer breeze, the rustling of the other apprentices fade away. I try to forget that all my new friends are watching me, ready to assess how much acting skill I really have, and that I'm so nervous, the tips of my fingers are starting to lose feeling. *You are Ophelia,* I tell myself. *You don't know any of these people, and you don't care that they're watching you. You're not nervous at all. You're miserable and wretched, and you've watched the person you love crumble to pieces right in front of you.* It actually helps me feel more grounded, and I start to think maybe there's something to this "becoming your character" thing after all. Maybe this is something I can incorporate into my performances forever.

When I feel sufficiently Ophelia-esque, I open my eyes and begin, focusing slightly above the tops of the other apprentices' heads. "*'O, what a noble mind is here o'erthrown!'*" I say. "*'The courtier's, soldier's, scholar's, eye, tongue, sword ...'*" Shakespearean language has never felt natural to me, and the words don't roll effortlessly off my tongue the way they did for Marcus, but I've practiced them enough times that I sound reasonably good.

Marcus leans over and starts rummaging through the bag at his feet. Whatever's in there makes a squeaking sound like Styrofoam rubbing together, but I try to ignore it. Where Ophelia is, there's no squeaking sound. "*'The expectancy and rose of the fair state,'"* I continue. *"'The glass of fashion and the mould of form . . .'"*

Something crunches against my collarbone, and I let out a little shriek as cold liquid starts dripping into my cleavage. My hand flies to my chest, and it comes away sticky and wet, sprinkled with bits of something hard and white. And just like that, I'm not Ophelia anymore. I'm Brooklyn Shepard, standing on a lawn in her favorite jeans and purple flats, gaping at the man who's throwing eggs at her.

"What are you doing?" Marcus shouts. "Why is Ophelia touching her chest? There's nothing on Ophelia's chest!"

I close my eyes and struggle to regain my composure, even though I can feel the egg soaking into the cup of my bra. *"'The observed—'* Um, *'the observed of all observers, quite, quite down! And I, of ladies most deject and wretched—'"*

Another egg explodes against my bare shoulder, and I pause to watch as the yolk slides all the way down my arm and drips off my fingers. Pandora giggles, and I begin to hate her with the fire of ten thousand suns.

"Be Ophelia, or what's the use of saying the words?" Marcus roars. "Act, dammit!" He throws another egg at me, and this one splatters across my thigh.

"And . . . *'and I, of ladies most deject and—'* Um, and— wretched—" But the monologue is gone. "I'm sorry. Can I start over from—"

Marcus throws a fourth egg, and this one hits me on the side of the head. At least half the apprentice company is laughing now, and white-hot fury flares up in me. I came here to learn how to *act,* not to be humiliated. I know I'm supposed to trust the process, trust the man who made this festival great. Everyone thinks he's a genius. But honestly, this is ridiculous.

I look over at Marcus—it's no use trying to pretend he's not there now—and try to judge the trajectory of his next egg so I can dodge it. But he's shaking his head sadly, like I've failed him. "Sit down, Brooklyn," he says. "You're done."

I sit back down with the other apprentices and try to pull myself together, but I'm so angry, my entire body is shaking. Zoe reaches out and squeezes my hand, and it makes me feel a tiny bit better, but not much. I send the universe visions of me smashing an entire carton of eggs over Marcus Spooner's smug head and watching the yolk drip off his stupid beard.

He doesn't throw eggs at everyone. While Todd does his monologue from *Twelfth Night,* Marcus lobs water balloons at him. He shoots rubber bands at a tiny girl named Natasha, and she shrieks like she's having her nails ripped out. During Jessa's performance, he sets off an air horn. He stands about two inches from Kenji's face, blocking him from the audience. He holds Pandora's ponytail like reins and turns her head back and forth at random intervals. During Zoe's monologue, he blasts the "I love you, you love me" song from *Barney* on an eighties-style boom box while performing interpretive dance moves. I half hope she'll crack up so it'll feel like we're even, but she doesn't. She doesn't even raise her voice over the music; she just performs quietly for the people who are close enough to hear.

Maybe I could've done that, too, if I'd had more time to prepare. Probably not, though.

Only four people make it all the way through their monologues. When Marcus is done torturing everyone, he heaves a world-weary sigh and slowly packs up his canvas bag. Then he says, "You all know which of your colleagues are real actors now. Watch them and learn to be better." I expect him to explain the next exercise, maybe one that'll teach us about focus, but instead he picks up his bag and walks away.

For a second we all sit there in silence. Then Jessa says, "That's *it*?" and a few people laugh nervously, which breaks the tension. Nobody seems sure if we're allowed to leave or not, but we all scoot toward our friends and start talking in low voices.

Zoe puts a hand on my shoulder. "Hey, c'mere. You've got shells in your hair."

When I was eight, I got Silly Putty in my ponytail while Marisol was babysitting me. It took her nearly half an hour to pick it all out, but I sat there happily the whole time, pleased to have her undivided attention. That's exactly how I feel now as Zoe combs her fingers through my sticky hair, careful not to pull as she picks out the fragments of shell. She's so focused on me that I become hyperaware of how I'm sitting, how loudly I'm breathing, whether I smell like egg. I'm suddenly not positive I put on deodorant this morning. When Zoe finally says, "There, you're done," it's kind of a relief, but I also feel weirdly let down.

It's been more than five minutes now, and since Marcus still isn't back, we decide it's probably safe to leave. As I head toward the dining hall with Zoe, Livvy, Jessa, Kenji, and Todd, I say what I'm sure everyone's thinking: "So . . . that was complete bullshit, right?"

I wait for everyone to laugh and say, *Oh my God, seriously!* But they're all quiet, and then Zoe says, "Well, yes and no."

"What do you mean?"

"His execution's definitely over-the-top, but I think Marcus's theories are actually pretty sound," Zoe says. "I really liked what he said about how acting is creating, not recreating."

"He's one crazy-ass dude, but he's kind of brilliant," Jessa says.

"Really? You guys thought that was a good class?" I try to sound confident, but now I kind of wish I hadn't said anything. From now on, I'm going to wait for someone else to express an opinion first.

"I mean, I don't think he taught us enough," Zoe says. "It doesn't really seem fair to point out our flaws without giving us any tools for how to correct them, you know?" It's big of her to say "us"; according to Marcus, she doesn't have any flaws.

"The whole thing *was* pretty gimmicky," Kenji says. "The guy's obviously supersmart, but I wish he'd show us the substance underneath the flashy stuff. I felt like he didn't bother because we're so low on the totem pole."

I still don't see why everyone thinks Marcus is so brilliant; all he did was distract us. Sutton and Twyla could do that. "What about that whole stabbing-yourself-in-the-leg thing? That was nuts, right?" I say. I want so badly to hear everyone confirm that I have the right opinion about *something*.

"I bet that's not even a true story," Kenji says. "Who even has a letter opener except, like, people from *Downton Abbey*? I think he was making a point about how there should be no limits on what you're willing to do for art, you know? And obviously there *are* limits, but maybe he was trying to tell us to push ourselves. The whole thing was probably supposed to be a metaphor about boundaries?"

"Yeah, that's what I thought, too," Zoe says, and everyone else nods.

This never even occurred to me, and I feel really stupid. "Well, I wish he'd work on his nonmetaphorical boundaries," I say. "I still have egg in my hair."

Zoe shoots me a sympathetic smile. "You got the worst of it for sure. Barney is nothing compared to being egged."

"I know he was trying to start things off with a bang, but I wish it hadn't been you up there," Livvy says. She probably means she's sorry I had to suffer, but what I hear is *I wish it had been someone who could've handled it better.*

"It was really brave of you to get up first, not knowing what to expect," Zoe says. "Marcus is going to remember that."

The rest of my friends agree, and I try to be gracious and thank them, but now I wish I'd never started this conversation in the first place. When someone takes a blind leap into the unknown, it doesn't necessarily mean she's brave. Sometimes it means she doesn't understand what she's up against.

6

My first rehearsal for *Señor Hidalgo's Circus of Wonders* is the next evening, and just walking into the Slice is a little disorienting. It's a regular black-box theater, except that if it were an actual box, it would be the kind two-dollar-pizza places give out to hold a single greasy slice. I can't even tell where the audience is supposed to sit. Pandora and Natasha are chatting with a couple of other apprentices in the corner, but I have no desire to talk to them, so I head over to the circle of folding chairs at the other end of the room. There's an upright piano pushed against one of the walls, and part of me wants to go over and play something to calm me down, but I don't want to be that girl who starts showing off before rehearsal even starts. I'm trying to stay positive—maybe *this* will finally be the Allerdale experience that clicks for me and makes me love performing. But after what my mom said about the quality of the side projects here, it's hard to be too optimistic.

"Hey," says a voice behind me, and when I turn around, there's Russell. "Brooklyn, right?"

"Yeah," I say. "Wait, you're not *in* this, are you?"

"Oh God, no," he says. "Nobody wants to see me perform, trust me. I'm doing the set."

I'm about to tell him I'm pretty sure nobody wants to see me perform, either, but I swallow the words down. "Cool," I say. "Do you know anything about the show?"

Russell sits next to me and stretches out his legs. "Nope. I haven't even met the director or anything. I hope he doesn't want anything crazy, 'cause my budget's only fifty dollars."

"Hey, thanks for helping me with the lighting stuff the other day," I say. "I would've been totally lost without you."

"No problem. You feeling more comfortable now?"

"Maybe a little." I haven't done anything too stupid during a crew call in the last couple of days, but I'm pretty sure that's because Solomon has stopped giving me jobs that require actual thought. Mostly I've been steadying other people's ladders like a human sandbag. At least the other actors who are on lighting crew first rotation show up every afternoon after their rehearsals, so I'm not the only one who's completely clueless.

"It takes a while, but you'll get it," Russell says.

I'm about to tell him I'll probably be assigned to another department by the time I feel comfortable, but before I can say anything, the door bangs open, and a guy in his twenties strides in. His square glasses are askew, and his dark hair is sticking up in a giant poof like he's been running his hands through it over and over. He looks so stressed out that if I saw him on the street, I'd assume he'd been in court all day, trying to get innocent people off death row. He plunks down in one of the folding chairs in a showily exhausted way.

"Gather round," he calls, his hands making weary sweeps through the air, and everyone sits. "My name is Clark, and I'll be your director for"—he pulls out a piece of paper and reads off it—"*Señor Hidalgo's Circus of Wonders.*"

Russell shoots me an incredulous look, and I raise an eyebrow back. If the director doesn't even know what's supposed to be happening in this room, that doesn't bode well for the rest of us.

"This play is a work in progress," Clark continues. "We're lucky enough to have our playwright, Alberto Muñoz, here to work with us and develop the play to suit this particular cast. Alberto, raise your hand." A skinny guy in blindingly white sneakers and slightly too-short jeans raises his hand across the circle, but he keeps his face tipped toward the floor. "Alberto will be here observing as we work together as an ensemble, and then he'll start developing some pages for the next time we meet."

"So . . . there's no script?" asks a guy with chin-length hair.

"We're going to develop the script *together*," Clark tells him, obviously frustrated.

"But, is there, like, anything? What's the play about?"

"It's about a circus of wonders," Clark snaps. He sounds bizarrely angry about it.

"But what are we working on, exactly, if there's nothing—"

Clark cuts him off. "I need everyone to go around and say your names and your special skills."

Nobody seems clear on what a "special skill" entails, but nobody seems to want to ask, either. Natasha says she can sing opera, tap-dance, or do both at the same time. One of the guys can do a back handspring, and another guy can bench-press a hundred and fifty pounds. The guy with the long hair says he can burp the alphabet. Pandora announces that she took a pole-dancing class last year, and I file that information away to tell Zoe later. I have a feeling she'll appreciate it.

When my turn comes, I say, "I'm Brooklyn, and I can play the piano."

Clark nods and makes a note on his pad. "Anything else?"

If the last couple of days have proven anything, it's that I'm not very special or skilled. I shake my head.

"Fine." Clark looks at Russell.

"Oh, I'm not in the show," he says. "I'm Russell. I'm your set designer."

"But there's not going to be a set."

"Well, there could be one, if you want. I could make you one."

Clark sighs heavily. "Using set pieces is insulting to the audience. If they can't use their imaginations, they don't deserve to be in the room. We'll do it all with lighting."

The girl sitting on Russell's other side says, "We really don't have that much lighting equipment to work with. I can try to—"

"I'm not *asking* you; I'm *telling* you," Clark snaps, and she goes silent. He turns back to Russell. "What are your special skills? I'm sure we can use you for something."

"Um. I also play the piano? And I'm pretty good at Auto-CAD and basketball. I don't know if those are special skills. It seems like maybe they're regular skills?"

"Everyone, on your feet," Clark says. "Let's see what you guys can do."

We scoot our chairs back against the wall and stand in a circle. Russell and the lighting designer stay against the part of the pizza slice where the crust would be and talk quietly to each other, and I kind of wish I could join them. Alberto settles himself in the point of the slice, the bite Zoe would save for last, and starts scribbling madly in his notebook even though we're not doing anything yet.

"Let's take some time to explore the space," Clark says. "Touch it, notice it, pay attention to how your body feels moving through it. There's no wrong reaction. Go."

It's so different from our master class yesterday that I actually snort. How is anyone supposed to learn to act here when we're getting such conflicting instructions?

"Is there something amusing, Brooklyn?" Clark asks.

"I, um. I'm just reacting to the space?" I catch Russell's eye, and he puts his hand over his mouth to stifle a laugh.

"Fine," Clark says. "Come on, people. I want to see some motion."

I start wandering around the perimeter of the room, dragging my fingers over the walls. They come away fuzzy and gray with dust; I doubt anyone has cleaned in here since the end of last summer. "Play with levels," Clark calls. "Nobody wants to watch you people *walk* all day." Bench-press guy gets down on the floor and rolls slowly in my direction, accumulating a film of grit and dust bunnies on his black T-shirt. I hop over him a couple of times, and he reacts by changing direction. Pandora rubs her body against the walls, making what she must think is a sexy face. In the corner, the blond guy swings on the rails of the low balcony that lines one edge of the triangle. One of the wooden rails breaks loose, and the guy is left clutching it like a club while he dangles by one hand. Three long nails protrude from the end like the spikes on a stegosaurus's tail.

"Oops," he says. Then he starts whacking the other rails like some kind of deranged percussion player.

"Destruction is creation," Clark shouts over the racket. "That was very organic. Are you getting this, Alberto? I'm giving you gold, man."

From his corner, Alberto nods furiously.

"The floor is made of tar!" Clark shouts so loudly, I jump. "You're wading through a lake of molasses!"

"Wait, tar or molasses, which one?" asks Natasha.

"I don't care! Make it happen! Make me see it!"

I try my best to move like I'm slogging through a lake of tar, but this whole thing is starting to feel more and more absurd. I'm all for theater being a collaborative effort, but it works a lot better when *someone* in the room seems to know what's going on. I tell myself this is only the first day, but there's no way walking around like my feet are sticking to the floor is going to help Alberto write a play.

Over the course of the next hour, we bounce like we're on the moon, run like we're being attacked by swarms of bees, tiptoe like we're on hot coals, and walk like various animals—

peacocks, elephants, cats, kangaroos. All of Pandora's animals involve making the same sexy face. Then Clark has us close our eyes and create a "soundscape." I think he's aiming for something like the time we created a rainstorm in elementary school by snapping and clapping and drumming on our thighs. But since he doesn't lead us at all, it ends up sounding like a lot of random humming and howling and popping that doesn't go together. When I open one eye and glance at Russell, he's got both hands buried in his curls like he might rip them out by the roots.

It's after eleven when "rehearsal" finally ends. Instead of giving us a pep talk about how well we're starting to bond as an ensemble, Clark picks up his clipboard, says, "That's enough," and walks out the door. Alberto gathers his notebook and pens and scurries after him, like he's afraid to be left alone in the room with us. I realize I haven't heard him say one word the entire evening.

The other six cast members and I look at each other for a minute, but nobody has anything to say. After a second, people shrug and start heading out. Nobody bothers to say good night.

Russell comes up next to me. "Well, that was ... something."

"That's one way to describe it," I say. "Your lighting designer friend looked like she was about ready to puncture her eardrums with a fork. I can't say I really blame her."

"Did you know it takes only seven pounds of pressure to rip your ears completely off?"

"Eew, *no*. And I wish I still didn't know that," I say, but at least I'm laughing. "This has seriously been the weirdest week of my life. Marcus Spooner threw eggs at me yesterday."

"What? *Why?*"

"It was at our master class; he was trying to teach us how to focus through distractions or something. He told us if we weren't willing to stab ourselves in the leg for art, we didn't deserve to be here."

Russell's eyes widen. "I'm sorry, I know the guy is supposed to be brilliant, but that is all kinds of messed up."

"I know, right? Thank you!" My voice comes out louder than I expected, but it's so reassuring that someone else has noticed that the emperor isn't wearing any clothes. "When I complained about it to a bunch of the apprentices yesterday, they were like, 'But Marcus is a genius, the whole thing was a metaphor, blah, blah.' I don't care if it's a metaphor! He threw *eggs* at me!"

"Did he actually teach you anything?"

I want so badly to be able to say yes, that even though it was difficult and humiliating, it also taught me lessons I'll carry with me for the rest of my career. I want yesterday's class to have proven that I made the right decision by coming to Allerdale. But it didn't, and I know I don't have to lie to Russell about it. He doesn't expect anything from me.

"Honestly?" I say. "No. Not at all."

"At least egg is good for your hair, right?"

I laugh. "How do you know that?"

"Olivier told me. He says his hair is so thick and soft

because he uses these egg yolk treatments on it. I mean, it sounds weird, but it's definitely working for him. You think I should try it?"

I want to laugh at his intimate knowledge of his boss's hair texture, but it seems too early in our friendship to tease him about his crush. So I say, "I can't say I recommend it, after yesterday. Your hair looks nice as it is."

"Thanks." Russell holds the door for me, and we head across the lawn toward the dorms.

"So, are you going to stop coming to rehearsals, since Clark doesn't want a set?" I ask.

"No, he'll probably change his mind. Plus, watching you all pretend to walk through a lake of tar was pretty glorious."

I shove his shoulder. "Ugh, shut up."

"Don't blame *me*," Russell says. "If you weren't so good at strutting like a peacock, I wouldn't be forced to keep showing up."

He flounces down the path in a ridiculous imitation of my peacock walk, twitching his butt from side to side, and I burst out laughing. "You're a terrible person," I say.

"But you're glad I'm not leaving, right?" He elbows me in the arm. "Admit it. You'd be supersad if I weren't around."

"I would. I don't think I could face this insanity without you."

Russell smiles and pats my shoulder, and the unexpected force makes me stumble forward. He's a lot stronger than he thinks. "Don't worry," he says. "I wouldn't leave you alone in there. I've got your back."

7

By the time I get back to the dorm, the warm, fuzzy feeling of Russell's companionship has worn off, and the futility of my situation hits me like a canoe paddle to the face. I'm not cast on the main stage. The master classes are humiliating bullshit masquerading as brilliant lessons in technique. My "show" is so nebulous that the person *writing* it doesn't even seem to know what it's about. So what am I doing here at Allerdale? Slinging a wrench all summer isn't going to teach me how to be a real performer or help me fit in with my family. I might as well be working at the Pinkberry down the street from my apartment. It would certainly make my back hurt less.

When I open the door to my room, Zoe's on the phone, but the second she registers the expression on my face, she says, "Hey, I've gotta go. I'll call you tomorrow, okay? Love you." She makes a kissing noise and hangs up. "You all right?" she asks. "How'd rehearsal go?"

I drop my bag onto the floor. "I think 'absurd' pretty much covers it?"

"Oh no. What happened?"

I tell her everything, imitating put-upon Clark and silent Alberto and Pandora's sexy animal walks. Zoe listens to the whole thing with wide, sympathetic eyes, but she's also laughing. She has this boisterous, unrestrained giggle that's way goofier than I'd expect from someone so put-together. When I'm done, I flop facedown onto my bed. "I'm glad my pain amuses you," I say.

"No, no, I'm sorry. I'm not laughing at you. The whole thing sounds awful. It's just, you looked *exactly* like Pandora when you did that sexy cat walk. She's in *Midsummer* with us, and that's her fairy walk, too."

"Well, enjoy my impressions while you can, because it's obviously the only acting I'm going to be allowed to do here."

"Aw, don't say that," Zoe says. "It's possible it'll get better, right? When Alberto finally manages to write a script, maybe—"

"It's not going to get better," I say. "The whole thing is a complete joke. Seriously, if they thought I wasn't good enough to be here, they should've rejected me. They didn't have to punish me with *Señor Hidalgo.*"

"Brooklyn, you're obviously good enough to be here, or you wouldn't be here."

She has no idea. "And yet I'm not allowed to set foot on the main stage unless I'm holding tools. I'm not even good at *that.* You should've seen—"

Zoe cuts me off. "Okay, that's enough." She stands up, and

I'm positive she's about to walk straight out the door and find someone better to hang out with.

"I'm sorry," I say. "I shouldn't bitch about this so much. I'll try to—"

"No, that's not the problem. Stand up."

"Why? Are you going to throw eggs at me?"

"Just do it!"

I stand, and she marches me over to the full-length mirror on her closet door. "Shoulders back, chin up," she says. "Look your reflection in the eyes."

I look at her reflection instead. "What are we doing?"

"You're doing what I say."

"So bossy," I complain, but I smile, and she smiles back. Her hands feel warm and steady on my shoulders. I make eye contact with myself, stand up straight, and lift my chin. Even the posture change makes me feel a tiny bit better.

"Good," she says. "Now say, 'I deserve to be here.'"

I turn all the way around and look at her. "Are you seriously making me do *affirmations*?"

Zoe spins me back toward the mirror. "Say it!" she orders.

It seems easier to get this over with than to argue. "Fine," I say. "I deserve to be here." It comes out sounding incredibly sarcastic.

"That is officially the least affirming thing I've ever heard in my life. You have to mean it!"

"But what if I don't mean it?"

"Brooklyn, that's the entire point of affirmations. If you say it enough times, you start to mean it." She points to the mirror. "Again."

"I deserve to be here." I try to sound more confident this time.

"Louder!"

"I deserve to be here!"

"Scream it! Let the whole dorm know!"

"I deserve to be here!" I shout at the top of my lungs, and then I burst out laughing, and so does Zoe.

"Good!" she says. "Now say, 'I am talented!'"

"I am talented!" I scream.

"I am beautiful!" Zoe yells.

"I am beautiful!" I repeat, but now all I can do is wonder if Zoe really thinks I'm beautiful. "Your turn," I say, because I need her to stop looking at me for a minute.

"Okay." She moves to stand beside me and squares her shoulders. "I can act over the Barney song!" she shouts. "I get to play Kim on the main stage! *I got into fucking Juilliard!*"

"I can hang a Source Four!" I shout.

"I have a fantastic ass!" Zoe screams, and then we're both laughing so hard, it's difficult to breathe. It's the kind of laughter that's almost painful, where you feel like your body is barely holding itself together, but the pain is so good, you don't want it to stop. My legs start to buckle, and I clutch at Zoe's shoulder to keep me upright, but she's equally weak-kneed, and we melt toward the floor together in slow motion. That makes everything even funnier, and I start hiccupping. Zoe's face is bright pink and wet with tears.

Jessa opens our door without knocking. "What the hell is going on with you people?"

"We are amazing!" I shout at her at the same time that Zoe screams, "We're hot, talented bitches!"

Jessa shakes her head. "Y'all belong in the loony bin."

She withdraws and shuts the door, and even though I feel weird for thinking it, I'm glad she's gone. I want this moment with Zoe to myself. My roommate buries her face in my shoulder as she struggles to calm down, and her hair drapes over us both like a curtain. When I glance up at the mirror, I like how our reflections look, all messy and sprawled and tangled together.

When she can speak again, Zoe says, "That was awesome. We should do that every day."

"We'd get thrown out of the dorm."

"But we'd feel so good about ourselves!" She giggles and wipes her damp cheeks. "Admit it, you feel a little better now, right?"

"I do, yeah." I don't tell her that the reason I feel better is because *she* sees me as this bright, shiny, better version of myself, not because I actually believe I deserve to be here.

Zoe sits back up. "Seriously, though, being in bad shows is part of the business. Those are your actor battle scars, you know? They're the stories you'll pull out at dinner parties forever. It sucks now, but it'll be hilarious later."

She's right; my entire family has war stories like this, and they're always laughing about them at Family Nights. The whole point of coming here was to be like them, and at least in this way, I finally will be.

"What's the worst show you've ever been in?" I ask.

Zoe settles into a more comfortable position on the floor. "Probably this student-written musical in tenth grade. The girl who wrote it was in love with our acting teacher, and the whole show was basically about him secretly being into her, too. I played her, and my then-boyfriend played the acting teacher, and then we broke up in the middle of the rehearsal process. And the *actual* acting teacher was the director, so it was basically this giant hurricane of awkward."

"Oh God," I say. "That might be even worse than *Señor Hidalgo*."

"Fortunately, my friend Brian was in it with me. I wouldn't have made it through without him."

"I've got an ally, too," I say. "Do you know Russell, that supertall guy from scenic? He's doing our set, and he's really cool. We talked a little bit after rehearsal."

"Oooh." Zoe sits up straighter. "No, I don't know him. Is he cute?"

I picture Russell's warm brown eyes and curls and strong arms. "Yeah, really cute. But also gay."

"Damn. Are you sure? I thought Carlos was gay when I first met him, and ... um ... he is *definitely* not." Her face turns a little pinker, and even though I'm the only other person here, I suddenly feel excluded from the conversation.

"I'm pretty sure about Russell. He knows about hair products, and he's totally into that guy who's doing the set for *Midsummer*. Olivier something?"

"Really?" Zoe wrinkles her nose. "Isn't that guy, like, fifty?"

"He's pretty attractive, though. Russell showed me a picture on his phone."

"Russell has a *picture* of him on his *phone*?"

I raise an eyebrow at her. "I know, right?"

"Yeah, definitely gay. That sucks."

"Why'd you think Carlos was?"

"This is going to sound awful, but he seemed too respectful to be straight. He looked me in the eyes when we talked, instead of trying to peek down my shirt. My last couple of boyfriends before him basically wanted a set of boobs to hang out with."

"Can I see a picture?" I ask.

"Of my boobs?"

I laugh. "Of your *boyfriend.*"

"I know. I'm just messing with you." Zoe pulls out her phone and opens a picture. Carlos has a stubbly beard, squarish black glasses, and those deep parentheses around his smile that are almost dimples but not quite. His teeth look incredibly white against the tan of his skin. Zoe's in the picture, too, wearing heart-shaped sunglasses and pressing her cheek against his. They look totally at ease with each other, and I'm flooded with an irrational wave of jealousy that there are people in the world who know Zoe so much better than I do. I want to skip ahead to a time when we've known each other for years, when we meet new people and they marvel at the depth of our friendship.

"He's adorable," I manage to say.

"Isn't he?" Even though she must've seen the picture a million times, Zoe's still practically glowing as she looks at it.

"How long have you guys been together?"

"About ten months. Are you dating anyone?"

I shake my head. "I was with this guy Jason for, like, five months this past year, but we broke up in April. He was really cute and sweet and everything, but we weren't into any of the same stuff. We kind of ran out of things to talk about."

Zoe nods. "That sucks. I'm sorry."

"It's fine; it was my decision. Plus, now I don't have to listen to my mom complain every single day about how he's not right for me."

"She didn't like him?"

"She thought he was nice. But he wasn't a theater person, and my parents kind of have this thing about how only theater people can really understand other theater people. My uncle's dating this financial analyst, and my mom will *not* leave him alone about it."

"Wait, *everyone* in your family's a theater person?"

"Pretty much."

"Wow, that's crazy. Are they all actors?"

Zoe's getting uncomfortably close to the truth. I wish I didn't have to be secretive with her when she's making such an effort with me, but I can't tell her about my mom right now, not when our friendship is progressing so well. Maybe I'll never have to tell her.

"They do lots of different stuff," I say. "Some of them sing opera or dance or direct or whatever, but pretty much everyone is an insanely talented performer. They all came to Allerdale, and they were all really successful, so that's why it sucks so much that I've basically failed here."

"You haven't failed, Brooklyn. You're being way too hard on yourself."

"We don't have to talk about it anymore," I say, hoping she'll take the hint and drop it.

"Okay." She shifts, and for a minute I'm afraid I've unintentionally ended the conversation altogether. But she just changes position so that we're both cross-legged and facing each other, knees almost touching. "Road trips, love or hate?" she asks.

It's so unexpected that I start laughing. "Um, hate, I guess—I can't drive, I have no sense of direction, and I have a really small bladder. Why do you ask?"

"Because I want to know more things about you."

I feel a small shift deep inside me, a little click, like something tiny has ignited. Zoe, with the Juilliard acceptance letter and the circle of admirers, wants to know more things about *me*.

"Oh," I say, because I'm too surprised to say anything else.

"Now you," she says, and I realize with a surge of happiness that this game could go on indefinitely.

"Okay," I say. "Um, leggings—love or hate?"

"Under dresses, love. As pants, hate."

"Me too!"

"*Cats,* love or hate?" she asks.

"The animal or the musical?"

"The musical."

I feel pretty neutral about it, but I say, "Hate," because I know every self-respecting theater person is supposed to hate *Cats.* "You?" I ask.

Zoe smiles sheepishly. "I kind of love it, honestly. It makes me nostalgic. I used to pin a scarf to the butt of a leotard like a tail and dance to the sound track every day when I was little."

I love that she answered that way. I also wonder if she was testing me.

"Sleeping till noon, love or hate?" I ask her.

"Love," Zoe says. "Sex—love or hate?"

I think about lying again, but that's already backfired on me once, so I decide to go with the truth. "Not applicable," I say.

"Really? You never did it with Jason?"

I shrug. "We did pretty much everything else, but I didn't like him enough for that. I'm certainly not, like, waiting for marriage or anything, but I at least want to be in love." I can tell my face is bright red, and I look down at my lap. "Is that weird?"

"No," Zoe says. "Of course not."

"How about you? Have you and Carlos . . ."

"Oh, yeah. Definitely love." The way she says it, kind of throaty and knowing, makes me feel like she's much older than me.

"My mom's horrified I've never done it," I say.

"She *wants* you to have sex? My mom would be horrified if she knew I had."

"My mom is super-open about that stuff. Like, too much sometimes. I mean, it's cool that we can talk about it, but I don't need to know exactly what she did on the roof of the theater building in college, you know?"

Zoe laughs and says, "Eew," and I feel like we're the same age again.

Livvy knocks on our door and pops her head in. "Hey," she

says, "a bunch of us are going to watch *Mean Girls.* You guys want to come?"

Even though Livvy can't possibly know she's intruding, shattering our fragile, intimate little cocoon, I'm furious with her for a second. I brace for the impact of Zoe saying yes and ending our conversation, but instead she says, "Go ahead and start without us. We're kind of in the middle of something."

I look down and pretend to adjust my sandal so she won't see how big my smile is.

Zoe and I play Love or Hate for what feels like hours. I learn that she loves the Muppets, paella, snow, *The Wizard of Oz,* and George Clooney, and that she hates high heels, jogging, juice cleanses, rompers, and the word "punctual." The game grows steadily more personal, and Zoe confesses that she loves chivalry even though it's outdated, and hates when directors correct the way she's delivering a line, regardless of whether they're right. I wish I could take notes on all the things I'm discovering about her.

When sitting on the floor starts getting uncomfortable, we sprawl on our beds and keep going. We never make it to Livvy's room. I've known Zoe only a few days, but in a lot of ways, I already feel closer to her than to anyone I know back home. There are plenty of people I'm friendly with, but we never have long, charged conversations like this, ones that actually *mean* something. Even after knowing me for years, those girls don't understand the things about me that Zoe inherently gets.

Around one in the morning, I ask Zoe's opinion on the

concept of love at first sight, and when she doesn't answer, I realize she has fallen asleep. I'm disappointed, but I love that she wanted to talk to me up until the very last moment that she could stay conscious. It reminds me of the times Jason and I used to fall asleep on the phone, doing that stupid "You hang up first. No, you hang up first" thing just to continue hearing the sound of each other's voices.

I turn off our lamps and match my breathing to Zoe's in the dark, feeling for the first time like I'm in the right place after all.

I'm exhausted when my alarm goes off at seven-thirty, but I still feel bubbly with happiness from last night's conversation. It's possible Zoe was being nice only because she knew I was upset, but she certainly *seemed* to enjoy our talk as much as I did. If the two of us are going to be good friends, maybe my summer at Allerdale will actually be worth something.

Zoe's rehearsal doesn't start until ten today, and I get ready as quietly as I can so I won't disturb her. I'm in such a good mood that I want to make other people happy, too, so half an hour before my crew call, I head to Kayla's Cakes in town and buy doughnuts for the lighting crew. The decor inside the shop kind of creeps me out—there are mounted taxidermy animals all over the walls and counters. But I'm sure the doughnuts will still taste good, and this gesture might finally earn me some respect from the tech people.

When I get to the theater, most of the crew is already

there, quietly smoking and sipping their coffee. But the second I put my pink pastry box down on the loading dock, everyone starts wolf-whistling and whooping. Douchebands pats me on the back. "Nicely done, new girl. Doughnuts the first week! I didn't think you had it in you."

I move away from him with the excuse of undoing the tape on the box; I want the crew to be friendly, but not *that* kind of friendly. "I mean, why wait when doughnuts are involved?" I answer.

"That's what I always say." Douchebands takes a chocolate one and crams it into his mouth.

Courtney reaches into the box and selects a coconut doughnut. "Congratulations," she says, which doesn't really make any sense, but at least she doesn't sound like she wants to kill me.

"Enjoy," I say.

"Oh, I will."

Solomon shows up and makes a beeline for the doughnuts. "You again?" she asks Douchebands.

He shakes his head. "Not today."

"Who brought these?"

"I did," I say, and I give her a big smile.

"Loud and proud," says a guy with dreadlocks. "Nice."

"Knock it off, Lamar." Solomon turns to me. "I respect a girl who learns the rules quickly. Thanks for the doughnuts."

"No problem," I say, but I'm really confused now. I'm clearly missing something here, but if there was a rule about doughnuts, wouldn't my family have told me?

"Get inside," Solomon says. "The designer's here, and focus

starts in ten minutes. Brooklyn, stick with Courtney today, okay? She'll show you what to do."

"Okay," I say, and when Courtney doesn't roll her eyes, I know I've taken a step in the right direction. I make a big show of attaching my wrench to my belt as I follow her into the theater, and she actually smiles at me. I consider asking her about the doughnuts, but I don't want to look completely stupid in front of her again, so I keep quiet.

Focus sounds like some sort of relaxation exercise my mom would be into, but it turns out to mean pointing the lights in the right directions and attaching gels, thin pieces of plastic that diffuse and color the beams. Courtney and I are assigned to the lights on the second catwalk, and the designer stands onstage, waving his hands around to indicate where he wants us to point them. I'm pretty slow and clumsy with my wrench, and my first couple of lights take so long, I can see the designer getting frustrated. But Courtney is surprisingly patient with me, and after a while, it starts to get easier. Every time one of the guys on the crew walks by, he smiles at me, which is a distinct improvement over the way they've ignored me all week. Courtney keeps snapping at them to leave me alone, and I wonder if maybe she's a little jealous.

By the time the day is over, I've successfully focused a bunch of lights by myself. As I leave, Solomon says, "Good work today," and I actually feel like it's genuine. It's the first time I've left the theater with a feeling of accomplished exhaustion instead of humiliated exhaustion, and all I want to do is tell Zoe about it.

I check the electronic call board on my phone and see that

she gets out of *Midsummer* rehearsal in twenty minutes, so I head over to Haydu to wait for her. The dance studio has a window set into the door, and through it I see the woman playing Titania, queen of the fairies, doing a monologue in the center of the room. Zoe and the rest of the fairies are running and leaping and spinning around her, gorgeous and graceful. When the choreographer stops the girls, Zoe leans over and says something to Livvy, who laughs. It's so unfair that all these people get to spend entire days in this room with her while I'm stuck in the catwalks.

Rehearsal finally ends, and everyone puts on their shoes and gathers their things. When Zoe heads toward the door, my hand flies up to make sure my hair looks okay, and then I immediately feel ridiculous. Why would she care how my hair looks?

"Hey!" she calls when she notices me. "What are you doing here?"

"I thought I'd see if you guys were done before I went to dinner."

"Aw, thanks for waiting," she says, like I have this whole other group of friends I could be eating with instead.

"I forgot my wallet," Livvy says. "Meet you guys there?"

"Sure," I say. As I watch her go, I wonder if being alone with Zoe will feel different now that we've connected on such a deep level. I wait for my friend to give me a hug or say something about how much she enjoyed our conversation last night, but she just heads toward the dining hall like everything's totally normal. I rack my brain for something fascinating to say.

"You guys looked really good in there," is what I come up with.

It's not exactly insightful, but Zoe smiles. "Oh, were you watching? How much did you see?"

"Not that much," I say. "There was a lot of leaping and spinning. It looked exhausting."

"It was," she says. "I could eat, like, six sandwiches right now."

None of this feels any different from how it would've felt yesterday afternoon, which is a little disappointing. I'm trying to think of a way to tell her how much last night meant to me, when she says, "Hey, where were you this morning? I woke up at eight-fifteen, and you were already gone."

"I left early so I could get doughnuts for the lighting people."

Zoe stops walking. "You brought *doughnuts*?"

"Yeah. I thought—"

She smacks me on the arm. "*Brooklyn!* We talked for *hours* last night! Why didn't you tell me?"

"Tell you what?"

"Tell me who it was!"

"I have no idea what you're talking about," I say.

Zoe claps a hand over her mouth. "Oh God," she says. "You don't know about the doughnuts, do you?" She sounds gleeful and horrified in equal parts, and my stomach drops like it does when someone says, *We need to talk.*

"I don't know *what* about the doughnuts?" I ask. "Just *tell* me."

"When you bring doughnuts in the morning, it means you

93

hooked up with someone the night before. It's like insurance. If you give someone a doughnut, they're not allowed to ask you questions, and if they find out who it is, they have to keep it a secret. I can't believe nobody told you."

Everything starts to click into place. The way Douchebands reacted when I said, *Why wait when doughnuts are involved?* Solomon's comment about following the rules. The way every guy who passed me in the catwalks today made a point of smiling at me. I stepped up and claimed those doughnuts like they were an accomplishment. I am officially the biggest idiot in the world. I can't *believe* my family told me about all the best nooks for secret sex but didn't bother to warn me about this.

"Oh *no,*" I say. "Was that in the welcome packet?"

Zoe laughs. "No, of course not. It's not, like, an official rule. My sister told me about it."

"And you didn't think you should pass that along?"

"I wasn't hiding it from you on purpose! I didn't even re-member it was a thing; nobody's brought them to rehearsal yet. I don't think accidental doughnut-buying is usually an issue. I mean, who randomly buys doughnuts for their crew for no reason? Nobody's that nice." She looks at me and smiles. "Except you, I guess."

"And now the entire lighting crew thinks I'm a slut. Fabu-lous." I sigh. "Okay. I'll tell them tomorrow that I didn't know and that—"

Zoe cuts me off. "No, absolutely not! First of all, hooking up with someone doesn't make you a slut. And second of all, why do you care what they think? I'd play it up, if it were me.

You should bring doughnuts again next week. It'll make you seem mysterious."

I roll my eyes. "Yeah, right. Nobody's going to believe I found multiple people to hook up with that quickly."

She looks confused. "Of course they will. Why would you say that? You're totally gorgeous."

I suddenly feel very warm. Is she *flirting* with me? Or is she stating what she believes is a fact? Either way, I can't quite meet her eyes.

She's not flirting with you, I think. *Get over yourself. She has a boyfriend.*

"Thanks for telling me before I made an even bigger fool of myself," I say. "People were so nice to me today that I probably would've started bringing them all the time. God, I'm so ridiculously naive."

Zoe puts an arm around my shoulders and pulls me closer. She's still all sweaty from rehearsal, but I don't even mind. "You're welcome," she says. "Stick with me, and that innocence will be gone in no time."

Rehearsals for *Midsummer* are kicking into high gear when we're called in for our second shot at *Señor Hidalgo's Circus of Wonders.* Since a bunch of our cast members are in both shows, we aren't even able to gather until ten-thirty at night, after the main stage rehearsal is over. I've already been in the theater for twelve hours, fetching gels and moving ladders and refocusing lights, and I'm not looking forward to another useless night of slogging through imaginary tar. But I'm a little heartened when I arrive and see that Clark is carrying a stack of stapled packets that look like scripts. Even having a couple of concrete scenes to read through would make me feel so much better about this production.

But when we settle into our circle of chairs and I look down at the "script" Clark has handed me, I feel the bizarre urge to laugh and cry at the same time.

SEÑOR HIDALGO'S CIRCUS OF WONDERS

my mind is a circus of wonders
wonderful circus of the mind
dark matter in three rings, circling, circling

*(THE ENSEMBLE becomes a series of concentric
circles, pulsing, nesting, pulling apart, linking
and unlinking)*

rings like a ringmaster
rings like a doorbell

(DING, DING, DING, THE ENSEMBLE becomes a doorbell)

rings on my fingers and bells on my toes

(jingle bells, jingle bells)

rings around my mind
like an iron band squeezing, squeezing, clamped
    around my brain
until the pain the pain the pain
the pain turns into rings
rings like saturn
my mind is a circus of planets spinning spinning
    spinning out of control

(THE ENSEMBLE spins out of control spins spins
spins EXPLODES)

```
explosion of light, explosion of the mind
the furious light of a supernova
my mind is a supernova
wonderful supernova circus
```

(THE ENSEMBLE coalesces into a writhing mass of fury)

```
I wonder wonder wonder wonder wonder
wonder wonder wonder wonder
wonder wonder wonder
wonder
```

(THE ENSEMBLE sings)

Okay, seriously, *what* are we supposed to do with this?

I glance up at our "playwright," who's sitting across the circle. He's looking down at his lap, tapping a pen against his leg with one hand and sliding his glasses up and down his sweaty nose with the other. He looks like the kind of person who would spend his time doing something comfortable and safe, like painting model airplanes alone in a basement. He does not look like someone whose mind is a furious supernova. Russell's sitting next to me, and I turn to give him a *Can you believe this?* look. The expression on his face is so horrified, I have to look away so I won't burst into inappropriate laughter.

"Um," says the guy with the long hair from across the circle. "I don't mean to be rude or anything, but how are we supposed to read this? It doesn't indicate who says what."

Clark runs his hands through his hair and heaves one of his world-weary sighs. "It's not a script. It's a jumping-off point. These are prompts, not lines. It's an *ensemble* piece. That means we create it *together*. Right, Alberto?"

Our playwright looks up like he's in the crosshairs of a rifle and nods quickly.

"I think it might be easier if—" the long-haired guy starts, but Clark cuts him off.

"If you want to do things that are easy, you shouldn't be here. On your feet, everyone! Start at the top."

We move our chairs back, stand in a circle, and stare down at our pages of text, but nobody does anything. After about ten seconds, Natasha says, "I don't really get what any of this means. Shouldn't we do some table work first and talk about themes and stuff? Like what Alberto's inspirations were for writing this?"

Alberto cringes back into his seat, and Clark shoots Natasha a death glare. "Who's directing this project? You or me?"

"I mean, you. But I don't understand your directions."

"I don't get it, either," says bench-press guy. "Like, here at the bottom of the page, it says we're supposed to sing. But *what* are we supposed to sing? We haven't had a music rehearsal or anything."

"Sing what you feel moved to sing! God!" Clark's voice comes out high and hysterical. Personally, I feel moved to run out of the room. I send the universe an image of the fire alarm going off so I can go spend this evening hanging out with Zoe, but it remains annoyingly silent.

So I do what I always do when I don't want to participate in a performance. I walk over to the piano, where I feel safe and comfortable, and I start playing. Nothing I know seems appropriate, so I improvise a low, creepy, meandering bass line to underscore Alberto's nonsensical words. Everyone seems to relax a little now that something is happening, and they start reading aloud, talking over each other and trying to make their bodies into doorbells and concentric circles and masses of fury. It's cool that my music is the thing that spurred everyone into action, but the result is still pretty abysmal. Clark nods like this is exactly what he wants from us, but I can't imagine how this random chaos is ever going to become a presentable show.

I stay at the piano for the entire rehearsal, playing with melodies to go with my bass line. I feel a little guilty that I'm enjoying myself over here while everyone else is yelling and contorting and writhing in a pile on the floor, but much more than that, I'm relieved to have found a way out. As I play, I try to remember every detail of the "acting" going on across the room so I can recount it for Zoe later. My body is here in rehearsal, but my mind is already back in the room, doing a dramatic reading of this "script" and reducing her to helpless, tearful laughter. It felt so awesome to have all her attention focused on me when I described last week's rehearsal. I can't wait to make it happen again.

Rehearsal ends as abruptly as it did last time; when Clark has had enough, he scoops up his clipboard and walks out. Alberto drops a pencil as he scurries after him, and the guy with the long hair pockets it on his way out the door. Pandora dials her phone as she leaves, and from out in the hall, I hear her say something about "amateur bullshit" and "meeting with company management."

Russell intercepts me before I can leave the piano bench. "My pain is like the rings of Saturn," he says.

"I feel more like a furious supernova, personally." I slump back against the wall. "What are we going to do?"

"I mean, what *can* we even do? We can't make a play until that dude writes a play."

"Do you think we could get the show canceled if enough of us complained? I'd honestly rather be in nothing than be in this."

"Well, you wouldn't be in *nothing*. What about your main stage show?"

"I'm not in one. Apparently I suck too much to be on the main stage." It's been long enough now that it doesn't hurt to say those words anymore.

Russell scoots me over with his hip and sits down next to me on the bench. "I'm sure you don't suck," he says.

"Trust me, I kind of do."

"Well, I guess I don't know for sure, since I've never seen you act. But you were good enough to get in here in the first place, and it's pretty competitive. Plus, you're a kick-ass musician." He puts his hands on the keys and starts trying to replicate the bass line I was playing. "I love this. Did you write it?"

I've never really thought of the silly little tunes I pick out as *writing* something, and I'm pretty sure nobody's ever called me a musician before, either. To everyone at home, I've always been just an accompanist. "Yeah," I say. "I made it up."

"It's really cool." With his other hand, Russell adds some chords, and they harmonize better than the ones I was using earlier. "What about this?"

"Ooh, nice." I start playing with a melody on the high keys, and pretty soon we've got an interesting little song going, melodic lines twining around each other in this cool, haunting way. Russell and I barely know each other, but somehow we're each able to anticipate what the other is about to do, like we've been making music together for years. My pulse speeds up, and my brain starts feeling busier, somehow, like I'm using more parts of it than usual. I'm always so self-conscious when I'm acting or singing, but it's totally different when I'm at the piano; I'm confident enough that I'm able to laugh off my mistakes like they don't even matter. What Russell and I are doing feels like playing in the most literal sense.

We finish the song by getting slower and slower, tapering off like a music box that's winding down. When the last note has faded away, we sit there for a second, motionless, still caught up in the web of what we've created together. Then Russell says, "That was *awesome.*"

"Wasn't it?" I feel weirdly giddy.

"You're really talented."

I shrug and smile. "Not the kind of talented that matters around here. But thank you. So are you."

"Are you a music major?"

"I don't start college till next year, actually, but I wasn't planning on it. I don't have any formal training or anything. My uncle taught me to play."

"That's cool. Is he a professional pianist?"

"No, he's a producer for the New York Musical Festival. He's really good, though, and we both get a ton of practice accompanying my family. They're all theater people, and everyone gets together every Monday night to eat dinner and get drunk and sing."

"Like, show tunes and stuff?" I nod. "Nice. Today's Monday; they're probably doing it right now."

I hadn't even noticed it was Monday; when you work seven days a week, it's easy to lose track. I picture everyone gathering without me—Marisol's belly getting bigger, Sutton and Twyla growing taller, Skye getting closer and closer to everyone. I must have my feelings painted all over my face, because Russell says, "You miss them, huh?"

"Yeah. A lot, actually."

"Play something for me." He moves over a little so I can have access to the lower keys, but his shoulders are so broad that he's still taking up most of the bench.

"What should I play?" I ask.

"I don't know, anything. *The Sound of Music.*"

I start laughing. "Really? *That's* the first thing you thought of?"

"Shut up and play it!"

I roll my eyes and play the introduction to "Edelweiss," and Russell starts to sing. His voice is rough and untrained, but he wouldn't embarrass himself doing karaoke or anything. Instead of the real lyrics, he makes up his own: "Crazy Clark, crazy Clark, never runs a rehearsal . . . We stand by, wond'ring why. Is this just universal?"

I smile and pick up where he leaves off. "This is so dumb, why'd I even come, when I could be sleeping? Crazy Clark, crazy Clark, you might make me start weeping."

Russell laughs and high-fives me. "Damn. A stellar pianist and a master of parody, *and* you have a pretty voice. You didn't list that stuff under your special skills."

I blush a little and look down so he won't see. "My uncle

and I make up silly lyrics all the time. He loves this kind of stuff. He once produced a parody of *Cats* that took place in a tattoo shop. It was called—"

"*Tats?*"

"Quick on the uptake," I say.

"Was it funny?"

"I thought so. My mom left at intermission. She thinks stuff like that is an insult to real theater."

"All theater is real theater. Except maybe *Señor Hidalgo's Circus of Wonders.*" He puts his hands back on the keys. "Let's do another one."

Russell may not be a performer, but he knows his musicals inside and out, and we work our way through song after song, cracking each other up with ridiculous lyrics. It feels so relaxing and familiar that when Zoe finally texts to ask where I am, I can't believe how late it is. Russell and I have been playing for almost an hour.

"Wow," I say. "I've gotta run."

"Meeting someone?" He says it casually, but I can tell he's asking if I'll have to bring doughnuts for my crew tomorrow. I can practically see him repressing a teasing eyebrow-waggle.

"Just my roommate," I say, but there's no *just* about it. She could be hanging out with anyone at all right now, but she wants to know where *I* am.

"Let's play together again sometime, okay?" Russell says. "This was really fun."

"Definitely," I answer, but I'm already halfway out the door, hoping Zoe will be up for another epic game of Love or Hate.

10

The timeline for the first show of the season is unbelievably short, and tech rehearsals for *Midsummer* start at the end of our second week at Allerdale. I'm excited that I'll finally get to be in the same room as Zoe twelve hours a day, but the performers and the run crew barely get to interact at all. I have only three jobs during the show—carry a chair onstage during a blackout, remove it during another blackout, plug in a set of twinkly LEDs on one of the moving set pieces—but I keep missing my cues because I'm too busy watching Zoe. It's impossible to take my eyes off her as she leaps and spins and climbs the set, which is made of giant, architectural-looking flowers. Her costume is a long-sleeved unitard, but the lighting makes it look like she's practically naked, decorated only with strategic swoops and swirls of glitter. Her hair is down, wound with tinsel and flowers. It doesn't seem possible that this otherworldly creature is the same girl who sat on the floor of our room with me and talked about sex and George Clooney.

Opening night is a huge success. The music and choreography are beautiful, the actors do a phenomenal job, and even though I'm standing in the wings with a headset on, it's easy to get swept up in the magic. When the curtain comes down at the end, everyone behind it squeals and jumps up and down, and despite the fact that I had practically nothing to do with the show, I feel that joyful, relieved swelling in my chest that a good performance always brings on. Zoe and Livvy and a bunch of the other fairies crush into a group hug, and I stand in the dark and watch them glitter.

The moment the curtain call is over, the whole cast rushes the wings and stampedes downstairs to the dressing rooms, chattering and laughing with high-pitched, adrenaline-spiked intensity. Livvy and Kenji and Todd high-five me as they zoom by, and even Pandora spares me a tiny, closed-mouthed smile. I position myself so Zoe will run into me before she hits the stairs, and my heart beats a little faster when I see her approaching. For a second I wish I'd gotten her flowers, but maybe that would've been weird.

"Hey," I call when she's within earshot. "You were really great. Congratulations."

"Thank you!" Zoe throws her arms around me, and I can feel how warm she is underneath her unitard. When she lets go after only a second and moves toward the stairs again, disappointment floods through me. We've barely gotten to connect lately, and I want more of her than this.

"Do you feel like it went well?" I ask, to keep her from leaving. "It looked fantastic."

"Yeah, it felt good!" She's looking back and forth between me and the rest of the fairies, like she doesn't want to be rude but also doesn't want to lose track of them.

"Go ahead," I say, even though it sucks, because I don't want to be the weight that ties her down when she obviously wishes she were somewhere else.

"Okay. I'm gonna go change. I'll see you at the cast party?"

I had assumed the cast party was an exclusive thing for people who were actually in the cast. "Am I invited?" I ask.

Zoe looks at me like I'm crazy. "Um, obviously! You worked on the show."

I'm about to say I hardly did anything, but then I remember I'm supposed to be trying to disparage myself less often. Plus, I really want to go. "Yeah, sure, I'll see you there," I say.

"Great! Common room of Dewald." Zoe blows me a kiss and runs off. Even in the dim blue lights of backstage, she sparkles.

My friends will probably take a while to make their way over to the party, and I don't want to show up alone, so I go back to my dorm to change out of my black run-crew clothes. Even after I'm ready to go, I wait fifteen minutes to make sure I won't be the first one to arrive. It starts to rain as I leave Ramsey, and I jog toward the party as quickly as I can, hoping my hair won't be frizzy by the time I get there.

The Dewald common room is huge, and it's decorated with the same giant, stylized flowers as the set; there must've been some left over. Russell waves to me from across the room, and

I'm heading toward him when a girl I don't know bounces up to me and extends a red plastic cup. "Midsummer cocktail?" she asks. She doesn't seem to care who I am or whether I belong here.

"Sure, thanks," I say. I've never really had any alcohol besides wine, but I guess tonight is a good night to start, so I take a sip. The drink tastes like pineapple mixed with nail polish remover, and I have to struggle not to cough. Hopefully I'll get used to it.

My friends are sitting in a circle on the floor with a bunch of other apprentices and non-equity people, and Zoe scoots toward Livvy to make room for me. Both of them are wearing tank tops and shorts, but they haven't bothered to remove their fairy makeup: lavender lipstick, glitter dusted across their cheekbones, feathery false eyelashes, and so much metallic eye shadow that I'm surprised they can blink. Zoe looks like a burlesque dancer who's ready to get on the subway after her show. Livvy looks like a little girl who raided her older sister's makeup drawer.

Zoe smiles. "Oh good, you already have a drink. We're playing Never Have I Ever."

I'm not a huge fan of games like this—I've never done any of the crazy things people come up with, and I'm not eager to seem boring in front of my new friends. But it would look much weirder if I refused to play, so I say, "Ooh, fun." These kinds of situations generate the stories that will get retold for the rest of the summer, and even if I can't really be part of it, I still want to be around to see it.

"Never have I ever smoked pot in my house while my parents were home," Kenji announces.

Three of the other guys and a non-eq girl with a choppy haircut drink, and everyone else laughs. "You drink if you've done the thing, right?" I whisper to Zoe.

She nods. "Haven't you played this before?"

"I have," I say. "Just checking." After the doughnut incident, I figure it's always safest to make sure of the rules. I want to take a sip of my drink so I'll have something to do with my hands, but then it would look like I was reacting to the pot question, so I spin the cup around and around on the floor in front of me instead.

It's Pandora's turn now, and she makes a big show of choosing her topic. "Let's seeee," she says. "Never have I ever had sex in a bathtub full of ice cubes."

Unsurprisingly, nobody drinks. Pandora looks around, gives a sly smile, and then raises her cup to her lips. Of *course* she would be that person who picks something weirdly specific in order to showcase how adventurous she is. Zoe rolls her eyes, and I know she's thinking the same thing.

"I'm sorry, you've had sex in a bathtub full of *ice cubes*?" says the next guy in line, a non-eq with a face so round, it's almost a perfect circle.

Pandora shrugs like it's no big deal. "It was hot."

"Hot like sexy or hot like too warm?"

"Both," she says. The guy nods slowly, and I can tell he's thinking about doughnuts. He clears his throat.

"Never have I ever had a crush on someone at this festival," he says, then immediately drinks. Pandora flushes with pleasure but keeps her own cup on the ground. The choppy-haired non-eq drinks, and so do Kenji and Todd, who share a sweet little kiss afterward. Russell drinks, and then he glances around the room, like he's checking to make sure no one saw him. I assume he's thinking about Olivier. It must suck when you have to see someone every day but you can't express how you really feel about them.

There's a sudden clap of thunder so loud that I feel it all the way to my core, and everyone squeals. The rain is coming down hard now, and the girl who played Helena in *Midsummer* starts closing the common room windows so the water won't blow in and wreck the decorations. I wish she'd leave them open. We rarely get summer storms like this in the city, and I love the raw power of them, the way they make you feel edgy and dangerous even if you're actually safe and dry.

It's my turn now, so I say, "Never have I ever cheated on my significant other."

One of the non-eq girls half raises her cup, then lowers it, then raises it again. "Does it count if your significant other knew about it and said it was okay?" she asks.

"That's not cheating," Zoe says. "That's an open relationship. Totally different."

"Oh, actually, wait," the non-eq says, and then she drinks anyway, and everyone laughs.

Another flash of lightning bathes us all in blue-white for a split second. The thunder is almost simultaneous, and this time the common room lights flicker and die. Everyone goes "Oooooh!" at the same time, and then we're all laughing and talking over each other much louder than usual, like our noise will chase away the dark. Cell phone screens blink to life everywhere and float around like a swarm of giant, rectangular fireflies.

It seems like our game is over; there's no point in playing Never Have I Ever if you can't see who's drinking. But then the choppy-haired non-eq digs an LED flashlight keychain out of her bag and tosses it into the center of the circle. It's not superbright, but when we scoot in a little closer, it's enough to see each other. Zoe's knee is pressing against my thigh, and I think about moving away to give her more space, but I don't.

"Whose turn is it?" Kenji asks.

"Mine," Zoe say. "Never have I ever kissed a girl."

Everyone but Livvy, Kenji, and I raise our cups. Zoe drinks, and I wonder if her kiss was for a show or a party game or just because she wanted to. I feel bizarrely let down that she hasn't told me that story yet in one of our late-night conversations.

"Never?" Todd's saying to Kenji across the circle.

"Babe, why would I kiss girls when I can kiss you?"

"I don't mean *now*. What about before you came out?"

"I came out when I was ten. You know that."

"I kissed a girl at a Halloween party last year," Pandora announces, though nobody asked her. "We were both dressed as sexy Hermione Granger."

I turn to Zoe, trying to think of a nonchalant way to ask who she kissed, and I find that she's already looking at me. It's probably the weird glow of the blue LED light, but her eyes look a little brighter than usual, a little more mischievous. Before I can speak, she reaches out and puts her hand on the back of my neck, her fingers cool and wet from the condensa-tion on her cup. And then, before I can process what's happen-ing, her mouth is on mine.

I've played Spin the Bottle before, and the kisses are al-ways either quick and perfunctory or incredibly showy per-formances designed to get a reaction out of the group. For a second, I'm positive this is the second kind of kiss; everyone around us starts whistling and screaming the way you do when you're slightly drunk and everything is way funnier than it should be. Zoe doesn't seem like the kind to beg for attention, and for a second I feel used and start to pull away. But she holds me in place, and I'm suddenly not sure whether she's kidding or not. I can't even figure out whether I *want* her to be kidding.

Zoe finally ends the kiss and opens her eyes. For a few sec-onds, she hovers a centimeter away from my lips, still so close to me that her false eyelashes brush my cheekbones when she blinks. I inhale the smell of her foundation and her grapefruit shampoo and her vodka-cranberry breath, and even though my heart is racing, there's nothing in me that wants this mo-ment to end. Across the circle, people are still whooping and hollering, but it feels like there's a barrier between us and them, like their voices are on the radio or underwater.

"There," Zoe says in a quiet voice meant only for me. "Now you've kissed a girl." She takes her hand off my neck and sits back up like nothing unusual just happened.

Because I have no idea what else to do, I pick up my cup and drink.

And then the world moves forward, like Zoe's kissing me

isn't a monumentally big deal. Livvy takes her turn, telling us that she has never hooked up with someone older than thirty, and then the girl on her other side says that she's never lied during a game of Never Have I Ever. But I'm not paying attention anymore. What did Zoe's kiss *mean*? Did it mean anything? Would I be disappointed if it turned out to mean nothing? Livvy hasn't kissed a girl, either, so why didn't Zoe kiss her? Was she looking for an excuse to kiss me?

I grab my phone, turn on the flashlight, and stand up. "I'll be right back," I say.

Zoe touches my ankle, and even that seems to mean something now that it wouldn't have meant two minutes ago. "You okay?" she asks.

"Yeah, of course." I hurry toward the bathroom, and she doesn't follow me.

Once I've made sure I'm alone, I set my phone on the metal ledge under the mirror and point the light at the ceiling so it casts a diffuse glow around the room. I'm breathing so fast, I'm starting to feel a little dizzy, and I brace my hands on the sides of a sink and force myself to calm down. I have no idea why I'm so worked up; I have no problem with girls kissing each other. Women kiss in front of me all the time. Theoretically, I believe nobody is totally gay or totally straight. It's just that I've never applied that idea to *myself* before. I've never even thought about kissing a girl. I certainly didn't expect to enjoy it.

Am I taking this whole thing way too seriously? Maybe Zoe's kiss only seems earth-shattering because it feels amazing to be chosen by someone so important to me. But maybe it wasn't about me at all; she could be the kind of person who will kiss anyone when she's a little drunk. In the morning, maybe she won't even remember that she did it. Or what if it was some sort of joke, something another apprentice dared her to do before I got to the party? I'm not sure I could stand that.

It didn't feel like a joke, though. It felt like she really wanted to kiss me. And if she wanted to do it again, I'm pretty sure I would let her.

I tell myself there's no way that's going to happen. The whole thing was probably a throwaway gesture; everyone here is overly affectionate with each other. Plus, Zoe has a boyfriend, and she's totally happy with him.

But it happened. I'll always know it happened, even if it never happens again.

I close my eyes and replay the kiss in painstaking detail, fixing it in my mind so I can pull out the memory whenever I need it. And then I lean in close to the mirror and inspect myself, trying to figure out if I look any different now that I'm a girl who has kissed another girl. The only evidence I see is a smudge of silver sparkles across my cheekbone. I leave them there. They match how I feel on the inside.

11

The moment I wake up the next morning, I start wondering if Zoe and I are going to talk about the kiss today. I grow increasingly nervous as I tiptoe around her sleeping form and get ready for my crew call, trying to predict whether things between us will be more intense and charged or more complicated and distant after last night. I'm afraid it'll be the second one; Zoe cheated on her boyfriend with me, and she'll probably feel pretty guilty about it now that she's sober. I decide to let her initiate the conversation, if we're going to have one at all. I don't think I could handle seeing a look of pity flash across her face if I brought it up and she had to explain that it can never happen again—or worse yet, that it didn't mean anything to begin with.

I'm a little relieved Zoe hasn't woken up by the time I leave. She isn't around at dinner, either, so I eat with Jessa, who spends the whole meal telling me a convoluted story about her ex-boyfriend. I see Zoe in the wings during the performance of *Midsummer,* of course, but it's not like we can have a private conversation there. She squeezes my shoulder on her way to the stage at the top of act two, and I spend the rest of the show trying to figure out whether there was a hidden message in the brief pressure of her fingers. *Sorry about last night? Don't even bother thinking about it?*

Or maybe *I want to kiss you again*?

I almost miss my cue, and the stage manager has to yell at me before I spring into action and plug in my LEDs.

I get back to the room before Zoe after the show and curl up with a book to wait for her, but I'm not even seeing the words on the page. When I hear her key in the lock, I frantically rearrange myself on the bed so I look as casually cute as possible, propped on my elbow with my hair hanging over one shoulder just so and my tank top riding up my stomach the tiniest bit. I toy with the end of my ponytail and look down at the novel I'm supposedly reading; I want her to walk in and think, *I can't believe how adorable she is when she's not even trying.*

But when I look up and say, "Hey," she doesn't even meet my eyes.

"Hi," she says.

"Did you have a good show?"

"Yeah, it was fine." Zoe drops her bag onto her chair, scoops up a binder from her desk, and starts paging through it so fast, she can't possibly be reading anything.

Is she trying to avoid me? I assumed that the worst possible scenario would be discovering that the kiss meant nothing; I never even considered the possibility that it would bring our entire friendship crashing down. Maybe Zoe confessed to Carlos and he told her to stay away from me. I have that bottom-dropping-out feeling I get when I go on the Cyclone at Coney Island, like my body has moved forward and left my stomach behind.

"How was the rest of your day?" I ask. I try to keep my voice bright and cheerful.

"I had my first *Birdie* rehearsal." When Zoe finally looks up from the binder, there's no embarrassment or anger in her eyes—there's only panic. I've never seen her look vulnerable before, and the way she's struggling to hide it makes her look heartbreakingly young and fragile. This obviously has nothing to do with me, and suddenly I can breathe again.

I sit up. "Was it bad? What happened?"

She sighs. "No, it was fine. I'm just . . . a little overwhelmed."

"Of course you are. Kim's a really big role, and it was your first day."

"I know, and logically, I'm sure I can handle the part. The songs aren't even that hard or anything. We started working on 'One Boy' this morning, and it went pretty well. But then I did 'What Did I Ever See in Him?' this afternoon with Julianna—she's playing Rosie—and she's . . ." Zoe sighs and drops her binder on the desk. "She's so professional. I mean, she *is* a professional, obviously. But it reminded me how much I'm not, you know? I don't even have any real training yet. How am I supposed to keep up with her?"

"Zoe, you're insanely talented," I say. "You'll totally be able to keep up."

"Thanks. I know it'll probably be fine. But . . . this is going to sound terrible, but I'm used to it being easy. I'm used to being the best. It was never hard for me to get leads at my high school. And here I'm, like, *so* far from the best, and it's going to be the same at Juilliard. What if I have to spend the entire rest of my life not being the best?"

A snotty little part of me wants to go, *Welcome to the club,* but I swallow down the words. Zoe has never really *needed* me before, and I want to show her how supportive I can be. Plus, listening to her spill her secret fears is making me feel close to her in a totally new way.

"You have tons of time to rehearse," I say. "The show doesn't open for six weeks. By then you're going to be even better than Julianna."

Zoe smiles at me. "You're sweet," she says. "I think maybe I'll feel better if I go to the practice rooms for a little while and look over what we did today."

"You can practice here. I don't mind."

"No, it's late. I don't want to bother anyone. I'll be back soon, okay? I'll try not to wake you up if you're asleep."

Of course I want Zoe to feel better, but I also don't want her to leave me. Before I even have time to think about it, I'm asking, "Do you want an accompanist?"

"Well, yeah. I'd love that. But nobody's going to be available this late."

"I'm available."

She looks up from gathering her things. "I didn't know you could play."

"Yeah. I'm pretty good, actually."

"It's really nice of you to offer. But I don't have the piano part."

"That's okay," I say. "I know it."

"Seriously? You know all of *Birdie* by heart?"

I shrug. "I mean, I probably don't know *all* of it. But I'm pretty sure I can do your songs."

I love the way Zoe's looking at me right now, like she's eaten an oyster and found an unexpected pearl lurking in the shell. "All right," she says. "If you're sure. Thank you."

She leads me downstairs and into one of the practice rooms, and by the time she closes the door behind us, I'm starting to panic a little. What was I thinking, setting her expectations that high? If I were in my own living room, accompanying Marisol or Christa, I have no doubt I could play most of *Birdie* from memory. But what if I choke in these new surroundings, when Zoe's counting on me? I can't stand the thought of embarrassing myself in front of her.

The room is tiny and windowless and much hotter than it is upstairs, and a bead of nervous sweat slips down my spine. I sit down on the bench and play some scales and arpeggios until my fingers feel limber and relaxed. "Okay," I say. "I'm ready when you are."

Zoe digs her music out of her binder and comes to stand right next to me. If she regretted last night, she'd probably try to keep some distance between us, right? "Can we start with 'One Boy'?" she asks.

"Sure."

I start playing, and by the time I'm through the short introduction, I already feel much better. I do know this song by heart; hundreds of songs are stored in my fingers, in my blood, in my DNA. I could play them while Marcus threw eggs at me. I could probably play them in my sleep.

I've never actually heard Zoe sing before, but the second she opens her mouth, it's obvious why she got into Juilliard. Her voice is sweet and pure, perfect for Kim, and she sings the song simply, without showing off or adding any unnecessary flourishes. When I accompanied Skye a couple of weeks ago, she stared off into the middle distance as she sang, like she was performing for an invisible, adoring crowd. But Zoe sings right *to* me, holding eye contact for so long, it unsettles and thrills me at the same time. If she can make me feel like this in a dingy little practice room, I can only imagine what it'll be like when she's onstage, backed by an entire orchestra. Everyone in the audience is going to fall in love with her. It's so easy to fall in love with someone while she's singing.

And then I start listening to the words.

"One boy, one steady boy,
One boy to be with forever and ever,
One boy, that's the way it should be . . ."

I've been waiting all day for a signal from Zoe about whether last night meant anything, and I think I finally have my answer. She's gently trying to remind me that she's straight, that she has a boyfriend, that they've been together for almost a year. How could I have assumed last night meant anything? She was drunk. I was there. It was a game. There's nothing to talk about.

There won't be any more kisses, and I can't believe how disappointed I am.

Somehow I manage to finish the song, and the second I take my hands off the keys, we both start talking at once. "You sound *awesome*," I say, and it comes out a little too enthusiastic, like I'm trying to mask everything I just thought.

But Zoe doesn't even notice, because she's too busy saying, "Brooklyn, that was amazing. You are *amazing*."

"Thank you," I say, and then I have to concentrate all my energy on not turning bright red.

"Seriously, why didn't you tell me you could play like that?"

"I don't know; it never came up. It's not a big deal."

"It *is* a big deal. You know not everyone can whip out some random musical from memory and play it perfectly the first time, right?" Her eyes bore into me, piercing and bright, like she's really *seeing* me for the very first time.

I shrug. "It's kind of like having a good sense of direction or a good ear for languages," I say. But now I feel like maybe my musical ability *is* kind of a big deal. Why didn't anyone at home ever tell me I was great at this? I've been playing the piano since I was six, and I've always felt like it was a cop-out. The bench was my place to hide. I've never even considered that it could be a place to shine.

"Can you play other shows, too?"

I laugh. "Yeah, of course. I know tons of them."

"Do you know *A Chorus Line*? *Phantom*? *Merrily We Roll Along*? *The Secret Garden*?"

"Sure," I say. "I can probably do stuff from all of those." I wonder if Zoe's imagining long nights locked up with me in this tiny room, singing her heart out while I play. Even if she doesn't want to kiss me again, I want to be indispensable to her in a way nobody else is. I send that image to the universe to help things along.

Zoe shakes her head in wonder. "Man, I can't believe you had this hidden talent the whole time I've known you. Makes me wonder what *else* you can do . . ."

Her voice is edged with the slightest hint of a tease, and I can't tell anymore if we're still talking about the piano. Maybe she wasn't trying to tell me anything with that *Birdie* song after all. The lyrics could be a coincidence; it's not like she wrote them. I wish I could *ask* her how she feels, but I'm not sure how to do that without sounding ridiculous. *Hey, straight roommate with a boyfriend, remember that time you put your mouth on my mouth? Can you explain the subtext of that to me, please?*

I should probably forget about the whole thing. Zoe and I are friends, and that should be enough for me. It was enough forty-eight hours ago. But now that she's standing six inches from me, flushed and glowing and looking at me like I'm something rare and exciting, it doesn't quite feel like enough anymore.

"Do you mind if we do it again?" Zoe asks, and for a second I think she's reading my mind. But when I look at her in alarm, she's holding up the music in her hand.

"Of course," I say. "We can do it as many times as you want."

12

We've been at Allerdale almost three weeks now, and I've settled into the routine. Drag myself out of bed at eight every morning. Slog through nine hours of boring manual labor with the lighting crew. Gulp down some food in the noisy dining hall. Sit backstage with a headset on and watch *Midsummer* for the billionth time. Drag myself back to my room. Lather, rinse, repeat. But the only part of the day that actually matters is from ten-thirty on, when I get to see Zoe. Sometimes we sprawl on blankets on the lawn with the other apprentices or watch movies in other people's rooms, and I know I should enjoy being part of the group. This is exactly the kind of bonding my family has been raving about my whole life. But I'm always relieved when everyone splits up at the end of the night and my roommate and I get to spend a little time alone. Life at Allerdale is starting to feel like one of those nature photographs where one antelope is in focus and the entire background is a blurry wash. Everyone else here is the grass and the trees and the sky. Zoe is my antelope.

We still don't talk about the kiss. I initiate games of Love or Hate and try to trick Zoe into saying something revealing, but she never does, and I'm too scared to ask her about it outright. When we're with our other friends, I compulsively dissect the way she interacts with them. Does she touch me more or less than she touches everyone else? When she loops her arm through mine, is it laden with meaning? Does she smile at Kenji and Livvy the same way she smiles at me? Most of the time, there's no difference in how she treats me, and every few days, I decide our moment in the Dewald common room was a fluke, and I vow to stop thinking about it. Maybe I've blown it out of proportion. Maybe I didn't even like it as much as I remember.

But every time I give up, Zoe turns to face me in the dark in those quiet moments before sleep and tells me something incredibly personal, and I start to wonder all over again if I'm special to her somehow. After she falls asleep, I stare at the ceiling and repeat her stories to myself so I won't forget a single detail—the day she lost her virginity, the way she held her grandmother's hand the night she died, the moment she realized she wanted to be an actor. She wouldn't entrust such important memories to just anyone, right?

I spend my days collecting stories to tell Zoe in return. The humiliating things that happen during my crew calls don't bother me nearly so much once I craft them into narratives that will make her laugh, even the way Douchebands keeps wiggling his eyebrows at me and talking about how he's hungry for doughnuts. When we spend our third *Señor Hidalgo* rehearsal learning basic sleight of hand so we can pull objects out of each other's ears, I'm able to laugh it off and concentrate on how I'll present it to her. After rehearsal, Russell catches me and asks if I want to play the piano for a while, but I tell him I have plans and head back to the room. I don't want to forget any of my good lines before Zoe has heard them.

But when I open the door, she's pacing the room and texting furiously, eyes wide and manic. "Did you *hear*?" she breathes.

"Hear what? What happened? Are you okay?"

"You're not even going to believe this. We have another master class tomorrow, and it's with"—she pauses for effect—*"Lana. Blake. Shepard."*

"What?" I say. "Are you serious?"

"I *know*, right?" Zoe flops onto her bed and hangs off it upside down so her hair trails onto the floor. "Holy shit, we get to meet Lana Blake Shepard tomorrow, Brooklyn. *Lana Blake Shepard.*"

I really wish Zoe would stop saying her name. "Where did you hear that?" I ask. Maybe it's another one of those wild rumors that are always flying around Allerdale. The other day, someone told me Rob Lowe was going to be in *Macbeth.*

"It's on the call board!"

I grab my laptop and pull up the electronic call board, and there it is in print: "Monday, July 14, apprentice company: vocal performance master class with Lana Blake Shepard, 1 PM."

"Oh God," I manage to choke. This is bad. This is so, so bad.

"What do you think we'll do with her?" Zoe asks. "Do you

think she'll like us? Should we go downstairs and practice our audition songs?"

I'm not even aware of having stood up, but I find myself holding my hoodie and my phone and moving toward the door. I have to talk to my mom immediately, and I definitely can't do it in here. "Where are you going?" Zoe calls. "I already told the other girls. Livvy's totally flipping out."

"I'm . . . I'll be right back," I say.

"Is everything okay?" she calls after me, but I let the door close and pretend I haven't heard her.

My mind spins itself into a froth as I head downstairs and out onto the dark lawn. I've misled my mom into thinking I'm in *Bye Bye Birdie.* I've misled everyone at Allerdale into thinking I'm a regular, worse-than-average actor who got unlucky with casting, not the freakish, talentless offspring of one of the country's best vocal coaches. By this time tomorrow, my cover will be blown with everyone, including Zoe. I've spent weeks trying to build up the trust between us, and when she finds out I've been keeping something so important from her, she might never forgive me.

I send the universe images of my mother having a fight with Marcus, of her Zipcar breaking down on the way to Allerdale, of her waking up tomorrow with a horrible case of laryngitis. But it doesn't help like it usually does, and I'm finding it more and more difficult to breathe. Why was I stupid enough to think I could keep anything a secret in a place like this?

When I finally manage to dial the phone, my mom picks up on the first ring, almost like she was expecting me. "Hi, sweetheart!"

"Mom. Why didn't you *tell* me?"

"Tell you what?" I can picture her wide-eyed, fake-innocent expression.

"That you're teaching here tomorrow!"

She squeals. "They finally announced it! I've been absolutely *dying* to tell you, but I wanted it to be a surprise. Isn't it wonderful?" When I don't respond, she says, "Brookie? You're not upset, are you?"

I'm about to say that I'm *very* upset, but it's not like I can explain why. "No, of course not," I say. "I'm really glad you're coming. I just wish I'd known so I could prepare."

"Oh, you don't need to have anything prepared in advance," she says. "You've done all these exercises before."

I try to figure out the best way to ask her to pretend we don't know each other while she's here, but then she says, "I can't wait to see you, sweetheart. I miss you like crazy," and I can't do it. She would assume I was ashamed to be associated with her. How can I let her think that, when I'm the shameful one in this equation?

So instead, I say, "I miss you, too."

"I'm teaching a class for the non-equity company right after yours, but I thought we could have dinner in the evening. Does that work for you? I know it's last-minute, but I was hoping to have some time alone with my girl."

Under normal circumstances, I'd love to have dinner with my mom. But twisting the truth on the phone is nothing like sitting across a table and lying straight to her face. I can try to avoid the topic of *Birdie* entirely, but I'm pretty sure anecdotes about *Señor Hidalgo* won't fill an entire meal. She's going to find out I wasn't cast, and I'll have to watch all the pride and excitement drain out of her face as she realizes her only kid is a liar and a failure.

I'm about to tell her I won't be able to make it because of an important rehearsal, but then I have a better idea. If I give my mom something else exciting and shiny to focus on, maybe I can keep the conversation away from my fictional main stage debut after all. "Can I bring my roommate?" I ask.

"The Juilliard roommate?" I can tell Mom's practically salivating, already preparing to add my friend to her entourage of talent. "Of course you can, Brookie. That's a wonderful idea. I can't wait to meet her."

I picture Zoe attending Family Night in my living room every week long after I've left for college, and a wave of jealousy hits me hard. But I force the image out of my head; I'll worry about that when it happens. Right now, I need a distraction, and Zoe is a perfect one.

"Great," I say. "I think you guys will really like each other."

"I'll make us a reservation at Spindrift in town. I love you, sweetheart. See you tomorrow."

"Love you back," I say, and then she's gone.

I stand there on the lawn for a couple of minutes after I hang up and try to pull myself together. Out in front of one of the other dorms, some non-eqs are practicing a song from *Dreamgirls,* and their voices sound ethereal in the quiet night air. When they mess up, they laugh and talk quietly and then try the harmony again. *This* is what I always pictured Allerdale would be like—a place filled with music and joy, where you can sing outside at night without the slightest hint of embarrassment, even if everyone can hear you. I thought this would be the place where I finally found myself, not just another place I'd have to hide.

There's loud, happy music on in our room when I come back in, and Zoe's shaking her butt as she digs through her dresser. "Hey, where'd you go?" she asks.

I take a deep breath. "Zoe, I have to tell you something."

She must hear the weight in my voice, because she turns off the music. "What's going on? Are you all right?"

"I'm fine. I should've told you this before, and I'm really, really sorry that I didn't, but ... Lana Blake Shepard is my mom."

Zoe sits down on the edge of her bed and blinks at me. "Wait. Seriously?"

"Yeah."

"Oh my God. Oh my *God*." She shakes her head like she's struggling to take this in. "Wow. Why didn't you *say* something?"

"I didn't want anyone to know," I say. "I was embarrassed."

"How is that *embarrassing*? She's, like, the coolest person ever."

"No, I mean, *she's* not embarrassing. But it's really embarrassing that she's my mom and I'm ... me. Everyone knows I wasn't cast in anything, and once people find out we're related, they're going to assume I'm here because she called in a favor." I swallow hard. "You're probably thinking that, too. It's okay if you are."

"No, of course not," Zoe says, but I'm not sure whether to believe her. I can feel all those *I deserve to be here*s packing up and slinking quietly out of the room.

"I wanted people to get to know me as *me,* not as Lana Blake Shepard's daughter, you know? Like, I know this girl whose dad died when she was twelve, but she never tells people about it until she knows them pretty well because she doesn't want to be 'the girl with the dead dad.'"

Zoe looks at me like I'm nuts. "This is *so* not the same thing."

"No, I know. I'm not explaining it well. I'm not saying my mom is, like, a tragedy. But it's really easy to get defined by one thing. Are you pissed I didn't tell you? Please don't be mad."

"I'm not *pissed,* Brooklyn. I just think it's a little weird that you lied about it."

"I didn't really lie. Nobody asked me if we were related. You asked if she'd done a workshop at my school, and I said no, because she hasn't." It's a lame excuse, and I know it.

Zoe shrugs. "Whatever. All I'm saying is, if Lana Blake Shepard were my mom, I'd tell *everyone.*"

Of course you would, I want to say. *Nobody would judge you, because you're the kind of daughter she deserves.*

"I can't believe I didn't figure it out on my own," she continues. "I feel so dumb now. I know your last name, and you kept talking about how you come from a family of theater people. What is it like living with her? Is it amazing? I can't even imagine."

I hate that she's asking the same question Skye asked

when she first met me, the same question *everyone* asks. I don't want anything about Zoe to be unsurprising. "I don't know; it's normal. She's the only mom I've ever had. I don't have anything to compare it to." It comes out a little harsher than I intend, and I sigh and sit down on my bed. I have to pull myself together. I was so worried about this revelation changing the dynamic between Zoe and me, but now I'm the one acting bitchy and making everything weird.

"Listen," I say more quietly. "My mom and I are having dinner tomorrow after she's done teaching all her classes. Do you want to come with us? I'd really love it if you would. She says she's looking forward to meeting you."

"She said that?" Zoe's eyes light up, and it hurts to see that kind of rabid interest on her face and know it has nothing to do with me. When Lana Blake Shepard is on the table, I'm no longer the most interesting person in the room, even when I'm the *only* other person in the room. "I'd love to have dinner with you guys. Thank you so much!"

Zoe springs off the bed and throws her arms around me like everything's suddenly fine between us again, but I can't even enjoy her affection because I feel like I bought it. I probably don't even deserve it; I'm using one person I care about as a sparkly, distracting bauble and another as a lure. I'm actually kind of a horrible human being.

I'm about to confess one last thing—that I need Zoe to pretend I'm in *Birdie* while we're at dinner tomorrow—when she says, "Have you told the other girls? Livvy's going to lose it."

I shake my head. "I was hoping maybe I wouldn't have to?"

"What, you want me to tell them?"

"No, I mean, maybe they don't have to know at all. Maybe my mom will treat me like everyone else, and then you and I can say we're going into dinner in town, and—"

"Brooklyn, they're not stupid. They're going to figure it out."

I put my head in my hands. "They're going to hate me."

"They're not. I don't hate you."

"But they don't know me like you do."

Zoe sits down on the end of my bed. "I'm sorry, but I think you're going to have to own it," she says. "If you don't tell them and then they figure it out, it'll be much worse than if you said something, right? Just act like it's not that big a deal, and maybe that's how they'll act, too."

"It's *not* that big a deal," I say.

Maybe if I repeat it enough times, I can convince myself it's true.

13

I mean to tell my other friends about my mom. I really do. But I keep putting it off, and by the time we're walking to Haydu Hall for class the next day, I still haven't said anything. Zoe keeps looking at me like, *What are you waiting for?* But I think there's still a chance I could get away with this, and I don't want to ruin everything if I don't have to. Every time one of my friends jokes around with me or asks my opinion about something, I soak it up and try to fix the feeling of camaraderie in my mind. If things don't go as I want them to, this might be the last time I'm allowed to be part of the group.

My plan is to drop my friends off in the classroom, say I'm going to the bathroom, and then wait for my mom in front of the theater—she loves making a grand entrance, so she's always late to everything. I figure we can get all the gooey "I love you, I missed you" stuff out of the way in private, and then she'll treat me like any other student the rest of the day.

I almost believe this is going to work, that everything's going to be fine.

And then we enter room 214, and Livvy whisper-screams, "Guys, that's her!"

My mom turns away from the piano, where she's been chatting with Pandora. When her eyes land on me, she breaks into a nine-thousand-watt smile and holds out her arms.

For a split second, I consider turning away and pretending I don't know her. It's possible she'd get the message and back off. But that's completely insane; that's not the person I want to be. So my mom is famous. Fine. Zoe's right; it's time for me to own it. If my friends think I bought my way into the company, I'll prove them wrong by rocking this workshop. My mom already told me I'll be ahead of the game today. I'll show everyone I do have Lana Blake Shepard's genes in me after all.

I deserve to be here, I whisper inside my head. And then I walk straight into my mom's arms.

"Brookie," she croons as she wraps me up in the folds of her voluminous dress. "I've missed you so much."

Despite all the stress her presence is causing me, she's my mom, and I love her, and it really is great to see her. I breathe in the familiar smell of her lotion and the cinnamon incense sticks she keeps in her closet.

"Hey, Mom," I say a little more loudly than necessary, in case anyone is confused.

I once saw one of those charts psychologists give autistic kids to help them parse people's facial expressions—cartoon face after cartoon face in neat little rows, labeled "angry" and "scared" and "sad" and "excited." When my mom finally pulls away and I look out at the rest of the company, it's a lot like scanning one of those charts. Livvy, Jessa, Kenji, and Todd are staring at me with total shock and disbelief, like they're not exactly sure who they've been hanging out with all this time. Pandora looks like she wants to punch me, but she always looks like that. Zoe has a huge smile on her face, and for a second I think she's proud of me for stepping up, but then I realize her eyes are firmly fixed on my mom. I don't see any expressions I'd label as "supportive."

"Is she for real?" Jessa mutters to Livvy, and I pretend not to hear.

My mom is totally oblivious. "Hello, everyone!" she says. "I'm Lana, and I'm thrilled that my dear friend Marcus has invited me to teach your vocal performance master class. I've had the privilege of teaching several Allerdale apprentice companies, but this one is particularly special to me, for obvious reasons."

Jessa leans over and whispers something to Zoe, and my roommate gives a half shrug and mouths, *I'll tell you later.*

"We'll begin with a guided relaxation exercise," my mom says. "Everyone lie down on your backs, close your eyes, and concentrate on my voice."

My friends will pepper me with whispered questions if I go anywhere near them now, so I lie down right where I am, next to Pandora and Natasha. My mom kicks off her shoes and starts pacing the room, and the sound of her barefooted gait is as familiar to me as the Manhattan traffic that constantly rushes by my bedroom window. "To attain optimal vocal technique, every muscle and tissue in your body must be a relaxed, supple resonator," she says in a lulling, steady voice. "We're going to relax each of our muscles, one by one. Start at the very top of your head. Picture your scalp melting like an Italian ice on a hot day. . . ."

My mom works her way through every muscle in the body—"Relax your abdominals. Let them sink right into the floor. . . . Relax your psoas. . . . Relax your vaginal muscles, if you have them. . . . Relax your sphincter. . . ."—and I try my best to get caught up in her spell and let go. But my mind is already skipping ahead to the exercises we're going to do next. She'll probably ask me to demonstrate something for the class. I let my leg muscles melt into the floor and prepare to embrace that opportunity, even though my stomach is tying itself into knots the way it always does when I have to sing at Family Night.

Then again, no matter what happens, this master class can't possibly be as bad as the last one.

When we're totally relaxed, we form a semicircle around the piano, and I position myself next to Zoe. Mom makes us yawn, paying attention to the way our airways open up. She makes us tense our shoulders like we're carrying heavy suitcases and then drop them. We shake our heads like horses as we do lip rolls to keep our neck muscles from tensing. I can tell some people are getting antsy to show off how well they can sing, but I like going back to the basics and reminding myself where my voice is supposed to come from.

When we finally do start to sing, we begin with simple arpeggios. "Feel the connections between the notes," my mom calls as she circles the room. "Pretend you're pulling a long, warm strand of taffy straight up from your diaphragm and out of your mouth." She pauses next to Pandora and lays a hand on her shoulder. "Not so much vibrato, sweetheart. These exercises are for you. There's no need to impress anyone." Pandora looks like she's swallowed a mouthful of lemon juice, and I have to bite my tongue to keep from laughing. Mom pauses next to Zoe for longer than usual, and when we're done, she says, "*Lovely,* dear." My friend shoots me an ecstatic smile, and it hurts to know I've never made her that happy.

The exercises get more and more complex over the next twenty minutes, and then Mom announces that we're going to take a short break. I'm not ready for my friends to confront me yet, so I link my arm with Zoe's and steer her toward the front of the room instead of heading out into the hall. "Mom, this is my roommate, Zoe," I announce.

"Of *course*! I should've known you'd be the one with the best tone in the room." My friend holds out her hand, but Mom ignores it and pulls her into a hug. When she lets go, Zoe looks so overwhelmed, I'm afraid she might faint. "I'm so thrilled to meet you," my mom says. "Thank you for being such a good friend to my Brookie."

"Yes. I mean, thank you! I mean, you're welcome!" I've never seen Zoe starstruck before, and it's completely adorable. Her words tumble out and trip over each other as she says, "This is seriously the best voice class I've ever had. I mean, I'm not saying my voice coach at home is bad. She's actually really good, but this is better? So thanks." She laughs. "Sorry."

My mom smiles. "Your coach taught you very well. You're extremely talented."

"Thank you!" Zoe looks at me like, *Can you believe this?*

"I hear you're going to Juilliard in the fall?" Mom says.

"Mm-hmm. I'm so excited."

"You're going to be a star," Mom tells her. "Juilliard is exactly where that voice belongs."

"I . . . *Wow.*"

My mom squeezes my friend's shoulder. "I've got to run to the ladies' room, but we'll have plenty of time to talk at dinner."

"I'm going to come with you, actually," Zoe says, and she follows my mom out of the room. I don't really want to listen to them flatter each other anymore, but I trail behind them anyway. As long as my mom is within earshot, nobody's going to confront me about her.

When class resumes, Mom hands out copies of "Anything Goes" by Cole Porter. We sing through the song a few times together, and when we all sound confident, my mom says, "As you see, anyone can learn a song. The notes, the words—those aren't difficult. The real meat of being a singer lies in being able to bring your own intentions and emotions to the text. Sometimes you discover things about a character that aren't apparent in the lyrics, and it's important to be able to express those things as clearly as what's on the page. What I'd like you to do is take 'Anything Goes' and create a narrative behind it, something that gives it *intention*. Are you singing it to your uptight mom so you can convince her to let you wear something revealing out of the house? Are you singing it to your girlfriend, who's about to dump you for another man? Think about which words to stress. Think about active verbs.

'Seduce.' 'Placate.' 'Dominate.' Let's take ten minutes to work, and then we'll perform for each other." She makes it sound like an adventure.

I've done this exercise a couple of times before, and I usually pick a jokey active verb that doesn't reveal anything about me. But today I want to do something that proves I belong here. I decide to sing about exactly that: proving myself, proving it wasn't all a lie when I screamed *I deserve to be here* into the mirror. *I may not have been a superstar right out of the gate,* I'll tell the apprentice company through Cole Porter's words, *but I have something to offer. I am worthwhile.*

I label the top of my handout with the word "VALIDATE."

I'm pretty sure my mom is going to pick me to go first, so I'm extra careful and deliberate about my emotional arc. By the time the ten minutes are up, I have some pretty solid ideas for how to make this song about me. When my mom gathers us back around the piano, my heart starts pounding and my lyrics sheet grows damp in my sweaty hand, but I tell myself I can do this, that I *want* to do this. If I don't make a good impression on the other apprentices now, I'll probably never have another chance.

"Let's get started," my mom says, and her eyes sweep over the group. When they land on me, I shift my weight and prepare to get up, even though I'm so nervous now that I feel a little dizzy. But then her gaze moves to my right and settles there.

"Zoe, would you like to go first?" she asks.

Okay, this is fine; I didn't really want my mom to single me out or give me special treatment. Guests always get to go first on Family Night, and this is kind of the same thing. Maybe she didn't want someone seasoned to go first and influence the rest of the group. But as Zoe moves to the front of the room, looking excited and full of emotional arcs, I can't help thinking there's something else going on here. Maybe my mom *does* want to start with the strongest example, and she knows I'm not the right person to deliver it.

"Should I tell you my active verb first?" Zoe asks.

"You can go ahead and sing." Mom turns to the rest of us. "Let's see if we can guess Zoe's intention."

The accompanist starts playing, and Zoe closes her eyes. When she opens them again, her whole physicality is different—she looks hopeful but vulnerable and unsure. Even though "Anything Goes" is a bouncy, confident song, Zoe sings it hesitantly, but with an undercurrent of quiet, tentative flirtation woven through every line. It's like she's trying to gauge someone's interest in her, but in such a subtle way that it wouldn't be too embarrassing if she were rejected.

My mom usually doesn't believe in applause during class—she says it changes the energy of the space—but she's the one who starts clapping when Zoe is finished. "That was marvelous," she says, and my friend's smile lights up the room. "You brought a whole new set of emotions to that song. Well done, Zoe." She turns to us. "Who wants to tell us what you thought Zoe was conveying?"

Livvy raises her hand. "She kind of made the lyrics sound like, 'I think you might like me, but I'm not totally sure.'"

Zoe beams. "That's exactly what I was going for!"

"Good," my mom says. "This is a wonderful example of

how a singer can really make a song her own. What was your active verb, Zoe?"

"My verb was 'assess,'" Zoe says. For a split second she glances at me, but I can't tell if it's on purpose.

My mom picks Todd next, and he sings the song like he's landed in a foreign country and has absolutely no idea what's going on; his verb is "bumble." Jessa sings it supersarcastically and explains that her verb is "scorn" and she's singing to a guy who cheated on her. Pandora unsurprisingly picks "seduce" and sings the song like she's trying to convince someone to cheat. Everyone sounds really, *really* good, and the longer I sit there waiting for my turn, the less confident I feel. Each time my mom calls up a new person, I find myself thinking, *Don't choose me, don't choose me.* I start to wonder if she's saving me for last. I hope she's not; I'm not sure how long I can hold this much tension in my body before something snaps.

I'm still waiting for my turn to perform when the choppy-haired non-eq from Never Have I Ever opens the door. "Oh, sorry," she says. "We'll wait in the hall."

My mom looks at her watch. "Wow. How is it three o'clock already?" she says, and I take a normal breath for the first time in an hour. "Time flies when you're surrounded by talent, I guess. Thank you all for giving me the privilege of listening to your unique points of view. It was such a pleasure to work with you."

I know I should be upset right now, but all I feel is relief that I don't have to sing in front of these insanely talented people. If I'm honest with myself, the second impression I made probably wouldn't have been any better than my first.

Everyone else here pulled off way better performances than I could've managed, even though I'm the only one who has done the exercise before. No matter how hard I try or how many master classes I take, I'm never going to be as good as they are. That should inspire me to work even harder, the way listening to Skye did on my last Family Night at home. But more and more, the thought of struggling toward something I'll likely never achieve is starting to feel exhausting. The entire point of coming here was to grow as a performer, but maybe nothing—not even Allerdale—is going to make me want this like I should.

If I never make it as an actor, will I be exiled from Family Night? I think about my mom saying, *Oh, my daughter? She's so mainstream. She's not like us,* and it stings like crazy. But it hurts just as much to lie and make excuses for myself and pretend to love something because I'm genetically predisposed to love it.

I'm so deep in thought that I don't even realize my mom's next to me until her hand lands on my arm. "That went so well, didn't it?" she says. "What remarkable people. You're so lucky to be in this group of apprentices, Brookie." She doesn't say, *You could learn so much from them,* but I hear it anyway.

"Yeah, definitely," I say, and it comes out sounding flat.

"Hey." She tilts my face toward her. "What's the matter?"

I can't tell her what I'm thinking, so I say, "Nothing. I just hoped I'd get a chance to perform, that's all." If I were a real Shepard, that's what would be bothering me.

My mom rubs my back. "I'm sorry, sweetheart. I didn't expect to run out of time. But you've done this exercise before, and this is the only chance I'll ever get to work with your classmates. You can perform for me later, if you want."

"No, that's okay."

"Well, the offer stands if you change your mind. I hope you're not too upset."

"I'll be fine," I say. "Have a good time with the non-eqs."

On the way out the door, I toss my handout labeled "VALI-DATE" into the trash.

14

I leave the classroom before my friends are done gathering their things, slip into the bathroom, and crouch down in the corner of the handicapped stall where nobody can see me. I'm going to have to face everyone sooner or later, but right now I'm feeling too fragile. I send the universe an image of my friends telling me it doesn't matter who my mom is or that I lied, that they like me for me. But I know deep down that's probably not going to happen. Not everyone is as understanding as Zoe.

As if I've summoned her, the bathroom door opens, and I hear Zoe's voice. "Brooklyn? You in here?"

I'm about to answer, but then I hear Jessa. "Why do you care? I don't get why you even hang out with her."

"She's funny and smart and supersweet," Zoe says. "And right now she's really upset, so be nice to her, okay?"

"*She's* upset? *We're* the ones who should be upset. Did *you* know Lana Blake Shepard was her mom?"

"I found out last night," Zoe says. "Why does it really matter, though?"

"Are you serious right now? It matters because she obviously bribed her way into this festival! I have tons of supertalented friends who didn't get in here, and *that* spoiled brat is taking up space because Marcus is friends with her mommy."

"Jess, you don't know that," Livvy says.

"Why else would she possibly be here? We've seen zero proof that she can actually sing or act or dance. She couldn't even get a part as a freaking *spear-carrier.*"

"It's not her fault she didn't get cast," Zoe says. "Plus, she's an amazing pianist. You should seriously hear her play."

The sink goes on, and Livvy says, "What is up with my hair today?"

Jessa ignores her. "If she's so good at music, she belongs at Interlochen! Allerdale is for actors, and she is *not* an actor. Her own mom didn't even want to watch her perform. Didn't you see how she called on everyone but her?"

"Brady and Adam didn't go, either," Livvy says.

"Jess, I really think we just ran out of time," Zoe says.

"Why are you sticking up for her? Don't you know she's using you?"

"How is she using me? She's my *friend.*"

"She wants people to see her with the Juilliard girl, obviously. She follows you around like a lost puppy."

145

Livvy giggles. "God, Jessa, you're kind of being a huge bitch right now."

"It's not bitchy if it's true."

"I *want* her to hang out with me," Zoe says. "What do you not understand about 'we're friends'?"

I can almost hear Jessa rolling her eyes. "Girl, you do what you want. But I wouldn't want some amateur hanging on to my coattails. Hey, Liv and I are going to Target later. You want to come?"

"I can't," Zoe says. "Brooklyn and Lana and I are having dinner."

"*Ohhhhh.*" Jessa says the word like it has about five syllables. "Okay. I get it now."

"Jessa, it's not like that."

"Whatever. I say good on you. If she's gonna use you, use her right back." And then the door swings open and bangs shut, and everything is quiet.

So I guess that's it; my days of being part of the group are over. No more raucous dining hall meals, arguing over which is the worst musical ever written. No more crowding around someone's laptop and watching dumb YouTube videos. No more late nights on the lawn. When those things were actually happening, I was always waiting for them to be over so I could be alone with Zoe. But now that they're not an option anymore, I realize how much I'll miss being invited.

Or maybe I was never really invited at all. Maybe I was just following Zoe around like a lost puppy.

At least she stood up for me. She didn't know I was here, so she didn't have to say the things she said. She really does like me, and it's not because I can bring her closer to my mom. And it's a good thing, too. If I don't have any shows or any friends, Zoe's pretty much the only thing I have left going for me at Allerdale. I better cling to her with everything I've got.

—

I spend the rest of the afternoon holed up in a practice room, playing overly dramatic sad songs. When I come back to the room to change for dinner, Zoe's waiting for me. She looks gorgeous in a strappy red dress and sparkly shoes. "Where were you?" she asks. "I texted you a million times."

Part of me wants to tell her I overheard her conversation with Jessa in the bathroom, but that would be embarrassing for both of us. "Sorry. I was in a practice room," I say. "There's no reception down there. Let me change, and we can go, okay?"

"Okay." Zoe smiles, a totally genuine smile, and it calms me down to see how excited she is for tonight. Honestly, even if she were using me to get closer to my mom, I'd probably let her.

We walk the five minutes to Main Street and find Spindrift, which is one of the three restaurants in town. The bistro turns out to be beautiful, all rough-hewn wood tables and tiny votive candles and chairs with swirly wrought-iron backs that are nicer to look at than lean on. Mom's already there when we arrive, halfway into her first glass of wine. "My girls," she says when she spots us. "Sit down. Get anything you want— appetizers, desserts, my treat."

"Thank you so much for inviting me," Zoe says as she

settles into her chair, and my mom says, "Of course, my darling," even though it was my idea.

"How were the non-eqs?" I ask.

"Oh, they were *wonderful.* No one topped you, though, Zoe. I was floored by what you did in class today."

Zoe turns pink. "Wow, really? I mean, *wow.* Thank you."

"When you get to New York, Brookie will give you my number, and we'll arrange a little audition, okay? No promises, but if I end up having space for another student, I'd love to teach you. If that's something you think you might want, of course."

"Oh my God, *yes.* I can't even—I mean—*yes.* Thank you. Thank you *so much.*" Zoe beams at me, and I smile back, but it almost hurts to do it. I can't even tell if I'm more jealous that she has captured my mom's heart so thoroughly or that my mom has captured hers.

"How's Dad? And everyone else?" I interrupt.

"Everyone's wonderful. Dad sends his love—he's at Glimmerglass this week. Marisol's due in three weeks—she's absolutely enormous—and your uncle's working on an absurd musical about online dating. It's called *Don't Kiss Me, Kate.* It's going to be intolerable."

"I think that sounds kind of hilarious," I say, and Zoe stifles a laugh and nods halfheartedly, like she kind of wants to be on my side but also doesn't want to contradict my mom. "Are you going to see it?"

"You could not pay me enough to sit through that." My mom takes a giant gulp of her wine. "You haven't said a thing about *Birdie* yet, Brookie; I need to know everything."

I suddenly realize I never told Zoe to pretend I'm in *Birdie* with her; I have no idea what I'm going to do now. I look around wildly, hoping for something to divert my mom's attention, and the waiter a couple of tables away catches my gaze and comes right over.

"Good evening," he says, sliding a bread basket onto the table. "Do you ladies know what you'd like to eat?"

"I think we need another—" my mom begins, but I cut her off.

"Yes, I'll have, um . . ." I haven't even looked at the menu, but I order the first thing my eyes land on. "The baked polenta."

Mom looks puzzled. "Since when do you like polenta?"

I'm not even completely sure what polenta is. "I thought I'd try it again," I say.

Mom starts peppering the waiter with questions about how the various dishes are prepared, and Zoe gives me a look like, *What is up with you?* I reach for my phone to text her, but Mom decides on an entree and starts paying attention again. The waiter takes Zoe's order and leaves.

My friend is clearly aware that I want her to do something, but she's not sure what, so she just starts talking. "*Birdie* has been so much fun. Jim Krowalzka is directing—I don't know if you know him—and I already feel like I'm learning so much. I don't know if Brooklyn told you, but I'm playing Kim, which is a great part and everything, but she's a little bit of a two-dimensional character, you know? But Jim's helping me really round her out and figure out what her motivations are. And Brooklyn's been helping me practice my songs. She's *such* a talented pianist." Even though she hasn't guessed right about what I need from her, I love that she's trying.

"Brookie, that's so nice of you, but I hope you're spending plenty of time working on your own music," Mom says. "You're here to grow as a performer, not as an accompanist."

Zoe's eyebrows crinkle. "Are there songs in *Señor—*"

I cut her off before she can blow my cover. "Don't worry. I'm concentrating on my own stuff, too. Zoe has a much bigger part than I do. The ensemble has a lot of downtime."

My friend looks thoroughly confused for a second, and then I see understanding click into place behind her eyes. "Right," she says. "They all sound really good, though."

"Well, I'm bursting with excitement. Dad and I can't wait to see you in your big Allerdale debut."

"Great," I say. I reach for the bread basket and stuff a roll into my mouth so I'll have an excuse not to talk for a minute.

My mom leans in and lowers her voice. "So, tell me all the *important* gossip. Any budding romances in the works?"

Zoe smiles. "I'm dating someone from home, actually. His name is Carlos."

"Ooh, what an excellent name. Is he an actor, too?"

"No, but he does play the guitar, and he has a really nice voice. He's going to Rhode Island School of Design in the fall to study animation."

"An artist! How delightful. Are you two serious?"

"Sort of," Zoe says. "It's a little complicated. We won't be in the same city next year, and we don't want to hold each other back or anything. So we're going to try to be flexible if we find ourselves wanting to date other people." She catches my eye for the tiniest moment, then looks away.

I try not to seem too interested, but this is the first I've heard of Zoe and Carlos having a flexible arrangement. I know it doesn't change anything between her and me, but my illogical heart does a little skip anyway.

My mom is nodding. "That's very mature, Zoe. Most people your age don't understand that love dies if you strangle it. I learned that the hard way a couple of times. Is he coming to visit at all this summer?"

"Yeah, he's actually coming in, like, two and a half weeks," Zoe says. "Sorry, Brooklyn. I meant to tell you that yesterday. You don't mind, do you?"

There is absolutely nothing I want less than to have Zoe's cute, guitar-playing, animator boyfriend staying in our room, but I force my expression not to change. "Of course I don't mind," I say. "I can't wait to meet him."

The waiter arrives with our food, and the plate he puts down in front of me contains a yellow square with some vegetables stacked on top. I take a tiny bite, and it's not terrible, but the texture is kind of weird and gritty. I wish I'd taken two seconds to actually look at the menu; Zoe's burger looks much more appetizing. As if she knows what I'm thinking, she turns her plate so the fries are toward me.

"Speaking of liking people," my mom says, "any summer sparks flying for you, Brookie?"

I look down at my plate. "Not really. The only guys I ever hang out with are gay."

"It doesn't have to be a *guy*. I was so in love with this girl the first summer I was at Allerdale. Her name was Madeline, and she had the sexiest legs you've ever seen."

"Mom," I say. *"God."*

"What? Don't get all uptight on me. I know there's someone here for you if you look hard enough. Zoe, will you please encourage Brooklyn to find a nice boy or girl to date, even if it's only a summer fling? She's so picky."

Zoe glances at me sideways. "Don't worry," she says to my mom. "I'm sure there are plenty of people here who would fall head over heels for Brooklyn if they knew she was available."

Suddenly my polenta doesn't taste nearly as disgusting.

Zoe gets up to go to the bathroom a few minutes later, and I'm sure my mom is going to take the opportunity to grill me about *Birdie*. But instead, she leans over and grabs my arm so hard, it hurts. "I knew it!" she whispers.

"You knew what?"

"She's totally into you."

"Mom," I say. I glance toward the bathroom, but there's no way Zoe could hear us from all the way over there. "She's not. We're just friends. She's straight. Plus, she's in a relationship."

"An *open* relationship," my mom emphasizes. "And she definitely wants to be more than your friend. It's blatantly obvious. There's no reason to be embarrassed, Brookie. I think it would be wonderful if something happened between you two."

"I'm not embarrassed," I say, even though my face is flaming. "It's just . . . there's nothing like that going on." But now all I can think about is how Zoe's lips felt pressed against mine, how her voice sounded when she whispered, *There, now you've kissed a girl.*

My mom rolls her eyes. "Sweetheart, I'm not blind. I see the way she looks at you."

"What? How does she look at me?"

"Like you're the brightest thing in the room. Like she wants to swallow you whole and then lick up the crumbs."

I start to say, *That's insane, no she doesn't.* But what comes out of my mouth is, "Really?"

"Absolutely. I couldn't be happier for you. She's a wonderful girl."

Zoe comes out of the bathroom and starts heading back toward the table, the silky skirt of her red dress swishing around her long legs. When she catches me watching her, she shoots me a brilliant smile.

"I know," I tell my mom. "She really is."

When Zoe switches off the light that night, I'm about to try to start a game of Love or Hate. But before I can come up with a question, she says, "So ... your mom thinks you're in the ensemble of *Birdie.*"

I bury my face in my pillow. "Ugh. Yeah. Sorry about that."

"Why are you apologizing?"

"Because I should've warned you that I wanted you to cover for me, and I totally forgot. And because it's your show, and I, like, co-opted it. Are you mad?"

"Of course not. Why do you always think I'm mad at you? I'm never mad at you."

"I don't know."

She rolls over to face me. "Why don't you tell your mom the truth?"

"I can't. She'd be so disappointed."

"Brooklyn, it's obvious how much she loves you. She's not going to love you less because you're not in a main stage show."

"I didn't really even plan to lie to her about it," I say. "It came out of my mouth one day, and now it's too late to take it back."

"But your parents are going to come up here next month to see you perform! What are you going to tell them when you're not in the show?"

"I'll fake the flu or a sprained ankle or something. It'll be fine." I sigh. "My whole family is so proud of me for being here, Zoe. Believing I'm actually successful for once isn't hurting them."

"They should be proud of you regardless," she says. "You're amazing."

"You know that's not true. My mom didn't even let me sing in the—"

"I don't mean at singing. I mean *you*. Like, as a person."

In my head, I burst into tears and laugh hysterically and set off fireworks and do a bunch of cartwheels, all at the same time. In real life, I somehow manage to say, "Thank you. So are you."

"Can I ask you something else?"

"Okay."

"That thing your mom said at dinner. The thing about finding you a nice boy *or girl*?"

I try to keep my voice light, like this conversation isn't a big deal at all. "Yeah, she says stuff like that a lot. She's really into me 'experimenting.' Sorry if it was weird."

"No, it wasn't. It was cool. I can't imagine my mom ever saying anything like that."

"But your parents are okay with that stuff, right? They wouldn't be upset if you liked girls?"

"No, they know I do," Zoe says. "I dated this girl Carina for a while junior year, and we talked about it then. They weren't thrilled at first, but they got used to it. Of course, then she decided she was straight and totally broke my heart."

Holy shit, my mom was right—Zoe really is bisexual. If I wanted something to happen between us, it's possible she might be kind of, sort of available to me. It's weird how everything suddenly looks a little softer and brighter when a "no" turns into a "maybe."

"Brooklyn?" she says, and I realize it's been way too long since I've said anything. "You're not freaked out, are you?"

"God, no, of course not. You just never said you liked girls."

"I didn't think it was important. Is it important?" Her voice is small.

"No, it's totally not. Like, half the people I know at home are bi."

"Right, okay." She's quiet for a minute, and then she says, "But ... you don't like girls, right? Even though your mom wants you to experiment?"

My heart is beating so hard now that I'm sure she can hear it across the room. People can probably hear it all the way down the hall. "I mean, I don't *not* like them," I say. "I've never really been attracted to a girl before, like, in the past, but I'm not saying it *couldn't* happen. If there were someone I, um, felt stuff for, I wouldn't discount it. Like, on principle, or anything. You know?"

It's probably the most inarticulate string of words I've ever put together. I half expect Zoe to burst out laughing and say, *I'm sorry, what?* But instead she says, "Yeah. I think I know what you mean."

"You do?"

"Yeah."

I can hear the smile in her voice, and even though we can't see each other in the dark, I smile back.

15

That Thursday is the closing night of *Midsummer* and my last day on the lighting crew, and on Friday morning, I switch to the scenic department. I don't know any more about building sets than I do about lighting, but this time Russell is there with me, so everything is less scary. He introduces me to the other scenic interns, and it's a relief to meet people who have no idea who Lana Blake Shepard is. The head of the scene shop gives me a bunch of huge Styrofoam balls and sets me to work covering them with blue and pink sequins for the *Dreamgirls* set. It's unbelievably tedious, but I don't actually mind—it's not dangerous, it doesn't involve any heavy lifting, and I can listen to music on my phone and think about Zoe all day. Whenever Olivier comes into the shop to check on our progress, I get to watch Russell light up and frolic in circles like a puppy. Since I'm too embarrassed to go to the dining hall and face the other apprentices, Russell and I walk into town every night and get sandwiches at Sammy's, where everything on the menu is named after a celebrity. The Tina Fey is particularly tasty.

The following Monday is the midpoint of the festival, and that means it's time for Pandemonium, the legendary mid-season party. We've all been working seven days a week for a month now, and this is the company's chance to go crazy and forget about our responsibilities for one glorious night. All through the season—and for my whole life, really—I've heard stories about people getting injured, destroying property, and hooking up with ill-advised partners during Pandemonium. Douchebands claims to have hooked up with fourteen different girls in one evening last year, and I'm pretty sure I believe it. The party is all anyone talks about, but nobody's more excited than me. On a night so centered around debauchery, it seems possible that something real could finally happen between Zoe and me.

Our directors and shop heads let us out early so we have time to get ready for the party. When I get back to our room, Zoe's blowing her hair dry in front of the mirror. She has on a tight white dress with a low back, which showcases the delicate branches and flowers inked onto her skin. I've never actually seen her whole tattoo, and I suddenly have an intense desire to know how far down it goes.

Zoe clicks the blow-dryer off and spins around. The front of the dress is cut much higher, but somehow that makes it even sexier. "Hey!" she says. "I was wondering when they were going to let you out. Jessa and Livvy are coming to get us in half an hour."

I have no desire to go to the party with Jessa and Livvy,

but I can't very well say that; Zoe still doesn't know I overheard their conversation in the bathroom. "You look really great," I tell her instead.

"Thanks; you're sweet. What are you wearing?"

I pull my favorite little black dress out of my closet and hold it up. It's the only appropriate thing I own, so I hope Zoe likes it; it's short and flirty and shows more leg than I'm used to. "Perfect," she says. "That's going to look gorgeous on you." She offers to curl my hair, and I sit very still in her desk chair, soaking up the feeling of her cool, quick fingers brushing my neck and shoulders. She lines my eyes in gold pencil, leaning so close, I can feel her breath on my cheek, and lends me the bright red lipstick she's wearing. When I'm thoroughly primped, painted, and dressed, and she pulls me over to the mirror.

"Look at us," she says. "We look spectacular."

"We really do." I'm not used to wearing this much makeup, and I look like a stranger to myself. It's weirdly freeing. I feel like I could do anything tonight and it would be totally fine, because it wouldn't really be *me* doing it. I stare at our reflections and try to fix them in my mind. Even if I can't be as brave as I'm hoping, I want to remember this moment, when we were sparkly and bright and alone together.

Livvy and Jessa burst into our room without knocking, and I start feeling awkward all over again; I've barely spoken to either of them since my mom's master class. They're both giggling and tottering in their heels, and when Livvy reaches into the red corset she's wearing and pulls out a flask, I see why. "You want?" she asks.

"Sure," Zoe says. She drinks, grimaces, and hands it to me.

Based on the face she made, I'm not sure I want what's inside, but I do want the courage that comes with it, so I take a swig. It tastes like lighter fluid that's been touched with a match, and fire flies up my nose and down my throat as I cough and sputter. Everyone laughs, and Zoe rubs my back.

"What *is* that?" I gasp when I can speak again.

"Whiskey," Jessa says. She's wearing this slinky silver thing that's more like a large handkerchief than a dress. "Little sips, Shepard."

I take another tiny sip to prove that I can, and it goes down better this time. "Good girl," Jessa says, and her smile looks pretty genuine as she takes the flask from me. I wonder for a second if she's gotten over all the stuff she said the other day, but I'm pretty sure she and Livvy are just caught up in the tipsy anticipation of the party. I smile back anyway. I'll take what I can get.

Pandemonium is already in full swing when we get there. The *Dreamgirls* set has been moved into the wings, and the stage and loading dock of Haydu Hall look like a New York City club. Rows of moving lights swoop around in a synchronized dance and shoot their colorful beams through the haze produced by a bank of fog machines. In the center of the stage, raised up on a platform, is an eight-foot-tall cage with a girl and two guys inside. All three of them are dancing like they're possessed, and for a second I think Allerdale has hired burlesque performers. But when the door swings open and the three of them spill out, laughing and whooping, I recognize them as non-eq company members. The music is so loud, I can feel the bass thundering through my chest.

Zoe grabs my hand and screams something. I have no idea what she said, but her eyes are bright and she's smiling at me like I'm the only person in the room, so I hold on tight and let her lead me. We snake through the writhing, sweaty crowd, dodging flailing limbs and flying hair, until we're right in the middle of the stage. When we reach the base of the cage, Zoe throws her head back, closes her eyes, and starts to dance. Normally it takes me a couple of minutes to fall into the rhythm of a dance floor, but here, everyone is so caught up in their own ecstatic motion that it feels like nobody's watching. I'm warm all the way through from the whiskey and the heat of the crowd. As the beat speeds up, I snake both arms up above my head, raise my face to the neon lights, and spin around and around. I feel free and fizzy and dangerous and lit up from the inside.

One song fades into another and another, and I lose track of time completely. Somewhere in this crowd is Livvy in her corset and Jessa in her handkerchief and Kenji and Todd and Pandora and Russell, but all that exists for me is Zoe. The crowd presses her closer and closer to me as we dance, and I don't back up to make room. Pretty soon she's got her hands on my hips and her body right up against mine, and everything in me goes, *Yes.* My arms have nowhere else to go, so I loop them around her neck. Our knees scissor together, and for a minute it's awkward, the movements of our bodies fumbling and unsynchronized. But Zoe looks straight into my eyes and smiles, and I find her rhythm and sink into it. I've seen girls dance like this before, rocking their hips back and forth like they're one eight-limbed, two-hearted animal, and I know doesn't necessarily mean anything. But I'm sure I've never felt this kind of connection to another person, even when Jason used to push me up against a wall and kiss me until I lost my breath.

A new song starts, one of those ubiquitous ones about freedom and summer and falling in love, and Zoe grabs my hand and leans in to say something. Her lips are so close, they brush my ear, but the music is loud enough that I can still barely hear her scream, "Let's go!"

I look at her like, *What?* She can't possibly want to leave already. But then she tips her head up toward the empty cage, and I realize what she means. Part of me is so not ready for this, but a bigger part is thrilled as Zoe leads me up the steps and behind the bars. The crowd cheers as she closes the door behind us and puts her hands on my hips, her front pressed to my back like she's spooning me. Everyone is watching us, but this doesn't feel anything like the kiss at the cast party. This doesn't feel like a game. It's suddenly very clear to me that after tonight, everything's going to be different between us.

I have no idea how long we dance in the cage, but by the time we're done, I'm soaked in sweat, and I'm delirious with exhibitionism and the feel of Zoe's skin. My legs are trembling a little, and I stumble in my heels and trip down the last two steps, but someone catches my arm and helps me balance. I look up, up, up into Russell's face.

"Thank you!" I shout, but I'm not sure he can hear me, so I give him a hug instead. I'm so happy to see him; I love everyone right now. Most of the company is dressed in leather and sparkles and booty-shorts and tulle, but Russell's in his standard T-shirt and jeans, and it's comforting. It reminds me that this evening is really happening, that it's not some crazy fever dream.

"You okay?" he hollers when I pull back. I nod hard, and he smiles. "You looked awesome up there."

It *felt* like we looked awesome, but it's nice to hear it confirmed by someone else. "Thanks!" I shout. "You should go next! Is Olivier here? You should make him dance with you."

"What?" Russell yells, and I shake my head. There's no way I'm going to make myself heard over this music.

"Do you want—" Russell starts, but Zoe comes up next to me and grabs my hand.

"Water!" she shouts.

I give Russell a little wave. "See you later," I yell.

There are big coolers of water on the loading dock, and Zoe and I gulp some down before we head back into the fray, grinning at each other like idiots the whole time. We pass Kenji and Todd near the edge of the stage, and they wrap us up in their sweaty arms and kiss our cheeks and grind with us in an exaggerated, hilarious way. Neither of them has really spoken to me all week, but now it's like they want me to be their new best friend, and I just go with it. Tonight, I don't care about whys or hows or what will happen tomorrow. Tonight, I belong with them.

I belong at this festival.

I belong with Zoe.

The party doesn't end until nearly three. When the music finally stops and the loading dock lights flicker on, Zoe's beside me in a moment, bedraggled and glowing. She slips her arm through mine and says, "Let's go home," and even though I'm way too warm, I shiver. Once we get back to the room, absolutely anything could happen. I'm pretty sure I'm ready.

Before anyone can trap us into a conversation, we slip outside and stumble across the lawn toward our dorm, clinging to each other and laughing as our heels sink into the dewy grass. Livvy's whiskey ran out halfway through the night, and the effects have long worn off, but I'm so tired that I feel tipsy anyway. There are people everywhere, but they all seem flat, like extras who have been hired to provide background noise for Zoe and me. She's the only one who feels solid and real. I'm hyperaware of the stripe of skin where my arm presses against hers.

Our heels click up the stairs, synchronized without us even trying. As we make our way down the hall to our room, Zoe giggles in the quiet, then claps her hand over her mouth and exaggeratedly shushes me. We're the first up here, so it's totally unnecessary, but I laugh and shush her back. It makes me feel like we're getting away with something delicious and forbidden.

I unlock our door—it takes me a couple of tries—and we push inside, both bumping our shoulders into the door-frame because we're not willing to separate long enough to go single file. Neither of us bothers to turn on the light, but the streetlamp along the path outside casts a soft glow over the room. Zoe steadies herself on my shoulder as she kicks off her shoes, then lets go of me to stretch her arms over her head. Her silver eye shadow is smeared, like a little kid at the end of trick-or-treating, and I have an unaccountable urge to press my lips to her eyelids. How much am I allowed to touch her, now that we're not performing for anyone?

She heads toward my bed and flops down onto her back, her hair splayed across my pillow. For a second I think she's still drunk enough that she's gone to the wrong side of the room by accident, but then she pats the spot next to her and says, "C'mere."

There's barely space for us to lie next to each other, and Zoe doesn't move over to accommodate me, so I end up on my side, curled toward her like a parenthesis. Our inside arms are pressed together from shoulder to wrist, and my top knee rests against her bare thigh. I close my eyes and try to memorize every place our skin is touching.

"Tonight was amazing," she says. She turns to look at me, and our noses almost bump. I feel a laugh rising in my chest at our clumsiness and sudden closeness, but she looks serious, so I swallow it back down. "*You* were amazing. I've never seen you let go like that. You're a great dancer."

"Really?" I ask, and she nods. "I loved it. I loved dancing with *you*." If there was ever a time for honesty, it's now, when we're both hazy and warm and not thinking too hard.

Zoe rolls away so her back is to me, and for a minute I'm certain I've said something wrong. But then she snuggles deeper into my comforter and mumbles, "So tired," and I realize she's planning to stay here all night. I'm not ready for her to go to sleep yet, though. Something started between us on that dance floor, and I need confirmation that it's real, that we can be like that even when we're alone.

Zoe's hair has slipped off her shoulder and pooled behind her, right next to my nose, and it still smells like grapefruit even after all the dancing. I sink my fingers into it near the nape of her neck and slowly drag them through to the ends, which are tangled and damp from sticking to her skin. Zoe tips her head back a little, and I wonder if I've pulled too hard. But when I retreat, she murmurs, "Mmm, no, don't stop."

I plunge back in, more confident now, and comb through the whole length of her hair, roots to tips, over and over and over. The room is totally quiet except for the soft, rhythmic shushing sound of my fingers. I drag my nails gently along her scalp, just to see what happens, and I'm rewarded with a soft, appreciative sigh that's almost, *almost* a moan. I wonder if she makes that sound when Carlos touches her other places, and the thought sends a nervous, satisfying warmth straight to my center.

In a fleeting moment of bravery, I sweep Zoe's hair to the side and run a single fingertip down the soft length of her neck. The top flower of her tattoo is right below where my finger's resting, and I trace the outline of it. I expect it to be raised a little, but it feels as soft and smooth as the rest of her skin. I trace the next flower and the next as they meander over her shoulder blade, down toward where they disappear under the back of her dress. Zoe's breathing more deeply now, and even though she's not facing me, I can tell how totally *with me* she is. There's something about holding her captive with my touch that bolsters my tiny spark of courage and builds it up into a small, constant flame.

I trace the top edge of her dress, back and forth, until I finally work up the nerve to grasp the tiny silver zipper. So slowly that it's almost excruciating, I pull it down. One, two, three inches of Zoe's inked back come into view as the zipper's teeth separate.

"Is this okay?" I whisper, and she nods. It's like she doesn't even want to speak for fear of tearing the web I'm weaving around us.

Her permission makes me hungry, and I slide the zipper down as far as it'll go, right below the edge of her underwear. I spread the fabric of her dress apart, revealing the expanse of her back, and when I slip my finger underneath the clasp of her bra, she shivers and nods again.

It comes apart, and for the first time, I can see Zoe's entire tattoo, a network of delicate branches and tiny pink flowers that reaches all the way down to her hips. It's absolutely gorgeous. I remember what she told me about the tattoo's symbolism—that life is beautiful but short, and you have to take advantage of every opportunity—and it makes me bold enough to reach out and run a fingertip all the way down her spine. Her back arches, and my breath catches in my chest. I've never felt so powerful in my entire life.

I start again at the very top and trace each flower and branch as slowly as I can, and I watch Zoe's body move as she breathes with me, all her attention focused on that tiny point where my skin and hers come together. Her skin is soft and slightly damp, and I'm not sure if it's from dancing all night or from what I'm doing to her now. When I reach her hips and there's no more ink left, I kiss her back once, right where I imagine the other side of her heart would be. I lick my lips and taste salt.

"Brooklyn," she whispers, and when she rolls over to face me, her pupils are so huge, they've swallowed all the blue in her eyes. She weaves her fingers through my hair at the base of my neck, and when she moves a little closer, I don't pull away.

"Can I?" she whispers against my mouth.

I answer by moving forward that last inch and closing the gap between us.

It's weird how you can spend countless hours remembering the feel of someone's lips and still be totally unprepared for the exquisite reality of them. Zoe's mouth is warm and lazy and sweet against mine, not urgent or aggressive at all, like it was during Never Have I Ever. This time it feels totally genuine, like she wants to take her time and drink me in. I expect kissing her to be different from kissing a boy, but it's really not, except that her face is smaller and smoother and fits in my cupped hand. Her cheeks are flushed, and my whole body heats up as I think, *I did this to you.*

She catches my bottom lip between hers and playfully bites me, and I gasp, which makes us both start laughing. Our mouths don't fit together when we're smiling, so we pull back a fraction of an inch and stare at each other, the kind of look I've been giving her for weeks when I thought she wasn't paying attention. This time, she looks back.

"Finally," she whispers, and my heart supernovas.

16

All we do is kiss. In the world of theater people, that barely even counts. But the next morning, I slip out of bed and walk to Kayla's Cakes, where I buy a single doughnut. I leave it on Zoe's desk while she sleeps in a tangle of sheets and silky hair and unfastened clothing. She's so beautiful, I can barely stand to look at her.

She chose me, I think as I watch the rise and fall of her chest, and it's more validating than any affirmation I could scream in front of the mirror.

I'm on my way over to the scene shop when my phone rings, and I smile when I see my mom's picture on the screen—for once, I actually have good news to share. But I barely manage to get both syllables of "Hello?" out before she starts talking.

"Brookie! I'm so glad I caught you! Marisol had the babies!"

"Oh my God, when?"

"Last night around four. I wanted to call you then, but I figured I should let you sleep."

Even though nobody can see me, I blush a little thinking about what I was doing at four in the morning. "She wasn't due for another two weeks, right?" I say. "Is everyone okay?"

"Everyone's perfect. The babies are just beautiful."

"What are their names? She didn't really name the boy Pierre, did she?"

"The girl is Jasmine, and the boy is Owen," my mom says. "Christa talked her out of 'Pierre' at the last minute. Honestly, I thought it was kind of cute."

"Are you at the hospital now?" I ask. "Can I talk to them?"

"Marisol's sleeping, and Christa went to get coffee, but they said to tell you they love you and they can't wait for you to meet the twins."

"I can't wait to meet them, either. I wish I could come home and see them right now."

"I wish you could, too," Mom says. "How's everything going up there? You sound a little tired."

I feel a goofy smile creep over my face. "Everything's good," I say. "Really, really good, actually. Pandemonium was last night."

"Oh! I forgot that was coming up! Did you have a fantastic time? Do they still have the cage? Did you dance in it?"

"Yes, yes, and yes," I say, and my stomach does a flip as I think about pressing against Zoe behind those bars. "I only have a couple of minutes right now, so I'll tell you everything later, but . . . um . . . I think you were right about Zoe and me."

"I knew it!" my mom shrieks. "Brookie, that's *wonderful.*"

I can't remember the last time I had her wholehearted approval for something I legitimately accomplished, and it feels like sinking into a warm bath. "It kind of is, isn't it?" I say. "I don't think there's anything superserious going on, because of Carlos and whatever, but she did say they have an open relationship, right? And I like her so much, and I think she really likes me."

"I like her so much, too. Wait till I tell Dad! Or do you want to tell him yourself?"

"It's okay, you can tell him." I'm at the door of the scene shop now, and I see Russell approaching from across the lawn. "Listen, I've gotta go. My crew call is starting."

"I'm proud of you, sweetheart," my mom says. "You've always seemed so resistant to dating girls. Allerdale is really opening up your world, huh?"

"I guess. I'll talk to you later, Mom. Give my love to everyone, okay? Tell Marisol and Christa I'll call them soon."

"I will. We love you back," she says, and I hang up.

Russell catches up to me, looking bleary-eyed and rumpled. "It should be illegal to make us come to work this early after Pandemonium," he says.

"Seriously. I hardly slept." I feel wide awake, but I think I'm running on pure adrenaline.

"Did you know ducks sleep with half their brains at a time so they can always be on the lookout for predators?" Russell says. He rubs his eyes and runs his fingers through his hair, which makes it stick up in a million different directions. It doesn't look like he washed it this morning.

"I did not know that about ducks, but it doesn't surprise me that you do." I reach up and pat him on the shoulder, and he gives me a weird look.

"What's with you?" he asks.

"What do you mean?"

"I don't know. You look so ... *happy.* Nobody's happy at nine in the morning."

Part of me wants to tell him what happened with Zoe—I think he'd be pleased for me—but another larger part loves having a secret with her. So I say, "I am happy. I have a new niece and nephew. They were born last night."

"Oh, wow. Wait, both at once?"

"Twins," I tell him. "Jasmine and Owen. So cool. Come on; let's go inside." I link my arm through his. He looks a little bewildered by my enthusiasm, but he lets me tug him toward the theater.

I spend the entire morning painting escape stairs black, but I barely register the work in front of me. All I can see are Zoe's eyes inches from my face, Zoe's tattooed back under my fingers, Zoe's hair sprawled across my sheets. A couple of times, I find myself singing without even realizing I'm doing it. At lunch time, I dash over to Haydu, where Zoe's in *Birdie* rehearsal, and peer through the window of the dance studio. It seems insane that we're both spending our days doing normal things like painting and learning choreography when such a seismic shift has occurred between us. I should be using this time to get food, but instead I wait outside the door for half an hour in case Zoe's choreographer gives them a break. I send the universe an image of us sneaking off into a stairwell and murmuring about how perfect last night was. But the girls are still dancing when it's time for me to go back to work.

I spend the afternoon replaying our kisses in my head until the memories are almost worn through. When the shop head releases me that evening, I'm out the door before Russell can even ask if I want to go to Sammy's. I haven't eaten in the dining hall in a week and a half, but my excitement about seeing Zoe eclipses all my awkward feelings about facing the other apprentices. The room is packed, but it takes me all of six seconds to spot her; having a crush on someone gives you serious tracking radar. Her table is full of people from the *Birdie* cast, including Kenji and Todd and Livvy, but at least Jessa's not here.

Everyone looks a little surprised to see me when I approach with my food, but Zoe shoots me a radiant smile and makes everyone scoot down so she can pull up a chair for me. Even though I've been thinking about her the entire day, I don't know how to act now that she's right here. Is she going to kiss me in front of all these people? I'm not even sure if I want her to or not. I'm relieved when she opts for a hug instead, but the way our breasts and hips and cheeks press together makes my face flame. I pull away much sooner than I want to.

"Thank you for the doughnut," Zoe whispers into my ear. "You are the sweetest."

"Of course," I say, and then she sits down and picks up the thread of Kenji and Todd's conversation right where she left off. I'm disappointed and relieved all at once.

I spend the whole meal trying to keep a normal, serene expression on my face while my knee presses against Zoe's under the table. I barely understand the conversation, anyway; missing ten days' worth of inside jokes at summer stock is like being off the grid for months back in the real world, and I know it'll be nearly impossible for me to catch up. But maybe I don't need anyone else, now that I have Zoe.

Time passes so slowly, I'm sure something's wrong with the Earth's rotation, but Livvy finally stands and gathers her trash, and everyone else follows. "My head still hurts from last night," she says. "I'm going to go lie flat on my back and watch *30 Rock*. Anyone want to join me?" She eyes me sideways, clearly torn between politeness and a strong desire not to invite me up to her room. In the end, her loyalty is to Jessa.

"We'll come," Kenji says.

For a second I'm afraid Zoe's about to say she wants to watch, too, but instead she says, "I'm actually gonna go to the practice rooms for a little while." She turns to me. "Do you have time to play for me? You don't have to, but—"

"Of course," I say before she's even done. "I mean, yeah, sure, I'm not doing anything." Going to the practice room is a brilliant strategy—if anyone caught us on the way back to our room, they'd try to talk Zoe into joining the group, and then we'd be stuck in we're-just-friends limbo for the rest of the evening. But no actor at Allerdale would ever try to talk someone out of rehearsing. This way, we can finally be alone.

Zoe and I practically run downstairs, and the second the practice room door shuts behind us, she has me pressed up against it. Her hands slip up the back of my shirt and then she's kissing me, fast and eager, like she can't get enough of me. "I've been thinking about this all day," she murmurs against my mouth, and she doesn't even give me time to respond before her lips are on mine again. I know I'm supposed to like this hungry urgency—I've been thinking about kissing her all day, too, and I love how totally focused on me she is. But this is way more intense than the slow, tentative way we touched last night, when everything was about closeness and warmth and the wonder of discovering each other for the first time. The way she's kissing me now makes me feel totally out of control, like I've been thrown into the deep end of the pool after one swimming lesson.

I draw back a little. "Hey, slow down," I say. "I'm not going anywhere."

She giggles. "Sorry. I didn't think I'd ever get to do this, and now that I can . . ." She trails off and shrugs, and the vulnerable way she's biting her lip is so adorable that it makes me want to pull her close again.

"Why did you think that?" I ask. "I haven't been able to get enough of you since the day we got here."

"I thought maybe we were just going to be friends, though. It seemed like you were straight, and when I kissed you at the *Midsummer* party, you literally ran out of the room. I thought I'd ruined everything."

I run my fingers through her hair. "I didn't run because I didn't like it," I say. "I needed a minute to figure things out, you know? I didn't know what it *meant*."

"It meant I wanted to kiss you, silly. What else could it have meant?"

"I don't know. We were playing a game. Maybe you were

doing it for attention, or to get a reaction out of everyone, or to freak them out, or—"

"*Brooklyn,*" she says. She touches my cheek, and I shut up. "You're overthinking this, okay?"

"I'm just saying, I wasn't sure—"

"Do you like it when I do this?" Zoe kisses me again, incredibly gently now. It's barely more than a whisper against my lips.

"Yes," I say.

"And this?" She pushes my hair aside and kisses my neck.

"Yes," I whisper. And I do, I do like it. I always liked it when Jason used to kiss my neck, so why should this be any different? It feels overwhelming and unfamiliar with Zoe, but I probably just need time to get used to it.

"Then enjoy it," she says. "Not everything has to mean something. We like each other. We like making out. That's all that matters. Okay?"

"It's more complicated than that, though, isn't it?" I say. "You already have someone else, and—"

"I don't want to think about him right now," Zoe says. "I want to think about you."

She leans back in and kisses me again, and I try to relax into it. But I keep thinking about the last time the two of us were in this practice room, after the *Midsummer* party, when she stared right into my eyes as she sang to me, and the tension between us pulled and stretched like taffy. There was something so exciting about that uncertainty, the not-knowing. Everything was full of possibility, and now that I know exactly what it's like to be pressed up against her, all of that is gone.

What's wrong with you? I ask myself. *Why are you thinking about being six inches apart when you finally get to touch her?*

Zoe pauses for a breath, and I take the opportunity to ask, "Are we going to tell people?"

"Tell them what?"

"That we're, um . . ." I make a vague gesture with my hand, because I have no idea what we are. Girlfriends? It seems way too soon to use that word. Friends with benefits?

"Hooking up?" Zoe offers. "What, you think we should buy doughnuts for everyone?"

"I mean, obviously we don't need to tell *everyone*. But what about Livvy and those guys?"

I'm not even sure how I want her to answer, but when she says, "Let's not tell them yet," relief washes through me. Everyone already thinks I'm using her to boost my social status, that she's using me to get in good with my mom. They wouldn't understand that what's happening between us is much purer and simpler.

"Okay," I say. "I'm good with that."

"It's nobody's business but ours, right?" she says, and I wonder if she's thinking about her conversation with Jessa in the bathroom, too.

"Right," I say. "Do you want to sing for a little bit, maybe?"

Zoe laughs. "I didn't bring you down here to *work*."

"Making music with you doesn't feel like work to me."

"No, not to me, either. But we can sing anytime, and there

are *lots* of other things we could be doing right now." Zoe toys with the strap of my tank top.

"I like it when you sing to me," I say. "You have such a pretty voice." I hope it sounds like I'm flirting, not making an excuse. But I need to know that not *everything's* going to be different between us after last night. Regardless of how much I like the kissing, I want it to be an added bonus, not a sideways shift.

Zoe presses her cheek against mine, and for a second I think she's going to ignore what I said. But instead, she starts singing very softly right next to my ear, sending tiny shivers dancing up and down my spine.

"Never know how much I love you, never know
   how much I care,
When you put your arms around me, I get a fever that's
   so hard to bear,
You give me fever . . ."

She grabs one of my hands from where it's resting on her waist and twines our fingers together, and she rests her other hand on my shoulder like we're at the prom. As she sings, she starts to sway, and I follow her lead as she dances us away from the door and into the center of the room. There's no space to do anything but turn in tiny circles between the piano bench and the wall, so that's what we do, wrapped in the warm, sultry embrace of her voice. It's sweet and romantic and beautiful, and I close my eyes and breathe her in.

This is exactly what I want right now. If I'm honest with

myself, this is *all* I want right now. This is a memory I can hold on to while I'm doing repetitive, menial tasks in the scene shop tomorrow, one that won't wear out quickly no matter how much I worry it between my fingers.

I know Zoe's probably humoring her naive, innocent, new sort-of-girlfriend. But I try not to think about it, and for a few perfect minutes, I am completely happy.

17

The entire week after Pandemonium is glorious. All day long, as I sort fake greenery and paint flats and glue endless sequins onto Styrofoam balls, my phone buzzes against my hip over and over:

> Can't wait to kiss you later

> Missed a cue bc I was thinking about how cute you are

> Learning a love song & pretending you're listening

It's really, really hard to keep the goofy smiles off my face.

I thought I wasn't going to get any acting experience at Allerdale, but pretending there's nothing going on between Zoe and me is harder than playing Ophelia while Marcus lobs eggs at me. Sitting next to her at dinner every night as we twine our feet together under the table and "accidentally" brush each other's thighs and elbows is exquisite torture. One night Zoe drops her fork on purpose and bites my knee while she's under the table retrieving it, and I squeal so loudly I have to pretend I saw a mouse. The two of us constantly burst into giddy laughter over nothing, and people start rolling their eyes over how many "inside jokes" we have.

We're probably being insufferable, but I don't even care. This kind of behavior has always driven me crazy in other people, but it doesn't seem nearly so bad now that I'm the one doing it.

Love or Hate becomes a thrilling, nerve-racking physical game that Zoe now initiates almost every night. Instead of discussing how we feel about performance art or ghost stories or moments from our childhoods, her hands and mouth wander across my body in the dark. Every time she touches me in a new way—her lips on my bare stomach, her nails on the backs of my thighs—she whispers, "Love or hate?" I whisper back, "Love," every single time, as if it'll drown out the anxiety that bubbles up inside me. Zoe knows doing this stuff with a girl is new to me, and she doesn't complain when I gently push her hands away before they can sneak too far up my shirt. But when she finally snuggles against me and drifts off, I always lie awake for hours, wondering if I'm doing this right. Honestly, I think I'd be satisfied if we never went any farther than we did after Pandemonium, but I know she doesn't feel that way. Every night, I try to silence the little voice in my head that accuses me of not giving her enough. I tell myself it's okay to need time. I tell myself I'll probably be ready for more tomorrow.

On the one-week anniversary of Pandemonium, I'm lying next to Zoe in bed, combing my fingers through her hair and recounting my *Señor Hidalgo* rehearsal, which involved two hours of performing "slam poetry." She laughs like she usually does, but she seems distracted, and when I pause to remember some particularly abysmal rhyme, she cuts me off. "Do you want to come out to dinner with Carlos and me tomorrow night?"

I freeze, silky blond strands tangled around my fingers. "What?"

"He's getting in around seven. Did you forget?"

"I mean, you haven't mentioned it all week, so I thought . . ." I trail off because my chest feels too tight to squeeze any more words out. Inside my head I say, *I thought you'd canceled the trip. I thought I was enough for you.*

"I should've reminded you," she says. "It's okay if you're not free, but I really hope you are. I want him to meet you right away. He's going to *love* you." She kisses the tip of my nose.

I pull back. "Does he *know* about me?"

"Of course," she says. "I talk about you constantly. You know that."

"I mean, does he know about *us*? About . . . the stuff we've been doing this week?"

"Yeah, I told him. We promised to be honest with each other. He's okay with it, I think."

"Really?" If I were Carlos, I wouldn't be okay with it. I've been with her for only eight days, and I already feel incapable of sharing her with anyone else.

"I don't know. I think it's different because you're a girl. I think he's relieved I haven't found another guy, honestly. So? Will you come? I really want you to."

I want her to work to convince me, so I say, "Won't you want time alone with him?"

"We'll have plenty of time alone. I don't have rehearsal on Friday, so we're driving up to the Catskills and going camping. We're coming back early Saturday morning."

I really want her to stop saying "we" and meaning her and someone who's not me. "Are we allowed to leave campus like that?" I ask.

"I don't see why not. If we don't have a crew call or a rehearsal, nobody cares where we are. It's not like they're doing bed checks or anything."

I have the day off on Friday, too, and it strikes me that if Carlos weren't coming, Zoe and I could've had an entire day alone together. I've never been camping before; she could've taken me. The idea of sleeping on the ground has never really appealed to me, but I'd be totally willing to sleep on the ground in Zoe's arms.

"Sorry. I thought I'd told you this already," Zoe says. "It'll be nice to have the room all to yourself, though, right? To have some privacy for once?"

She's trying too hard, and it's obvious she's aware of how weird this situation is. She probably just doesn't want to acknowledge that I'm upset, since that would validate my feelings.

"I'll come to dinner tomorrow," I say. Knowing Zoe and Carlos are alone together would probably be even worse than watching them interact.

"Good. I'm so glad. I think you're really going to like each other."

I fake a yawn and roll away from her, and she doesn't make any effort to keep me awake like she usually does.

The next day's crew call feels endless. I spend the entire time sorting washers by size and giving myself an ulcer thinking about the evening ahead. Russell asks if I want to hang out later, and I seriously consider saying yes and ditching Zoe and Carlos. But that's the cowardly way out, and I know Zoe will respect me more if she thinks I'm mature enough to handle this open relationship thing. I ask Russell if we can hang out over the weekend instead.

When I get back to the room to change for dinner, Zoe's perched on her bed in a short turquoise dress. "Hey!" she says, chirpier than usual. "He's, like, ten minutes away. Will you be ready by then?" She gets up and gives me a quick kiss on the cheek, but when I put my hands on her waist, she pulls away and starts messing with her already-perfect eye shadow in front of the mirror. Maybe making out with me feels more like cheating now that Carlos isn't across the country.

"Sure," I say. I rummage through my closet and try to find an appropriate meeting-your-girlfriend's-boyfriend outfit. Should I wear something sexy, so she'll feel torn about who she'd rather go home with? Something conservative, to make things easier for her? I give up and choose a random dress printed with flying birds.

When Zoe's phone rings, she starts bouncing up and down on her toes. "Are you here?" she squeals. "Where are you?"

I hear the tinny murmur of his voice through the speaker,

and then Zoe says, "Okay, perfect. We'll meet you downstairs in a minute." She hangs up and looks at me, her face all lit up from the inside. "Come on!" She reaches out to take my hand, but it doesn't feel personal. It just feels like she wants to hold on to something. I let her lace her fingers with mine anyway.

Carlos is coming around the corner of the building when we get outside, and Zoe lets go of me and runs to him. He's a little shorter than I expected, but he's solidly built, and when she does a flying leap into his arms, he catches her like she weighs nothing. Her legs twine around his waist, and her skirt rides up so much, I can see her underwear, but she doesn't seem to care. I don't want to watch them kiss, but I can't look away, either.

It feels like forever before Zoe hops down and beckons me over. "Carlos, this is Brooklyn," she says, like that's all the introduction I need.

Carlos's face is open and kind, and he takes off his mirrored sunglasses to look me in the eyes when he shakes my hand. "It's so good to meet you, Brooklyn," he says. "I've heard wonderful things about you."

I wish he'd stop acting friendly and considerate so it would be easier to hate him. "You, too," I say.

I'm hoping Zoe will make a joke that'll get everything out in the open and make us all feel less weird, but instead she says, "My two favorite people in the same place. This is the best."

"You ladies ready for dinner?" Carlos asks, and Zoe nods and takes his hand. She reaches for mine with the other one, but I start fixing my ponytail and pretend not to notice. I'm not going to walk on her other side like we're her parents, swinging their boisterous, euphoric little kid between them.

Zoe chooses the same bistro where we had dinner with my mom; this place is apparently a magnet for awkward situations. At least I now know not to order the polenta. I have more than enough time to peruse the menu, actually; Carlos wants to tell Zoe what's going on with all their mutual friends back in Boulder, people whose names I've never heard. Considering that the two of them talk every day, I can't imagine where all this news is coming from. When they finally wrap up the gossip session, Carlos turns to me. "Tell me all about you," he says. "Are you in *Birdie* with Zo?"

"No," I say. "I'm not good enough for the main stage." I know I'm being annoyingly self-deprecating, but I want Zoe to jump in and tell Carlos how great I am.

She takes the bait. "Brooklyn's basically a professional pianist. She can play *anything* by ear. She knows, like, the entire thing of every musical. It's ridiculous."

I look down at my menu and smile. "Not *every* musical."

"Pretty much every musical. I bet you never look at the music when you play for your family."

"Almost never," I concede, and it comes out sounding both modest and confident, like the way Zoe said "Juilliard" on the day we met. I'm pretty pleased with myself.

"Your mom is that famous voice teacher, right?" Carlos asks. "What's her name?"

"Lana Blake Shepard," Zoe supplies.

"Right. Do you really think you can get Zo an audition when she moves to New York?"

I hate that Carlos seems to be under the impression that Zoe likes me because I'm *useful.* It's one thing for Jessa to think it, but it's totally different with someone who knows Zoe so well. Hasn't she cleared this up yet? "It's not up to me," I say. "But my mom basically already offered her a spot in her studio. She loves Zoe. When I told her we were together, she was thrilled out of her mind." I sit up straight and look Carlos right in the eye when I say it. *Did you hear that? I'm serious enough about us that I've told my parents.*

Carlos doesn't seem bothered at all. "That's so awesome. Zo's spent the entire last year talking about Lana. When she found out she was moving to New York, it was one of the first things she mentioned." All I hear is, *I was there when Zoe got into Juilliard, and you weren't.* I picture Carlos and me as two rams, butting each other with our big curved horns.

When the waiter comes, I order a burger, medium rare. I need to fortify myself with red meat if I'm going to wage a subtextual war all weekend.

Zoe orders, then gets up and heads toward the bathroom. "I'll be right back," she says. "You kids play nice, okay?"

Carlos smiles at her and says, "Why wouldn't we?" He's not acting like I'm a threat to him at all, which means one of us is misreading this situation. I desperately hope it's not me.

As soon as she's gone, he leans toward me. "So, listen . . . Zoe and I haven't seen each other in more than a month, and we were wondering if maybe . . . could you give us the room tonight? And maybe on Saturday, after we get back from camping? You can obviously sleep there tomorrow, while we're gone." He looks apologetic, but I can tell it's not really a request.

I don't know why I'm surprised; obviously Zoe and Carlos want to be alone tonight. They're not exactly going to lie chastely side by side and catch up on Boulder gossip while I sleep six feet away. In a couple of hours, they're going to have *sex*—full-on, naked *sex,* where no body parts are off limits and nobody pushes anyone's hands away. Maybe if I were satisfying her even a little, she would've canceled his trip.

I can't be upset with Carlos for any of this. It's entirely my fault he's here.

"Sure," I say, and my voice comes out scratchy and hoarse, like it had to claw its way up my throat. "You can have the room. That's fine."

"Thanks, Brooklyn." Carlos puts his hand over mine and gives it a grateful squeeze. "Zoe said you were cool. I can see why she likes you so much."

Half of me is going, *Zoe likes me so much!* and the other half is going, *I really wish my girlfriend's boyfriend would let go of my hand.* I flash him a quick smile and pull away.

When Zoe comes back from the bathroom, she slides into her chair and beams at us. "What'd I miss?" she asks. "Did you guys bond?"

"Yup," Carlos says at the same time that I say, "You didn't miss anything."

Zoe turns back to her boyfriend, full of questions about his summer job, and I slide my phone out of my purse and text Russell.

> You still free tonight?

18

The rest of dinner is excruciating. I spend the first half cataloging every detail of how Zoe and Carlos interact. It's obvious she likes him better than she likes me, but I want to know exactly how *much* better. Of course, that quickly becomes exhausting. By the time I'm halfway through my burger, I'm too worn out to pay that kind of attention, and I settle for keeping my eyes on my plate and making sure my mouth is always too full to talk. The second the check lands on the table, I plunk down a twenty and stand to leave.

Zoe looks up at me. "Where are you going?"

"I told Russell I'd meet up with him."

She makes a pouty face. "Can't you meet him later? We're going to get ice cream at Moo-Moo's. They have that blackberry chocolate chip you like." I'm not sure why she's trying to get me to stay; she obviously wants to be alone with her boyfriend.

"No, thanks. I'm too full for ice cream." I sling my bag over my shoulder, certain my head is going to explode if I stay here one more second. "Have fun camping tomorrow."

"Won't I see you back in the—" Zoe starts, but Carlos puts his hand over hers, and she stops talking. I guess they're one of those couples who can communicate telepathically. "Thanks, Brooklyn," she says instead.

"See you Saturday." Zoe moves to get up and hug me, but I can't handle her arms around me tonight; it'll only feel like a consolation prize. I pretend I don't see how she's reaching for me, and I walk out of the restaurant.

I'm not even twenty paces down the street when my phone chimes with a new text:

> You're not mad, are you?

No, I write back. *Have fun.* I add a smiley emoticon, glad she can't see my actual face.

The phone chimes again immediately.

> You're the absolute best. xoxoxo

I want to feel like I'm in control of *something,* so I don't reply.

I go straight to the dorm and stuff my laptop, a book, pajamas, toiletries, a towel, and a change of clothes into my duffel bag. It's probably way too much stuff, but I don't know what time they're leaving tomorrow, and the last thing I want is to show up when they're still in bed, sleepy and naked. I try not to even look at Zoe's bed as I pack, so I won't think too hard about what's going to happen there in a couple of hours.

Russell texts me his room number in Dewald, and I head over. I assume he'll have a roommate, too, but when he opens his door, I'm surprised to see that the room is a tiny single. The walls are covered in black-and-white posters of architecture, and there's a small drafting table set up in the corner and a pile of unfolded laundry on the bed. I kind of expected the room to smell musty or sweaty, like Jason's always did, but instead it smells like detergent.

"Hey," he says. "Come on in. What's with all the stuff?"

I plunk my bag on the floor and sit on the edge of his bed. "I got sexiled," I say.

"Oh, man. That sucks. Wait, who's Zoe dating?"

Me, I want to scream, but instead I say, "Someone from home. He's visiting from Colorado. Carlos." His name comes out of my mouth like it's a synonym for "slimy" or "chemotherapy."

"Is he terrible?" Russell asks.

"No, he's fine. He's actually really nice. I just . . . I want to sleep in my own room." *With my own girlfriend.*

"Where are you going to sleep tonight?"

I shrug. "The lounge in Ramsey, I guess. I know we're not really supposed to, but I don't think anyone ever checks."

"Those couches are kind of short, aren't they? Do you want to stay here?"

I look around. "Where?"

"You can have the bed—I washed the sheets today. I can crash on the floor. I have a sleeping bag."

I search his face for signs that he's just being polite, but he kind of looks like he *wants* me to stay. "Really?" I ask.

"Really. It's no big deal."

"Thank you," I say. "And, um, do you think maybe I could sleep here on Saturday, too? Zoe and Carlos won't be around tomorrow, so I can have the room then."

"Of course you can. It'll be cool to hang out. Let me fold this stuff, and then maybe we can watch a movie or something."

"Sounds perfect," I say. I'm too distracted to talk, and I don't want Russell to notice how preoccupied I am.

He takes his time folding his laundry into superprecise squares, and I try not to look; we're not close enough to know what patterns are printed on each other's underwear. I've learned enough uncomfortably intimate things already tonight. When Russell's done, he joins me on the bed, facing his giant desktop computer. We pick a silly buddy cop movie—I can't deal with watching people have actual feelings right now—and switch off the light. A few minutes into the movie, Russell wraps a friendly arm around my shoulders, like he knows I need to be comforted, and I snuggle against his side. It makes me feel tiny and warm and protected. I'm not able to forget about Zoe and Carlos, exactly, but knowing someone's here for me numbs the pain a little.

When the movie ends, Russell doesn't move, and his breathing is so deep and steady that I wonder for a minute whether he's fallen asleep. I'm about to slip out from under his arm and go sleep on the lounge couch after all, when he clears his throat. "Did you know there are more heavy metal bands per capita in Scandinavia than anywhere else in the world?"

I snort. "That is ... not as surprising as it probably should be."

"Damn. I was trying to blow your mind." He thinks for a minute. "Did you know female kangaroos have three vaginas?"

"*What?* No. That *does* blow my mind." Russell laughs, and he's so close that the sound rumbles through me like when you stand too close to the speakers at a concert.

"Hey," he says. "You seemed upset earlier. Was it the sexiling, or is something else bothering you?"

It's nice that he noticed, though it's also annoying that Russell is so much more in touch with my emotions than Zoe, who should be paying the closest attention. "Thanks, but I don't want to talk about it, if you don't mind," I say. "I feel better now that I'm here. You and the movie and the kangaroo vaginas totally helped."

"Kangaroo vaginas—the cure for what ails you."

I laugh and sit up. "We should get some sleep. Are you sure you'll be okay on the floor?"

"Yup," he says. "I don't really fit in that bed anyway."

"I feel bad. I can still go to the lounge if—"

"Brooklyn," he says. "Shut up and let me be nice to you."

I shut up.

He goes to brush his teeth, and I change into my pajamas and climb into his bed, which has dark blue sheets and a striped comforter that screams "boy." It's a little pilly and not nearly as soft as my green polka-dotted bedding, but at least it smells clean. Russell comes back from the bathroom wearing square glasses that look really cute on him, and he spreads out his sleeping bag right next to the bed like he's guarding me from something. I offer him the only pillow, but he lets me keep it and balls up a couple of sweatshirts under his head instead. When he turns out the light, I expect things to get awkward, but they don't. Lying there in the dark with him feels surprisingly comfortable.

"Russell?" I say.

"Mm-hmm?"

"Road trips—love or hate?"

"Love," he says. "Before I got this gig, my sister and I were talking about driving across the country this summer. We still might do it next year. Why do you ask?"

"No reason. It's a game someone taught me."

"Oh, okay." Russell's quiet for a second, and I think that's the end of it, but then he says, "Emo songs about how love is a lie and people always disappoint you—love or hate?"

I laugh; that's a really good one, much more creative than anything Zoe or I ever came up with. "Most of the time, hate. But in that first week or so after a relationship ends, love. When you actually feel like love is a lie, there's nothing like a good angsty song to validate you."

"You don't really think love is a lie, though, do you?"

Right now I think love is a big confusing snarl, but I say, "No, of course not."

"Good. That would be a depressing way to live."

"Looking at other people's vacation photos, love or hate?"

"Fewer than fifty, love," Russell says. "More than fifty, get over yourself, nobody cares. Marathoning a TV show you know is objectively bad but that you can't seem to stop watching, even though you have no idea why—love or hate?"

"Hate. I have to take my guilty pleasures in small doses or it makes me feel gross. Like, I actually feel physically sticky." Russell makes a snorting sound, and I say, "What?"

"I don't believe in guilty pleasure," he says.

"Oh, come on. Are you telling me there's not one single thing you secretly love?"

"Of course there is. But I think that if you like something, you should just like it. You don't need to apologize for it or explain yourself to anyone. Why should liking something make anyone feel *guilty*?"

"You're right," I say, and I wonder if he's thinking about Olivier.

With Zoe, I was always satisfied playing this game with normal topics like amusement parks and sad books and the idea of having children. But Russell pushes me to come up with quirkier, funnier, more creative topics: guessing the killer right from the beginning of a mystery, sticking your hand out the window while you drive, that feeling of falling you get when you're right on the edge of sleep. I had thought Zoe's and my new version of Love or Hate was as good as the old way, but now that I'm playing this game with words again, I'm surprised by how much better I like it. Having someone really *listen* to me actually makes me feel closer than touching does.

When you start dating someone, people always say you've become "more than friends." But now, as I laugh with Russell,

I'm less sure that what Zoe and I have now is more than we had before.

I hear him roll toward me in the dark. "Hey, Brooklyn?"

"Yeah?"

"What are you doing tomorrow?"

I hadn't planned to do much of anything besides sulking in my room and hoping Zoe came home early. "Nothing, really. Why?"

"I was thinking of driving around the Hudson Valley a little bit and checking out some of the other weird small towns around here. You want to come?"

"Is there a group going?"

"No, it would just be us."

For a second I feel disloyal to Zoe for even thinking about it; first I'm playing our game with someone else, and now I'm considering spending my day off alone with Russell. But she's the one who should feel guilty; she's across campus having sex with someone else right now while I'm having an innocent pajama party with my gay friend.

"That sounds really fun," I say. "I'd love to."

"Great. Maybe we could grab breakfast at Kayla's first? I've been meaning to try their scones."

I tell him I can't wait, and for a few minutes, I'm proud of myself. If Zoe gets to have fun without me, I get to have fun without her, too. But as I try to fall asleep in an empty bed for the first time in eight days, I can't help missing her.

19

The next morning is bright and sunny, and Russell and I pick a random direction and set off down the highway. We stop in every town we pass and investigate the weird little shops—the one that sells knives carved from animal bones, the bookstore full of tomes about conspiracy theories, the antiques shop with the dresses that were supposedly owned by Audrey Hepburn. We buy a baguette and some cheeses with fancy names and have a picnic next to a half-dry creek. We play Love or Hate. We think up titles for silly Shakespeare-musical mashups, like *A Midsummer Night's Dreamgirls* and *The Lion King Lear* and *Thoroughly Modern Macbeth*. Russell tells me you can write a thirty-five-mile-long line with the average pencil and that it's illegal to burp inside a church in Nebraska. When we get back to Allerdale in the evening, we grab dinner at Sammy's and spend a couple of hours messing around on one of the practice room pianos.

It should be a perfect day. Instead, I spend the entire time missing Zoe.

The scenic crew and I start loading the *Macbeth* set into Legrand early on Saturday morning, so I don't see her again until we're all called in for a surprise company meeting that night. The second Russell and I walk into Haydu, she calls my name from across the room, and a smile breaks across my face when I spot her waving and gesturing toward the seat she's saved for me. She looks a little tanner from hiking, and it's strange and terrible that she could change even a little bit in the two days we've been apart.

"I'm going to sit with Zoe," I tell Russell. "You want to get dinner after the meeting?"

He looks surprised; we've spent so much time together the last couple of days that I guess he expected me to sit with him. But when he says, "Sure," he doesn't sound upset at all. "I'll meet you out front when this is over." He smiles at me and then heads straight for Olivier, who's chatting with Barb near the stage.

I bump into a bunch of people as I hurry over to Zoe; I can't get to her fast enough. When I sit down, she hugs me close, and even though the arm of the chair is digging into my side, even though I *know* I should be pissed at her, I never want her to let go.

"Hey," she says close to my ear. "I missed you."

I think, *No you didn't,* but what comes out of my mouth is, "I missed you, too. Where's Carlos?"

"He's showering. Hopefully this meeting won't take long. Do you know what it's about?"

"No," I say, and I try not to think about the reasons Carlos might need to shower at six in the evening. "Hopefully it's nothing bad. Did you guys have fun camping?"

"Yeah, it was great! The Catskills are *gorgeous,* and the hike we did was supereasy after what we're used to at home. Look at this!" She digs out her phone and shows me a picture taken from the top of a small mountain.

I scroll through her photos: trees, a lake, Carlos with a makeshift walking stick, Zoe eating a granola bar, about fifteen selfies with their faces pressed together, a few shots of them kissing. Then come the photos of Zoe setting up their tent and Carlos roasting marshmallows over a campfire. When I get to one of Carlos shirtless in a red sleeping bag, I hand the phone back. "Looks really nice," I say.

"What'd you do while we were gone?"

Before I can answer, Bob Sussman jogs onto the stage. "Good evening, warriors for art!" he shouts. "Is everyone having a good summer?"

The whole company cheers, and Bob smiles so hard, I think his face might split down the middle. *"Wonderful,"* he says. "I am *so* pleased to hear that."

"How's your summer, Bob?" someone shouts from the front row, and everyone laughs. If someone asked Marcus Spooner a question like that, he'd probably give us a lecture about how happiness is detrimental to acting, then throw a few cream pies at us for good measure.

"My summer has been *spectacular!*" Bob answers. "Thank you for asking! It's such a delight to see all of you. The work you've done over the past six weeks has been phenomenal.

Some of our long-time donors have told me they think this might be the very best season Allerdale has ever had, and that's all down to you. Thank you for making it so special."

Everyone applauds, and I find myself smiling. I know I've had nothing to do with making this season special, but it's impossible not to feel included when Bob is talking.

"I have a very exciting announcement for you tonight," he continues. "This coming Monday, right here in Haydu Hall, Allerdale will hold its first twenty-four-hour play festival!"

Everyone breaks into enthusiastic murmurs and whispers, and Bob beams like a benevolent dad. "I'm so glad you're excited as well! The goal of a twenty-four-hour play festival is, of course, to write, rehearse, and perform original short plays within the span of a single day. You will form groups of eight or fewer, and starting at 12:01 AM on Monday, you will gather to create your own fantastic original work. At eight PM that same day, you will perform those ingenious creations right here for an audience of donors and subscribers. The only rules are that you may not begin work on your play until the clock starts, and the work you perform must be memorized and completely original. Your whole group is not required to perform, as long as you all contribute to the creative process. Do something you've never done before! Experiment! Be bold!" Bob is bouncing on his toes now, so buoyed by his excitement that I think he may achieve liftoff.

My phone vibrates with a text from Russell:

> Want to try one of our mash-up musicals?
> Midsummer night's dreamgirls, maybe?

OMG YES, I text back, and my brain floods with adrenaline at the prospect of creating a whole parody musical with him. Writing, rehearsing, and performing a play in less than a day sounds insane, but I know the two of us can make it happen. In a weird way, it feels like the most doable thing I've been asked to accomplish since I got here.

"You're free to start forming your groups now," Bob says. "Please write your names down on this sign-up sheet, and have *fun,* you brilliant people! I can't wait to see what you come up with!"

Everyone starts talking at once, and Zoe grabs my hand. "Should we work alone, or should we ask Jessa and Livvy and those guys to work with us? It might be easier to get ideas if we have more people. Then again, if it were just us, we could—"

I cut her off before she can say anything about being alone with me in a rehearsal room. "Russell and I already have an idea for something we want to write, actually," I say. "But I'd love it if you'd work with us. All of you, actually—we're going to need a bunch of people."

A crinkle appears between her eyebrows. "Wait, how do you guys already have an idea? Did you know about this in advance?"

"No, it's something we've been kicking around. He texted a minute ago to ask if I wanted to work on it for this. See?" I hold up my phone, as if I'm required to prove it.

"Oh," Zoe says. It's like she had no idea until this moment that I had a life separate from her. "What's the idea?"

"It's a Shakespeare-Broadway musical mash-up, like a parody. We were thinking of maybe doing *A Midsummer Night's*

Dreamgirls, since everyone knows both shows. We'd keep the general story from *Midsummer,* and we'd rewrite the lyrics from a bunch of *Dreamgirls* songs to be about the *Midsummer* characters." Russell and I haven't actually discussed the logistics of the mash-up, but it's very clear to me that this is how it should work, and I know he'll agree.

For a second, I'm afraid Zoe's going to say that's a dumb idea, that she'd rather do something else. If she's not into it, I'm afraid I'll back down and let her take the lead, like always, and being in charge for once is suddenly really important to me. Fortunately, she starts laughing. "That's really funny. I'm definitely in. Want me to round up everyone else?"

"Yeah, that'd be perfect," I say. I can write a twenty-four-hour play with no problem, but there's no way I could find a cast without Zoe. None of the other apprentices take me seriously anymore. Maybe this play festival is exactly the opportunity I need to show Jessa and Livvy and Kenji and Todd that I'm worth something.

Zoe gets up. "Okay, I'll be right back."

"Should I come with you?"

"No, I can do it myself." Her tone is light, but she obviously thinks it'll be easier to talk them into working with us if I'm not there to screw things up. "Why don't you put our names down on the sign-up sheet?"

"Shouldn't we wait until they say yes?"

"They'll say yes. I'm very convincing."

She could just as easily have said, *It's a really good idea. I'm sure they'll go for it* or *How could they not want to work with you?* But she's trying to help me, so I try not to be annoyed that she's making this all about her. "Okay," I say. "Thanks."

"When I'm done, we'll pick up Carlos and go get some dinner in town, okay?"

And that's all it takes for my annoyance to get the better of me. How rude is it to assume I have nothing better to do than be a pathetic third wheel? "I can't go out with you guys tonight," I say, struggling to keep my voice even and pleasant.

"Why not?"

"Because I'm eating with Russell."

Zoe looks confused. "I thought we weren't supposed to start working on the show until midnight tomorrow."

"We're not working on the show; we're hanging out. He's my friend. And I'm sleeping in his room tonight so you and Carlos can . . . you know."

"Oh," Zoe says. "It's just that I already told Carlos you'd come with us. We barely got to hang out with you the other day, and he wants to get to know you better."

I can't believe she's making me argue with her about this. She has to know how much it sucks for me to see them together. "Carlos isn't going to care if I'm there or not," I say. "He wants to see you, not me."

I wait for Zoe to make it right by saying, *I care if you're there.* But instead she says, "All right. I guess I'll see you tomorrow, then." She sounds disappointed, but not disappointed enough.

As she walks away from me, I try not to feel too disappointed, either.

20

I lie awake for hours after Russell falls asleep on the floor that night, my mind chasing its tail like a hyperactive puppy. Is Zoe mad at me for ditching her and Carlos? She did me a favor by convincing the other apprentices to work with me on the play festival, and maybe I should've gone out with them in return, regardless of how uncomfortable I felt. Then again, she's handled this whole Carlos situation so badly that maybe I don't owe her anything. If her boyfriend was going to fly out here, she really should've talked to me about it beforehand and laid down some ground rules, right? I shouldn't have been exiled to Russell's room, and Carlos shouldn't have been the one to ask me to go. All of that was Zoe's responsibility, and she totally dropped the ball.

I send the universe an image of myself yelling all those things at her, but it doesn't make me feel any better. I don't want to fight. All I want is for Carlos to leave so she can be mine again.

I spend my whole crew call on Sunday debating whether to confront her. Maybe if I don't say anything, the weirdness will fade away on its own. It might be too early in the relationship for me to complain; everything still feels fragile between Zoe and me, and I don't want to ruin our last three weeks at Allerdale. But she'll be in the city starting in September, and situations like this are bound to happen again. Isn't it better to confront a problem before it becomes a precedent?

I still haven't decided what to do by the time I get home on Sunday evening. When I unlock the door, I find Zoe sprawled on my bed, staring at the ceiling; she's not even listening to music or anything, and her mascara is smeared like she's been crying for hours. How am I supposed to bring up my hurt feelings when she looks so listless?

"Hey," I say quietly. "Is he gone?"

"Yeah."

"Are you okay?"

"I guess," she says. "Come here?" She reaches out a hand to me, but she looks so hesitant, like she's not sure whether I even want her anymore. It's ridiculous to feel sorry for her when I'm the one who's hurt, but she seems so miserable that I can't help it. She's my Zoe, and she needs me.

I sit down on the bed and gather her into my arms, and she curls against me. "Are we okay?" she asks in a very small voice.

It's the perfect opening to say all the things I've been

thinking, and I almost do it, but then I chicken out at the last second. "I think I'm okay if you are," I say.

"I barely slept all night 'cause I kept thinking about how pissed at me you probably were. Having him here was awful for you, wasn't it?"

It's really nice to hear her admit it. "Yeah, it kind of was," I say.

"I'm so sorry, Brooklyn."

"It's okay. I know it's complicated. And I know I'm allowed to see other people, too, if I want."

She looks up at me, startled. "But . . . you don't want to, do you?"

I think about telling her I do, so she'll know how I've been feeling all weekend, but the last thing our relationship needs is more drama. "No," I say.

"Good. I know it's unfair, but I want you all to myself." She sighs and puts her head down on my chest. "Loving two people at once is so confusing."

I suddenly feel like I've downed fifteen shots of espresso. "Wait," I say. "You *love* me?"

"Of course I do. Don't you know that?"

She looks up at me with those pretty sunflower eyes, and it becomes very easy to forget all about Carlos. Guys I've dated have told me they loved me before, and I've said it back; Jason and I started saying it after a couple of months. I thought I was telling the truth, but the way I feel right now is so different that it makes me want to call him and take it back.

"I love you, too," I say, and the smile that breaks across her face could power a city block.

"So you're not mad?"

"I'm not mad," I say.

"And you still want to do this?" She cups my cheek in her hand and kisses me, soft and sweet.

"Yes," I whisper against her mouth.

"Good. I was so afraid that I'd screwed things up and lost you."

I *know* I shouldn't let everything I feel fade away. We'll have to talk about Carlos eventually. But no relationship is perfect, and *my girlfriend loves too many people* seems like something I should be able to handle. Dating Zoe is the one thing I'm doing right this summer, and I'm not willing to give it up over this.

So I pull her closer and say, "You didn't lose me. You can have both of us."

—

We stay in bed until the shadows start to lengthen, holding on to each other and murmuring silly, pointless things that feel important because they're interspersed with "I love you"s. When Zoe's alarm goes off at seven-thirty, she buries her face in my shoulder and groans. "I have a stupid costume fitting. I don't want to let go of you."

I kiss the top of her head. "I'll still be here when you get back."

"Will you come with me?"

I'll probably be in everyone's way, but Zoe finally wants me near her again, and I don't want to let go, either. "Sure," I say.

She holds my hand all the way to the shop. When we get there, she changes into a flouncy yellow dress and stands in front of a three-way mirror while a gray-haired woman pins her hem. There are only two costume people still working—everyone else is probably at dinner—so I wander through the organized chaos of the shop without fear of being a nuisance. The shelves that line the walls are packed with spools of thread, ribbon, trim, and buttons in every conceivable color, and there are half-naked dress forms everywhere, clad in Shakespearean doublets and sequined evening gowns. In one corner, shoe boxes are stacked all the way up to the ceiling, each one neatly labeled. The lulling whir of sewing machines and box fans fills the air, underscored by the oldies station playing on a tiny radio. It's nicer than I expected in here; maybe I won't mind working wardrobe for *Macbeth* next rotation.

I'm inspecting a pair of blue satin pantaloons when Zoe comes back out in her normal clothes and slips an arm around my waist. "Hey," she says. "All done. You want to see something cool?"

"Of course," I say.

She grabs my hand, leads me to the back corner of the shop, and pushes back a faded maroon curtain to reveal a staircase. "Come on," she says. "Costume storage is up there."

"Are we allowed to go in?"

"Probably not," she says, but she's already on the third step. I take a quick look around the room, but nobody's watching us, so I follow. This isn't exactly a daring escapade, but Zoe's enthusiasm makes everything feel like an adventure.

We emerge into a big, dusty space crowded with a maze

of clothing racks. The one closest to me is labeled "1920s Women" and holds more flapper dresses than I've ever seen in one place. The next one over has military uniforms on one end and Victorian gowns on the other. I finger the beaded hem of a black-and-silver dress. "This place is *amazing*," I say.

"Isn't it?" Zoe disappears down an aisle and emerges a minute later wearing an enormous red Kentucky Derby hat with feather plumes. "What do you think?" she asks. "Does it bring out my eyes?"

"Oh, for sure," I say.

"Here, I got you one, too."

She tosses me a hideous, wide-brimmed gold hat covered in cloth roses, plastic cherries, and a fake bird. I pull it on and adopt a terrible British accent. "Daahhh-ling, won't you join me for tea and crumpets in the parlor?"

Zoe swaps her hat for one of those furry Russian ones with giant earflaps. "No time for tea! Fetch me the sled dogs!" she growls in a baritone voice, and we both burst out laughing. I love that even after everything we went through this weekend, we can still be silly together. It makes me feel like things are going to be okay between us after all.

Zoe pushes deeper into the room, opens a plastic bin labeled "Undergarments," and pulls out a lacy purple bra so big, she could probably fit her entire head into one side. "Oh my God, look," she says. When she fastens it over her T-shirt, the empty cups sag down so low, they almost touch her waist. She sidles up to me and shimmies her shoulders. "Do my giant purple bazooms turn you on, baby?"

I laugh. "That thing would probably fit Barb."

"Can you even imagine? I bet she sneaks up here at night and parades around in it." Zoe tugs a flouncy red petticoat up over her shorts, then pulls something out of the box that looks like three U-shaped neck pillows sewn together. "What do you think this is?"

"It goes under a bustle," I say. "Here, give it to me." I tie it on over my jeans and shake my butt so the pillows bounce up and down. "It matches my hat, don't you think?"

"So hot," Zoe says. "Now all you need is this." She grabs a purple velvet cape with a dragon embroidered on the back and drapes it around my shoulders. I complete the ensemble with a huge, blingy dollar sign on a long gold chain, and she nods her approval.

"Perfect," I say. "I'm ready for my close-up."

Zoe grabs the two sides of my cape and uses them to pull me up against her. "Is this close enough?"

"Almost," I say. "Maybe a tiny bit closer?"

She runs her hands down to my waist and over the pillows. "Mmm, a cape and a butt pad. Exactly what I look for in a girl."

"I've always had a thing for furry earflaps, personally." She leans in to kiss me, but my dead-bird hat bonks her in the forehead, and we both start giggling. She tips the brim up and tries again, and this time it goes better. I love that she's willing to risk kissing me when someone could come up here at any moment and catch us, and I pull her tighter against me. Now that this weekend is finally over, I never want anything to come between us again.

After a minute, Zoe pulls away and runs her thumb gently

over my cheek. "You," she whispers, "look absolutely ridiculous."

"Says the girl with the dead wombat on her head."

"Take a picture with me," she says. "We need to commemorate our hotness."

She pulls out her phone, and we lean our heads together and make sultry faces. Zoe clicks and clicks and clicks, like she can't get enough of documenting us. When she ducks under the brim of my absurd hat and snaps a photo of herself kissing my cheek, the joy that wells up in my chest makes me feel like I might pop and scatter bits of velvet and red crinoline and plastic cherries everywhere.

It wouldn't be the worst way to go.

———

At ten minutes to midnight, Zoe and I head over to Haydu to get our rehearsal room assignment for the play festival. Everyone's there, clutching blankets and snacks and psyching themselves up for the all-nighter ahead. Most of the company's wearing T-shirts and yoga pants, but a few people are taking the sleepover thing to the next level—Pandora's in a lacy shortie pajama set that definitely isn't appropriate for anywhere but the bedroom. Our cast looks wide awake and ready to work, and they greet me with friendly smiles. Even Jessa seems to be making an effort to set our differences aside for the night. I wonder what Zoe said to them.

Russell introduces himself to everyone, then turns to

me and holds up his hand for a high five. "Ready to kick some ass?"

"Ready," I say. Even though I'm nervous, I *do* feel ready, now that things are good between Zoe and me again.

Bob reads off our rehearsal room assignments, leads us in a countdown to midnight, and then sends us off to "make some brilliant theater." The seven of us set up camp in Haydu 107 with some party-sized bags of Doritos and a whiteboard. I'm crunching on chips and waiting for someone to suggest a starting point, when Jessa turns to me and says, "You're supposed to be our director, right? So, what do we do?"

I've never really been in charge of anything before, and I realize I have no idea how to begin. I glance at Russell for help, but he nods like I should go ahead and take the lead. "Okay, well, um, we have people here from both shows, which is really great," I start. "Maybe the *Midsummer* cast could give us a refresher course on the basic story, and then you could walk us through the *Dreamgirls* sound track, Jessa? How does that sound?"

The words come out timid and hesitant, but Zoe says, "Sure, sounds good," and when she and Livvy and Kenji and Todd start listing *Midsummer* plot points on the whiteboard, I start to relax. When we're done listening to the sound track, Russell and I lead a discussion on which parts of the *Midsummer* story we should keep and where we should insert our parody songs, fitting the text and the music together like a puzzle. It's challenging, but it's really fun, too, and it occurs to me that this is the first Allerdale-sanctioned activity that hasn't felt like work. I can totally do this.

We agree that Zoe, Livvy, Kenji, and Todd should play the four confused, manipulated *Midsummer* lovers. Zoe will double as Titania, queen of the fairies, and Russell will make a brief appearance as Puck, who just has to run across the stage and administer a love potion. Jessa will play Bottom, the actor who gets his head swapped for a donkey's and gets drawn into a brief love affair with Titania. I'll be the accompanist instead of appearing onstage, but for the first time, I don't feel like I'm trying to hide behind the piano. I'm excited to show the whole company how well I can play.

When it's time to start working out the parody lyrics, Russell and I sit down on the bench side by side, but it's hard to fall into our usual rhythm with so many people watching us. I never think twice about singing when I'm alone with him, but performing even the smallest snippets in front of the other apprentices makes me feel sick with nerves. My back is to Jessa, but I imagine the triumphant looks she's probably exchanging with Livvy and Zoe every time I open my mouth—*See, I told you she didn't deserve to be here. No wonder her mom didn't let her perform in class.*

I stop singing and clear my throat, and Russell breaks off in the middle of a phrase. "You okay?"

"Yeah," I say. "My allergies are acting up. You'll have to forgive my voice tonight."

"I think you sound fine," he says.

"Thanks, but I really don't." Behind me, Jessa coughs, and I can't tell if it's a subtext-laden cough or a genuine one.

"Well, I don't exactly sound like Beyoncé, either, but it doesn't really matter as long as we write some great lyrics, right?" Russell starts playing again and sings another little snippet. "What do you think about that?"

I know he's probably just trying to make me feel better, but he's totally right. Tonight I'm a songwriter, not a performer, and the only thing that matters is how funny and clever I can be. Aside from the people in this room, nobody will ever hear me sing our lyrics. I shoot him a grateful smile, and I dive back in.

Soon Russell and I are working together like a machine, caught up in our own little world as we toss ideas back and forth and try to outdo each other. Though we've encouraged the rest of the group to contribute, they all keep quiet, and pretty soon I completely forget they're here. Writing with Russell is even more fun than writing with Uncle Harrison, and the process feels so completely right that the time flies by. When I glance at my phone after we've finished our third song, I'm shocked to see that it's five in the morning.

I turn around to check on the cast and find them sprawled on the floor, their heads pillowed on each other's stomachs. Kenji and Todd are spooning, both fast asleep, and everyone else seems to be struggling to stay awake. "You guys should go home and nap," I tell them. "Meet back here at eight?" They all nod blearily, struggle to their feet, and shamble off. When Jessa pats my shoulder on her way out and says, "Good stuff, girl," I feel way more validated than I probably should.

Zoe comes up next to the piano. "You ready to go?"

There's no way I'd be able to sleep right now; my mind is overflowing with ideas, and I want to get them all down before they float away. "I'm not actually that tired," I say. "I think I might keep working. How're you feeling, Russell?"

He rubs his eyes. "We can probably knock out one more song before I crash."

Zoe looks disappointed. "Well, at least come outside with me for a second?"

A sliver of sunlight is starting to peek over the horizon when we step out the front door of Haydu. Even though I know everyone is up and working, it's quiet enough that it feels like the whole campus belongs only to us. Zoe laces her fingers through mine and stands so close that our arms touch all the way up to the shoulders. The air is cool, but her skin is warm, and I hold on to her as I listen to the sounds of the birds waking up.

"You were awesome in there," she says. "Totally in charge. It was so sexy."

"It was?"

She turns me to face her and wraps her arms tight around my waist. "Absolutely. You're suuuuure you don't want to come back to the room and nap with me?"

"I should really keep working," I say. I try to sound resigned to it, and I hope she can't tell that I'd honestly rather be at the piano than in bed with her right now.

She sighs and makes a pouty face. "It's no fair that Russell gets to hang out with you all night and I don't."

"Night's already over. And if I don't write, you guys will have nothing to sing." I touch her cheek. "Get some sleep, okay? And bring me some coffee when you come back? And maybe a doughnut?"

"If you want a doughnut, you better earn it, Shepard."

"Later," I tell her.

She gives me a quick kiss. "Fine. Later. I definitely won't be lying naked in your bed while you're doing boring work, so don't think about that. It would only be distracting."

I smile, but my stomach is twisting uncomfortably. I want Zoe to say the perfect thing right now—that I'm a talented songwriter, that our parodies are hilarious, that my work makes her respect me and proves I belong at Allerdale. I want to go back to the way we connected earlier today. But now she's focusing on all the wrong stuff, and it makes her seem so disappointingly normal. I know *everything* she does can't be new and sparkly and endlessly fascinating, but I hate that she doesn't surprise and delight me every time we talk anymore. I hate that I care.

She gives me a mischievous smile back, and then she turns and heads toward Ramsey, hips swinging. She doesn't turn around, but I can tell she knows I'm watching her. She's as beautiful and sexy as ever, but as much as I hate to admit it, I'm a little relieved to see her walking away from me.

21

By the time we gather in Haydu that evening to perform our short plays, I'm running solely on caffeine and adrenaline. I napped this afternoon while the cast worked on their lines, but I kept waking up to jot down more ideas, so it wasn't exactly restful. I could really use more coffee, but I know my hands will shake if I have any, and then I won't be able to play the piano. The whole company looks to be in the same exhausted-manic state as me; everywhere I turn, I meet too-wide smiles and glassy, crazed eyes. Even though I feel pretty awful, it's kind of cool to be as wrung out as the rest of them—it proves I've worked as hard as they have. This is exactly the kind of Allerdale experience my family has been talking about my whole life, and now I'm here, right in the middle of every-thing.

Our group is scheduled to perform last, and I'm pretty sure everyone's going to be asleep by the time we get up onstage.

"Pinch me if I start to snore," I tell Zoe, who's sitting next to me dressed in a bedsheet toga. A few seats away, Jessa holds the donkey head from *Midsummer* on her lap and idly strokes its nose.

"Do I get to choose *where* I pinch you?" Zoe asks.

Russell sits down in the empty seat on my other side. "You ready for this?" he asks.

"I think so." I want to express how much it means to me that we got to create this show together—the one truly creative moment of my summer—but I'm too tired to organize those ideas into coherent sentences. So instead I nudge him with my shoulder and say, "Thanks. Seriously."

"Thank *you*," he says back, and I know he gets it.

The lights go down, and Bob bounds onto the stage in a bright yellow bow tie, looking so fresh and rested that it's hard not to hate him. He explains the rules of the festival to our audience, and then the first group of non-eqs gets up and performs a singsongy, rhyming chant accompanied by a lot of stomping and clapping and body-slapping. I think it's about a truck stop, but I'm not totally sure. Three apprentices do a play about a stripper who accidentally gets sent back in time to the home of Sylvia Plath. Pandora's group does a moody piece about a breakup, heavy on keening and garment-rending and light on dialogue. Most of the plays aren't *good,* exactly, but they're all pretty entertaining, and watching them makes me even more frustrated with *Señor Hidalgo.* Every single group has come up with something more cohesive in the last twenty-four hours than Alberto has in six weeks.

By the time it's our turn, I'm so exhausted, I don't even have the energy to be nervous. We get a huge round of applause as we make our way up to the stage, but I can't tell if it's because our cast is popular or because everyone's glad the night is almost over. I take my place at the piano, and as Zoe, Livvy, Kenji, and Todd group together center stage for our opening number, I feel a surge of love for my cast. Part of me can't even believe how much we've accomplished today.

Our show starts with the lovers singing a parody of "Steppin' to the Bad Side" as they head off into the magical woods, represented by the fog pouring out of the hazers. Russell does his brief cameo as Puck, poisoning Titania's and Lysander's eyes so they'll fall in love with the first living creatures they see. He also turns Bottom's head into a donkey head, and Jessa sings a parody of "I Am Changing" as she makes her transformation. The lovers fall for the wrong people and sing our parody of "Love Love You Baby" before eventually sorting themselves out. Bottom gets her normal head back and sings our version of "And I Am Telling You I'm Not Going" to Titania. When I look up from the piano, I see Bob in the front row, laughing so hard, there are tears running down his cheeks.

Our cast finishes up with a parody of "One Night Only," and then Zoe pulls me out from behind the piano for a full-group bow. I grip her hand on one side and Russell's on the other as a wave of applause breaks over us, and it's insanely satisfying to know that I created something everyone loved. I know this is probably the only time in my life I'll get to bow on the Haydu stage, and I stare out into the audience's smiling faces and soak it all up. I wish my family were here to see me succeed at something. Uncle Harrison really would've appreciated this.

The houselights come up, and the seven of us stumble into the wings, where we crush into a group hug with the donkey head squished in the middle. Jessa's arm is tight around my shoulders, and even though I know her affection is probably temporary, I hold out hope that we can at least be friendly again, now that she sees I'm actually good at something. Everyone's talking at the same time, and I close my eyes and stay very quiet, trying to fix this perfect feeling of belonging in my memory.

Bob comes bounding backstage and claps us on the shoulders, and we break apart. "The stars of our evening!" he cries. "That was absolutely *brilliant*! I can't remember the last time I laughed so hard. How did you come up with the idea?"

"It was all Brooklyn," Zoe says.

I smile and look at the floor. "Russell and I wrote most of it together."

"Well, it was fantastic. I'd love to see a full-length show in this format one day."

"Thanks," Russell says. "We'd be happy to write you one anytime. Have your people call our people."

Bob laughs. "I will, I will," he says. "Congratulations to all of you." As he walks away, he pumps his fist in the air and shouts, "Warriors for art!"

There's a formal reception set up in a tent outside, and everyone heads in that direction. But when Zoe tries to steer me into the crowd, I resist. "I think I might go back to the room and sleep," I say.

"What? No, you can't leave! We need to celebrate!"

"I can't think of anything more celebratory than being unconscious right now," I say. "You should go to the reception, though. Have some champagne for me."

She plants her hands on her hips like a defiant six-year-old. "Absolutely not. You wrote a brilliant short play, and I am not letting you leave until you've celebrated."

"Zoe, I really can't deal with all those people—" I start, but she cuts me off.

"Wait here, okay? I'll be right back."

I'm too tired to fight with her, so I sit down in the wings, lean against the wall, and wait. My eyelids feel very heavy, so I decide to rest them for a few seconds, but I've barely had time to blink before Zoe's shaking my shoulder.

"Brooklyn," she whispers. "Wake up. I got us dessert."

I open my eyes and see her holding up a napkin-wrapped bundle. Everyone's gone, and the theater around us is completely silent. The ghost light sits in the center of the stage, casting its eerie blue-white glow onto the side of Zoe's face. "Did I fall asleep?" I ask. "How long have I been sitting here?"

"I don't know, fifteen minutes? You looked so peaceful, I almost didn't wake you." She sits down next to me, her shoulder pressed to mine, and I feel her shiver. "It's cold in here. I wish they wouldn't crank up the AC so high."

"I know somewhere warmer," I say. It's a Herculean effort to struggle to my feet, but if we're going to celebrate, we might as well do it right. "Follow me."

I lead her to the back of the stage and up the metal spiral staircase to the catwalks. The air is filled with that burning dust smell I've come to associate with stage lights, but it's toasty-warm, and I love being up here alone with Zoe. We settle down directly above the first row of seats, and she unwraps her napkin bundle, which is full of fancy little chocolate brownies and lemon squares and pecan rolls. I can't remember the last time I ate anything besides Doritos, and I stuff one into my mouth. "Oh my God, this is so freaking delicious," I say.

"I can't believe I've never been up here before." Zoe grabs the plug of the light above her head and looks at the piece of gaffer's tape holding it together. "J5," she reads. "What does that mean? What do you think would happen if I unplugged it?"

"Nothing would happen, except this light wouldn't turn on during the show tomorrow. J5 is the circuit number." I grab her hand. "Leave it alone."

"Oooh, the *circuit* number. Look at you, Little Miss Technical." Zoe pokes me in the side, and I giggle, but I'm kind of proud that I knew something she didn't.

We're both quiet for a minute, and I nibble on a tiny brownie and listen to the soft, comforting hum of the dimmer rack. "I love theaters when they're dark and empty like this," I say.

"I love theaters more when they're full of people cheering for us," Zoe says.

"I love theaters even *more* when they're full of you and me eating tiny delicious brownies *after* people cheered for us."

"I love theaters most when they're full of you and me eating brownies *and* making out," Zoe says, and she leans over and kisses me softly. There's more *I love you* than *I want you* in it, and it feels perfect.

I'm reaching out to pull her closer when I notice that the acrid smell of burning dust seems to be getting stronger. "Do you smell something weird?" I ask.

Zoe laughs. "Are you trying to tell me I need a shower?"

"No, I'm serious. It kind of smells like something's burning. But maybe it's—"

I don't even get to finish my sentence before the fire alarm goes off.

"Oh *shit*," Zoe shouts over the deafening buzzer, and we both leap to our feet and run for the spiral staircase. The smell gets worse as we near the ground, and as we dash down the center aisle toward the lobby, I notice smoke pouring out from under the black velour curtain at the back of the stage. I cover my mouth with my shirt and try to get a better look at where it's coming from, but Zoe pulls me forward.

"Should we call 911?" I yell.

"We need to get *out*!"

We burst into the cool night air and run for the tent full of patrons, looking for Bob or Marcus, but everyone has heard the alarm and is already stampeding in our direction. Barb stalks toward us like an angry bull, and Bob scurries behind her, shouting into his phone.

"Were you two inside?" Barb bellows when she spots us.

Zoe looks terrified. "Yes, but we didn't do anything, I swear!"

"Is there anyone else in the building?"

I shake my head. "Not that we saw, but we were only in the auditorium."

"Did you see smoke or flames?"

"There was a lot of smoke. It was coming from upstage left."

"Smoke upstage left!" Barb yells to Bob, and he repeats it into the phone.

The whole company and most of the donors have caught up with us now, and everyone's talking at once. "Back up!" Barb shouts, her voice like a megaphone. "Move away from the building! This is not a drill! The fire department is on the way. Seriously, guys, *move away from the building!*"

We back across the lawn and gather together in a tight knot. "That's our stage for *Birdie*," Zoe says. "What are we going to do?"

"Maybe they'll put it out quickly," I say. "It probably looked worse than it is. The theater will probably be fine."

But the glassed-in lobby is growing hazy with smoke by the time the police arrive a few minutes later, and it doesn't look like everything is going to be fine. In the next few minutes, two fire engines and two ambulances arrive and drive straight up onto the lawn, digging deep ruts into the perfectly manicured grass. The way the spinning blue and red lights wash over the company reminds me of Pandemonium. Firefighters spill off the trucks and surround the theater, shouting things like "working structure fire" and "flake the line out" and "upgrade to next alarm," and then they start unrolling hoses and strapping on masks and air tanks. Even from here, I can see flickers of flame when they open the theater doors and charge inside. Almost the entire company is taking photos and video on their phones, but I don't want to document this. I stand very still with my arms wrapped tight around me, watching the theater burn.

Putting out the fire takes way longer than I expected. Pandora and Natasha cling to each other and wail as they watch firefighters rush in and out of the building, and I wish I could duct tape their mouths shut; everyone's already upset, and they're making things worse. Zoe cries silently, and I put my arms around her as a few men climb up onto the roof and cut into it with saws, releasing spirals of smoke into the night air. Everything reeks of charred wood and burning synthetic fabric, and it's getting harder to breathe, but nobody makes a move to leave.

After about forty-five minutes, the firefighters finally get the flames under control, and we applaud as they emerge from the building, blackened from head to toe. Water streams out of the sooty lobby and soaks into our shoes as they remove their air tanks and start packing up their gear. Bob confers with the fire marshal, and when he finally heads in our direction, everyone starts shouting questions at the same time. Barb lets out an ear-piercing whistle to make us shut up.

"My dear, brave company," Bob says. "What a tragedy that you had to witness the death of our beautiful theater. But nobody was hurt, and we can all be grateful for that." I've never seen him look defeated before, and it's heartbreaking.

"What started the fire?" calls one of the non-eqs.

"We'll know more once we've done a thorough investigation, but it looks like the hazer shorted out backstage and ignited the curtains." Zoe and I exchange a startled look; if we hadn't used the hazer for our show tonight, would the theater still be standing? Is this all our fault? I wait for Bob to ask to see our group alone in his office, but he doesn't even glance at us. "I'm sure this goes without saying," he continues, "but you *must not* enter the theater again for any reason. It has sustained major structural damage, and you could be seriously injured. A contractor will board up the building tomorrow."

"But we're supposed to load in *Birdie* on Saturday," Livvy says.

Bob looks pained. "I'm afraid that won't be possible. Haydu will be out of commission for the rest of the summer."

Zoe grips my hand. "Is the show going to be canceled?" she asks.

"Hopefully not," Bob says. "My esteemed colleagues and I will talk over some possible solutions tonight, and we'll all reconvene in Legrand for an update at eleven tomorrow morning, okay? In the meantime, be safe and get some sleep. It's been a long day, and everything's under control now."

He tries to smile at us, and we try to smile back. But as we watch him turn away from the charred remnants of Haydu Hall and head toward his office, flanked by Barb and Marcus, it's impossible not to worry.

22

I wake up the next morning to the sound of my phone ringing. It's barely seven, and I don't recognize the number on the screen, but no one ever calls this early unless it's an emergency. Maybe something happened to my parents. I'm suddenly wide-awake.

"Make it stop," Zoe mumbles. She pulls my pillow over her head as I hit talk.

"Hello?" I choke. My throat is scratchy from all the smoke I inhaled last night.

"Good morning," says a calm, pleasant man's voice. "Is this Brooklyn?"

"Yes. What's wrong?"

"This is Bob Sussman, the managing director. I'm so sorry if I woke you, but we'd appreciate it if you could join us in my office as soon as possible."

I struggle into a sitting position. "What? Why?"

"I'll explain everything in person," Bob says. "Can you be here in twenty minutes?"

I throw on some clothes, and my mind starts spinning as I trudge across campus in the early-morning quiet. Have they decided the fire is my fault after all? Am I about to get kicked out of Allerdale? If I am, at least I went out on a high note, plus my parents will never know I wasn't really cast in *Birdie*. Maybe this is for the best. Then again, leaving Allerdale three weeks early means leaving Zoe three weeks early, and I'm not sure I can stand that. We've barely had any time to be together.

I push into the main office, ready to plead my case, and find Russell sitting outside Bob's closed office door. "Hey," he says. "What are you doing here?"

"I don't know. They told me to come in as quickly as I could. What are *you* doing here?"

"Same."

I sit down next to him. "Do you think we're in trouble?"

"What? No. Why would we be?"

"I mean, Bob said the hazer burned down the theater, and we're the ones who used it last, right? So doesn't that kind of make it our fault?"

"*We* didn't know it was broken," Russell says. "If we hadn't used it, they would've turned it on for *Dreamgirls* today, and the same thing would've happened. Right?"

"I guess." I pick at the hem of my shorts. "Tell me something weird to distract me?"

"A group of weasels is called a boogle," he says. "Everyone has a unique tongue print. The largest recorded snowflake was fifteen inches across. Is this helping?"

"Not really. But I do love the word 'boogle.'"

The office door opens, and Bob sticks his head out and beams at us. "You made it! Come in, come in." He certainly doesn't seem angy with us, but I can't imagine why we'd be here unless we're in trouble. I take a deep breath and follow Russell inside.

Bob's office is cluttered and cheerful, the walls crowded with framed Allerdale show posters and children's drawings. Barb and Marcus are seated on either side of the desk, and the third-rotation stage managers, Lauren and Magdalena, are crammed into narrow folding chairs against one of the walls. Russell and I sit down in the two remaining seats, and Bob boosts himself up onto his desk like a little kid and plunks down right on top of a pile of papers. I see the word "INSUR-ANCE" poking out from under his thigh.

"I'm sure you're wondering why we've called you here," he says.

"Yeah," Russell says, at the same time that I blurt out, "Are you kicking us out?"

Bob laughs. "No, of course not! Far from it. We have a proposal for you, actually. You two were the brains behind *A Midsummer Night's Dreamgirls,* correct?"

I nod. "I mean, the cast helped. But yeah, we wrote pretty much all of it."

"Wonderful. As you know, we're in a bit of a bind right now. We're down a performance space, but we can't cancel any of the actors' contracts or shorten the run of either *Birdie* or *Macbeth.* We considered trying to run the shows in repertory in Legrand, but we don't have the resources or the crew to do that many changeovers. So we wondered if the two of you might be interested in helping us create a *new* show, one in which the actors from both casts could perform."

We're both silent for a minute, and then Russell says, "Wait. You want us to write another mash-up?"

"*Precisely!* A full-length one, this time. We were thinking the original *Macbeth* actors could perform most of Shakespeare's text as planned, and you two could rewrite all the lyrics to the songs from *Birdie* to fit in with Shakespeare's story. Whenever it was time for a song, the *Macbeth* actors would leave the stage, and identically dressed *Birdie* actors would take their places and sing. That way, everyone can be included, and everyone can play to their strengths."

"It's not a perfect solution, of course," Marcus says. He's obviously disgusted by the whole idea.

"But it's the best one we can think of on short notice," Bob says. "What do you two think?"

Russell and I look at each other, and the stunned expression on his face mirrors my feelings exactly. This whole Shakespeare-musical mash-up thing was supposed to be a silly joke. And now *this* is happening?

Bob must take our silence for reluctance, because he starts talking again. "We wouldn't be able to compensate you properly for all your hard work, and I'm sorry about that, but we can offer you a small stipend. And you'd be released from any prior obligations, of course—crew calls and assistantships and whatnot. We'd need you in rehearsals full-time."

"I'd get to withdraw from *Señor Hidalgo's Circus of Wonders*?" I ask.

"Do you have a large role?"

I sneak a glance at Russell, and we both bite back a laugh. "Replacing me shouldn't be a problem," I answer.

"Perfect. Consider it done. So? What do you say?"

No more ridiculous ensemble work and slam poetry and pretending the floor is made of tar. No more gluing sequins or sorting screws. No more master classes that reinforce my lukewarm feelings about performing. I'd get to be in charge of something again, to immerse myself in work-that-doesn't-feel-like-work for more than a fleeting twenty-four hours. I'd get to mess around on the piano with my friend all day every day, and I'd get *paid* for it. For the last three weeks, Allerdale could be exactly what I want it to be.

"I'm in if you are," Russell says. His fingers are tapping his thighs like they can't wait to get to a keyboard.

"Let's do it," I say. "We can call it *Bye Bye Banquo.*"

Russell and I arrive late to the company meeting and lurk near the back of Legrand as Bob makes an announcement about the new show. People congratulate us over and over as they pass us on the way out the door, and a couple of girls even ask us to make sure they get solos. I hear a lot of grumbling, too— two non-eqs from *Macbeth* complain that their serious show is being "tainted" with songs, and a few girls from the *Birdie* ensemble bitch about how they'll need to learn all new chore-ography. But the only reaction I really care about is Zoe's. Her beautiful lead role is being snatched away from her, and I'm afraid she won't take the news well. Even though none of this is my fault, I'm so involved in the new show that I'm scared she'll blame me anyway.

But when she spots me near the theater door, she breaks into a huge smile and throws herself into my arms. "Holy crap, Brooklyn, I'm *so* proud of you!"

"Thanks," I say. "It doesn't even seem real yet. How are you feeling about the whole thing?"

"It totally sucks, to be honest. We've put so much work into *Birdie,* and it seems kind of unfair that we have to start completely over and the other cast barely has to change anything. But at least I've got someone on the inside who'll make sure I still get lots of stage time, right?" She bats her eyelashes at me.

I have no idea if I'll get any say in casting, but I say, "I'll do what I can."

Zoe grabs my hand. "We should go celebrate. We have the whole day off. Let's go somewhere special."

I can't believe she's finally offering this *now.* "I would really, really love to," I say. "But Russell and I have meetings with the directors and designers all day."

Her face falls. "Oh. Right. You're all important now. Maybe we could go out for dinner, at least?"

"I doubt we'll have enough of a break to go anywhere. I'm sorry."

"All right," she says, and I can tell she's struggling not to sound annoyed. "Just text me when you're done for the night, I guess, and I'll figure something out?"

"Okay," I say. "Thanks for being flexible."

"It's fine. Write us something great, okay?" She's smiling, but I know her heart's not in it. I tell myself it's enough that she's trying to be happy for me, even if she doesn't totally mean it. She's not used to my having priorities at Allerdale other than her.

Russell and I spend the whole day in production meetings, discussing the logistics and structure of *Bye Bye Banquo* with the directors, stage managers, and design team. At first I'm too intimidated to speak much, but people keep asking for my opinions like they really matter, and I finally start to relax and concentrate on the show instead of what everyone thinks of me. When my ideas go up on the whiteboard right next to the directors' and Bob's and Marcus's, I feel that same pure joy that always breaks across my family's faces when they sing. This is so much better than performing, and I never want it to end.

But my euphoria stutters to a halt when the meeting finally wraps up and I look at my phone for the first time since this morning. It's nearly eleven, and I have four missed calls from my mom and six texts from Zoe asking where I am. My mom can wait—I emailed her about the fire last night and told her everyone was fine—but Zoe's going to be *pissed* that I'm running so late. I text her that I'm on my way home, then practice apologies in my head as I walk back toward Ramsey. She probably planned something special for us even though she was upset, and I've paid her back by ignoring her all day. I'm the worst sort-of-girlfriend ever.

When I get to the dorm, she's waiting for me on the front steps in a little black dress with a flouncy, fluffy skirt. "Hey," I say as I rush toward her. "I'm so, so sorry I didn't get out until now. I know wherever you were going to take me is probably closed, and I totally suck for ruining our night, but you look *really* pretty, and I'm—"

Zoe smiles and puts a finger to my lips. Weirdly, she doesn't look upset at all. "It's okay," she says. "Close your eyes."

I do, wondering if she's going to put a present in my hands, but instead she slips a blindfold over my eyes. "What are you—" I start, but she shushes me again.

"Follow me," she whispers. She takes both my hands, and I let her lead me.

It's hard to gauge how far we walk, but by the time Zoe stops me, the Allerdale background noise is gone, and all I can hear is the wind and the soft, musical chirping of crickets. Zoe runs her fingers down the sides of my face and brushes her lips against mine. "Ready for your surprise?" she asks.

When I nod, she unties the knot at the back of my head, and the blindfold falls away. We're at the top of a small, secluded hill, far from the lights of the theater, and there's a flowered blanket spread out on the grass. Arranged in the center are a baguette, a wedge of cheese, a bowl of strawberries, and two doughnuts on a paper plate. A bottle of champagne sweats in the humid night air and glistens in the light of a cluster of votive candles, a couple of which have blown out.

"I couldn't get them to all stay lit at the same time," Zoe says. "It's too windy. Do you like it?"

The whole thing is kind of a cliché, but it turns out even cliché stuff is perfect when it's the first time someone does it for *you.* Jason's definition of "romance" was buying me a bunch of half-dead daisies from a bodega. Zoe put some serious effort into this, and it makes me so happy, I'm afraid I might cry.

I pull her into a hug. "I love it, Zoe. Thank you. How did you get champagne? Do you have a fake ID?"

"No, I swiped it from the fridge in the green room."

"Won't someone notice it's gone?"

"Who cares? You deserve it. You're a *professional playwright,* Brooklyn Shepard." She tugs me toward the blanket. "Come on. Let's drink it."

We settle onto the blanket, and I eat a strawberry while Zoe wrestles with the champagne cork. "I can't believe you did all this for me," I say.

"Of course I did." The cork pops free, and froth overflows and streams down Zoe's arm. "Shit, I forgot glasses. We'll have to drink out of the bottle." She grips it by the neck and lifts it. "To Brooklyn and her complete and utter amazingness!"

She drinks and passes the bottle, and I raise it above my head. "To us!" I say, and she echoes me. When I take a sip, the bubbles explode on my tongue and warm my stomach, and I suddenly understand why people use champagne for celebrating.

"So, tell me *everything,*" Zoe says. She settles back on her elbows and shoves a huge bite of doughnut into her mouth, and for the first time since before Carlos got here, I feel like she's really listening to me. I tell her everything I can remember about our production meeting, and by the time I'm done talking, most of the food and two thirds of the champagne are gone. My head feels light and fuzzy, like there's a thin layer of cotton batting right behind my eyeballs.

"What'd your mom say when you told her you're writing the new show?" Zoe asks.

At the mention of my mom, everything starts to feel less bubbly and bright. "Um . . . I actually haven't told her yet," I say.

"Oh my God, call home right now! She'll still be awake, right? Where's your phone? Put it on speaker. I want to hear how she reacts."

"No, it's okay. I'll do it later."

"I don't have to listen if you don't want me to, it's fine. You should call, though. You must be dying to tell everyone."

It's weird how Zoe knows me so well in some ways and doesn't understand me at all in others. "Honestly? Not really," I say.

"Why not?"

I shrug. "You've met my mom. You know how she is."

Zoe looks confused. "Um, yeah. She loves you like crazy and she's supersupportive."

"She is when you're doing things she approves of."

"Why wouldn't she approve of you writing a show for a world-renowned festival? That's insane."

"Because I'm not performing in anything," I say. "That's what's important to my family. Plus, my mom hates parodies. You heard how she talked about my uncle's online dating musical when we were at dinner. It's better if I let everyone think I'm in the ensemble and then 'get sick' at the last second. They'll never know the difference."

"That sucks, though. This show is important to you, right? You seem way more excited about it than anything else you've done here."

"Yeah," I say. "This is way better than being onstage, honestly." It's the first time I've ever admitted it out loud. I take another gulp of champagne, and I'm not sure if the fizzy rush that goes through me is from the bubbles or the words.

"Then I don't get why your family would be upset," Zoe says. "It's not like all of them perform. Your mom teaches, and your uncle's a producer, and you said your dad directs, right?"

"Yeah, but my parents proved they were good enough to be onstage before they did other stuff. My uncle's the only one who doesn't have some sort of performance degree, and I know everyone thinks less of him for it."

"I just don't see how anyone could think less of you for writing a show," she says. "What you're doing is ridiculously impressive."

"That doesn't matter, though. I'm still failing at the career they want for me, you know? They're going to find out I'm not good enough eventually when I don't get into any acting schools, but is it so bad if I want them to believe I fit in for a little longer?"

"They're your *family*. Of course you fit in."

"I don't, though." I sigh. "Sorry, I didn't mean to get all angsty about it. I'm totally ruining our picnic. I think maybe I'm a little drunk?"

"It's fine, don't worry. C'mere." Zoe lies back on the blanket and holds out her arms to me, and I sink down and settle my body against hers. It's weird how comfortable and familiar it already feels to lie like this, our limbs all tangled together.

"Let's not talk about it right now," she says. "Let's focus on the good stuff, okay? I bet I can cheer you up."

"I bet you can, too," I say, because no matter what's wrong, Zoe can always make me feel like I'm worth something. I wait for the pep talk to start, but instead she leans in and starts kissing me, warm and deep and unhurried. Her mouth tastes like champagne and chocolate frosting, and I tell myself this is good, too. I'm in the most romantic situation ever with a gorgeous, fascinating girl who loves making out with me. This is exactly what I *should* want, isn't it?

Zoe runs her fingers through my hair and kisses the spot where my ear meets my jaw. "Feeling a little better now?" she whispers.

"Yes," I say, because I'm trying to trick myself into believing I do.

She pulls away and sits up, and for a second I think maybe she's done kissing me for now and is ready to talk again. But then she straddles me, slips the straps of her dress off her shoulders, and pulls it down around her waist, eyes locked on mine the whole time. She isn't wearing a bra.

"How about now?" she asks, her voice low and sultry.

My throat seizes up, and it's suddenly very difficult to swallow or speak. It's not that I don't like what I see; Zoe's skin is so beautiful in the candlelight that she almost looks more like a painting than a person, and her breasts are perfect. But there's this sudden metallic tang at the back of my throat that overpowers all the fluttery feelings I should be having, the same panicky sensation I always get when the subway train stops in a tunnel between stations and I don't know how long it'll be before we start moving again. I'm not sure what's wrong with me; I've seen plenty of breasts in my life, and none of them have ever scared me.

Then again, I've never been expected to *do* anything with them, either.

"Um," I manage. I wish I hadn't drunk all that champagne. Or maybe I haven't had enough?

Zoe laughs, so low and deep, it's almost a purr. "It's okay," she says. She takes my hand and tries to guide it toward her chest, but I resist.

"We shouldn't— I mean, someone could come out here and see—"

"Brooklyn. Nobody's coming. We're completely alone." She leans over and kisses me again, those warm, naked breasts hovering *right above me,* and I kind of wish I could sink into the ground. "Anyway, I don't care who sees," she murmurs against my mouth. "I just want you to touch me. Okay?"

If I were Carlos, I'd flip her onto her back, strip her dress off the rest of the way, and kiss every inch of her body. She probably misses his mouth and his hands and all the *things* he did to her three days ago. He already has more of a hold on Zoe than I do, and I'm afraid that if I don't cooperate right now, I'm not going to be allowed to keep her. If touching her and losing her are the only two options, I'm sure I can swallow down my discomfort. I love her, and she's done everything she can to make me happy. I owe her this.

Zoe sits up a little and takes my hands again, and this time I let her put them where she wants them. Her breasts are a little fuller and heavier than mine, but they basically feel the same, and I tell myself I can handle this. I trace the outer curves with my fingertips, and she closes her eyes and makes a little humming sound that tells me I'm doing something right. Before I can think too hard about it, I brush my thumbs over her nipples, and she sucks in her breath and arches her back. It makes me feel incredibly powerful, like the night I traced her tattoo, but this time all I want to do is put some space between us. That night in my bed didn't feel sexual at all, somehow; it felt like a wordless way of discussing how we felt about each other. There was no end goal, just a wash of tingly warmth and closeness and magic. But what Zoe's asking me for now feels totally different.

I move my hands down to her sides, into safer territory, hoping she'll notice something is wrong. But instead, she grabs one of my hands and moves it to her inner thigh, way up under the tulle lining of her skirt. Her skin is as hot and damp as a feverish forehead. She reaches down and starts undoing the buttons on my shirt, and I reflexively start to sit up. "What are you doing?"

"What do you think, silly?" She pushes the fabric out the way with one finger and exposes my bra, which is light blue with darker blue polka dots. It's not sexy at all, but this isn't what I expected to be doing when I put it on this morning.

"Ooh, cute," she says.

I pull my shirt back into place. "Zoe . . . I don't . . ."

She sits back, the tulle under her skirt scratching my legs. "What's the matter?"

"I just . . . I don't think I can do this right now."

"Of course you can." She moves toward me again and

presses her hips against mine. "Come on, Brooklyn. Can't you tell how much I want you?"

"I mean, I . . . I don't feel ready, I guess."

Zoe deflates a little. "I'm not trying to have sex with you," she says. "I'm trying to take your shirt off. It's not a big deal."

"I know, but . . . I don't know. It feels like too much."

"Really? We've been hooking up for two weeks, and all you've really let me do is kiss you."

The things I've done with Zoe feel so momentous to me that it's weird to hear her belittle them like this. "You know I've never been with a girl before," I say. "I need to go slowly."

"Carina had never been with a girl before, and we were doing a lot more than this after two weeks," Zoe says. "And you've done all kinds of stuff with guys, right? So I don't get why it's different."

It's true; if she were a guy, my shirt would be in a crumpled heap on the ground right now. "I don't know why it's different," I say. "It just is."

"Are you not into me?" It sounds like a challenge, but Zoe's face looks vulnerable all of a sudden.

I touch her cheek. "Of course I'm into you," I say, but even as the words are coming out of my mouth, I start to doubt them. I love her, and she's beautiful, and I want to tell her everything and be with her all the time, but that's not really the same thing, is it? I don't need to touch her at all for those things to be true. I *definitely* don't need to put my hands up her skirt.

"I'm really sorry, but can we put this on hold for right now?" I ask. "I worked for fourteen hours today, and I'm kind of drunk, and I'm so tired. I don't feel like myself."

It's a total cop-out, and I know it, and I'm sure she knows it, too. But she says, "Okay," climbs off me, and pulls her dress back on. It's embarrassing how much better I feel once she's covered up.

"I didn't mean to ruin everything," I say, and it comes out choked.

"You didn't," she says. "It's fine." But instead of lying back down with me, she stands up and starts packing up the leftover food.

"Are you okay?" I ask, even though she's really the one who should be asking me.

"Yeah. It's late, though. We should go back."

"Probably." I start blowing out the votive candles, and once we're in the dark and she can't see my face, I let a couple of stray tears escape. I thought it might ease the tightness in my chest to get them out, but it doesn't help at all.

We're silent all the way back to Ramsey. Zoe and I each have a free hand, but she doesn't reach for me, and I don't reach for her, either. When I come back to the room after brushing my teeth, she's lying in her own bed for the first time in weeks. I want to tell her she can still sleep over here with me. Curling up together, warm and safe, doesn't make me uncomfortable at all. But I know I've hurt her, and the least I can do is leave her alone to lick her wounds.

I pull my blanket up over me and switch off the light, and we lie there in the dark, awake but separate. Neither of us even says good night.

23

It's like the entire world has been flipped onto its head. For the last six weeks, Zoe has made me feel confident and worthwhile, like I was doing everything right by being myself, and being in the theater has made me feel exactly the opposite. But now I can't wait to get to Legrand for *Bye Bye Banquo* every morning, and I try to stay there as late into the evenings as I possibly can. I tell myself I'm hiding in the rehearsal studios because Russell and I have so much work to do. But deep down, I know I'm avoiding being alone in the room with Zoe.

I expect her to be sulky after our failed picnic, and I spend days waiting for my punishment to start. But the other shoe never drops—if anything, Zoe's even kinder than usual. She moves back into my bed the next night, gives me sweet little kisses, and whispers that she loves me, but she doesn't try to take off my clothes again. She brings me offerings whenever I have breaks from rehearsal—iced coffees, doughnuts, funny notes folded into origami shapes—and she surreptitiously holds my hand under the table while we eat dinner. This is exactly the friendship-plus-more situation I've been wanting from her, and I know I should be happy. But I can't relax into it, because I never stop wondering how long this reprieve is going to last. We'll be living together for only a few more weeks, and there's no way Zoe's going to let them pass without trying to push things forward again. It feels safer to stay in public, where we have to act like we're nothing more than good friends.

Fortunately, it's easy to stay out of the room. The music director cedes more control of *Bye Bye Banquo* to Russell and me every day, and eventually he abandons the piano altogether and lets us teach our parody songs to the actors ourselves. Being in charge is a challenge at first, mostly because it's hard to act confident enough that people twice my age will accept me as a leader. But after a few days, I find my rhythm, and I start to love the feeling of shaping a show into exactly what I want it to become. After rehearsals, the cast always unwinds at a pub called the Bronze Pineapple, and I'm surprised and pleased when they invite Russell and me along right from the first night and treat us like part of the group even though we're not actors. Even Jessa jokes around with me when she joins us after her *Dreamgirls* performances. Zoe's always there, too, of course, standing close enough to me that she can unobtrusively touch my hand or my waist while she chats with the cast. We usually stay out late enough that I can feign exhaustion and go to bed the minute we get home without seeming like I'm rejecting her.

I know this comfortable limbo won't last, but I try to enjoy it while I can.

And then I get to the Bronze Pineapple on Saturday night and find that Zoe is already there, waiting for me at a table for two instead of with the other actors near the bar. The whole time we've been at Allerdale, I've been the one waiting for Zoe's undivided attention while she finished her important work, and it's weird to be on this side of the equation. It's flattering that she wants to be alone with me, but it also puts me on edge.

She slides a ginger ale across the table as I approach. "Hey! This is for you. Sit with me for a while?" She sounds casual, but her smile looks too-bright and pasted-on.

I sit down across from her anyway. "Of course," I say. "Thanks for the drink."

A waitress comes over and drops off a spiral wire stand holding a cone of curly fries. "Those are for you, too," Zoe says. "I know you always want salty stuff after rehearsal."

I'm starting to get really nervous now; it's like she's buttering me up before she delivers bad news. I wonder if she's cheating on me or something—I mean, with more people than Carlos. But I force a smile anyway and say, "You're the best. Here, have some."

We eat the fries and chat about nothing while I wait for her to drop whatever bomb she has in store for me. But there's no big revelation, and after a few minutes, I can't stand the suspense any longer. "So . . . why are we all the way over here?" I prompt. "Is there something you want to talk to me about?"

She shrugs. "Not really. I just miss you, I guess."

"You saw me this morning in rehearsal, silly. We were together for, like, six hours."

"You know what I mean. You're never really around anymore."

I reach across the table and take her hand. "I'm sorry. We start rehearsing onstage tomorrow, and there's been so much work to do. It's not like I'm avoiding you or anything." I've never told her an outright lie before, and it takes everything I have to maintain eye contact.

"It kind of seems like you are, a little," she says.

"No, I've just been really tired and overworked. I'm sorry if it's getting in the way of us."

Zoe turns my hand over and runs one finger along the inside of my wrist. "You're not working right now."

My heartbeat speeds up, but I force my voice to stay bright and cheerful. "No, I'm eating these delicious fries you bought me because you're the nicest person ever." I almost say *nicest girlfriend ever,* but I'm still not sure if I'm allowed to use that word.

"When you're done, maybe we could go hang out."

"We *are* hanging out."

"Maybe we could hang out *alone.* Back in the room."

"You don't want to bond with the cast?"

Zoe rolls her eyes. "Brooklyn, I'm with those people twelve hours a day. I'm so sick of them. I want to bond with *you.* Unless you don't want to."

"No, I do." I glance over at Russell and send him a telepathic message to come save me, but he's having an animated discussion with Olivier in the corner and doesn't even notice me.

I eat my fries as slowly as possible, but there's only so long I can make them last. Zoe has already paid our bill, and she's on her feet the second the basket is empty. "Ready?" she asks.

If she had suggested we abandon the group and hang out alone four weeks ago, I would've been out the door before she was even done asking. It seems so wrong that I feel more apprehension than excitement now. I'm suddenly nostalgic for the night we yelled affirmations into the mirror, when our friendship was heavy with possibility but nothing was expected.

But I still say, "Ready."

Zoe slips her arm around my waist the moment we're outside, and as we walk back to Ramsey, her fingers stray down until they're tucked into the back pocket of my skirt. Every so often she gives my butt a gentle squeeze, and I make myself smile, but if she's acting like this in public, it's going to take some serious effort to deflect her advances once we get home. I check my phone to see if it's late enough that I can claim exhaustion again, but it's only ten-thirty. I consider saying I don't feel well, and then I wonder when I turned into the kind of person who fakes illness to get out of kissing her girlfriend.

The door of our room has barely shut behind us before Zoe has me pressed up against it, her teeth tugging at my bottom lip and her hands sliding up my sides, under my shirt. After a minute, she walks me backward toward the bed and lowers me down onto it, and even through my anxiety, I'm impressed by how smoothly she does it. I wonder how much practice she's had. Before I can even catch my breath, her mouth is on my neck and her hands are creeping up over my ribs, pushing my shirt out of the way and tugging my bra down. I'm pretty sure my heart is going to burst straight up out of my chest, but I close my eyes and try to stay calm. *Just let her touch you,* I tell myself. *What's the worst that can happen? Pretend she's a guy if you need to.*

The thought is so startling that my eyes snap open. Being touched by someone I love should feel natural, like it used to feel with Jason. It shouldn't be something I need to pretend away or get used to. If I'm really attracted to Zoe, I shouldn't like her better when she's six inches away than when she's right on top of me. I've been telling her I'm not ready, that it's not the right time, but maybe there's never going to be a right time.

I tug my clothes back into place, and Zoe sighs with frustration. "Brooklyn, what's the problem now?"

"I'm really tired . . . ," I say, and it sounds lame even to me.

"It's ten-forty-five. That's why I wanted to come back early, so you wouldn't be tired for once."

"Can't we talk for a little while or something?"

"I don't want to talk. We talked for an hour at the bar. Right now I've got an extremely hot girl in my bed, and I want to take advantage of it, okay?" But she doesn't say it like it's sexy; she says it like I owe her something. Her hand glides up my thigh, under my skirt, and I squirm away.

"But we never talk about anything *important* anymore. Don't you miss the conversations we used to have? Sometimes

I wish we could play Love or Hate like before, when I felt like you were actually paying attention to me."

"I *always* pay attention to you," Zoe says. "I'm not thinking about anything but you right now."

"But you're thinking about *this*." I gesture vaguely to my body. "You're not thinking about what I'm saying."

Zoe sits up. "So, what, you want me to stay on the other side of the room and pretend we're just friends?"

"We can still be more than friends if we're not touching every second."

"We're *not* touching every second, Brooklyn! We don't touch *ever*. You've barely let me kiss you all week, and I've been trying so hard to be accommodating. But I watch you all day in rehearsal, and you're so adorable and smart and sexy, and all I want to do is put my hands all over you. So when we're alone, I want to be *with* you. What's the point of even being together if you don't want that?"

"Are we even really together, though?" I know I'm latching on to the wrong thing, but it feels like the easier argument to have. "What about Carlos? It's not like you wanted to touch me when he was here. I don't want to be your backup relationship."

Zoe sighs and looks at the ceiling. "We talked about this last week, and you said you were okay with it."

"Well, yeah, 'cause you were so upset, and I knew that was what you wanted me to say. But honestly, it was pretty weird being kicked out of my own room and knowing you were in here having sex with him when we had hooked up for the first time like a week before, and—"

"You don't even want to hook up with me, though! Every time I try, you tell me to stop. Are you seriously telling me that it's because of Carlos? What if I broke up with him? Would you let me touch you then?"

"It doesn't matter, 'cause you're not breaking up with him, are you?"

"It *does* matter. Answer the question."

I grab a pillow and hug it to my stomach. "No, okay? It's not totally about Carlos. It's mostly about me not being ready and you pushing me."

"But are you ever going to be ready? You said you did everything but have sex with Jason, so I know you're not scared. And I know you're not playing hard to get, because that's not the kind of person you are. So what exactly is the problem here?"

I think about that first night when Zoe saved the best bite of her pizza for last. She's not impatient; she loves delayed gratification. But she needs to know that perfect bite is coming at the end of the wait, and I know I can never give her that.

I take a deep breath, then another. The inevitable moment is coming when I'm going to ruin everything between us, and I want to hold it off a little bit longer. But if we don't have this conversation now, we're going to have it tomorrow or next week, and it's never going to hurt any less.

"I don't think I'm into this the way I thought," I say.

Zoe doesn't answer, and I feel like I have to fill the silence, so I keep talking. "I think you're the absolute best. It's nothing about you, or not liking you, or not thinking you're attractive. I think you're really attractive. But I think maybe it was better when we were just good friends, and we could tell each other everything and hang out all the time but we didn't have to worry about all this complicated . . . *stuff,* you know?"

Zoe's quiet for a few long seconds, and then she finally says, "It's because I'm a girl, right?"

"I don't know," I say. "Maybe."

"Jesus, Brooklyn. I asked you flat-out if you liked girls weeks ago, and you gave me some vague answer about how you could *maybe* like them under the right circumstances, and then you let me kiss you! Why didn't you just say no?"

"This isn't about liking *girls,* though. I really thought I liked *you* that way."

"But it turns out you don't," Zoe says. "Oops. But no harm done, right? It's not like anyone else here has feelings." I've never heard her be sarcastic before, and it hurts more than I expected.

"Zoe, it's not as straightforward as you're making it sound. It's not like I feel this way on purpose. Haven't you ever been totally obsessed with someone and thought you were attracted to them and then figured out later that it was actually platonic?"

"No," Zoe says. "When I'm attracted to someone, I know. It's not hard to tell. I look at them and I think, 'I want to have sex with that person.'"

"But it doesn't feel that different to me. I want to be with you all the time. I want to learn everything about you. I want to be the best version of myself, because that's how I want you to see me. I always know exactly where you are in the room. That's how a crush feels, except without all that . . . other stuff."

Zoe stands up and towers over me on the bed. "You're the one who started that 'other stuff!' *You* unzipped *my* dress after Pandemonium. It's not like I made you. Were you just messing with me to see if you could? Is this some sort of weird power thing?"

"No! Of course not. I didn't even mean for this whole thing to be, like, *sexual* at first. I felt so close to you, and I wanted to get closer and express how much you meant to me, and then it kind of got out of control and turned into this, and . . . I don't know."

"But you seemed like you liked it! Were you faking this entire time?"

"No! I love kissing you, Zoe. And I really tried to be okay with doing other stuff, but it makes me really uncomfortable, and I feel like if it's this hard, it's probably not right."

Zoe rakes her fingers through her hair. "I can't believe this is happening again. You're *exactly* like Carina. I put myself out there, and I let myself fall for you, and then I find out you're using me like some experiment you can throw out when it doesn't go the way you planned! I'm not here for you to toy with while you figure out who you are or whatever! I was actually invested in this, and you should've told me you weren't, so I didn't make a complete ass of myself!"

"Zoe, I didn't *know*! How was I supposed to know I didn't like something when I'd never done it?"

"You let me *throw* myself at you! When I think about the stuff I said to you . . . God, you fucking straight girls trying to find yourselves. I'm never going to learn, am I?"

Zoe picks up her messenger bag and starts cramming

things into it—pajama pants, toiletries, a book. Her face is red and splotchy, and I want to wrap her up in my arms and tell her to calm down, that I'll make it all okay. But I can't be her solution right now, because I'm the problem.

"What are you doing?" I ask from the safe little island of my bed.

"I'm going out." She tries to shove a bottle of shampoo into the bag. It's too big to fit, but she leaves it poking precariously out the top.

"Where?"

"I don't know, Brooklyn, okay? Somewhere you're not. I want to be by myself."

"Okay," I say. "I'm really sorry."

"Not as sorry as I am." She slings the bag over her shoulder, and the bottle of shampoo falls to the ground, but she doesn't bother to pick it up before she storms out. It's still rolling around on the floor, trying to find its equilibrium, long after she's gone.

24

I lie awake most of the night, crying and waiting for the sound of Zoe's key in the door, but she doesn't come home. When my alarm goes off at seven, I feel like I've had about thirty minutes of sleep, and even after a shower, my eyes look red and puffy. I know I have to pull myself together; we're moving into the theater today and attempting a stumble-through of act one with the orchestra. Under normal circumstances, I'd be super-excited about seeing all our hard work up on its feet. But last night's conversation has colored everything, and all I feel is sadness and desperation and dread. It's like I've finally made it to the top of a mountain, only to find that the beautiful view I was promised is shrouded in thick, gray fog.

I'm psyching myself up to walk over to the theater and face Zoe when my phone rings and my mom's picture pops up on the screen. I've been dodging her calls for days, but right now I really need to talk to someone who loves me, so I answer.

"I finally got you!" my mom says. "Where have you been? I've been trying to get in touch with you all week!"

"I'm here," I say. My voice comes out flat.

"Sweetheart, what's wrong? Is everything okay?"

"Yeah. I'm just really, really exhausted."

My mom makes a sympathetic noise. "Third rotation is so hard. It's okay, Brookie. Things will calm down a little after opening night. Tell me about this new show they're cobbling together. Is it any good? The email Bob sent said they're combining *Macbeth* and *Birdie* into one thing, but I can't imagine how that's even possible."

Here I was, thinking my parents wouldn't find out about the new show unless I told them myself. I've been a complete idiot; of course the Allerdale administration would notify all ticket-holders about the change in the programming. At least my mom doesn't seem to know what my role in the new show is, and there's still plenty of time to put my fake-illness plan into action later this week.

"It's kind of like a mash-up," I say. "We left most of the *Macbeth* text intact, but we're inserting songs from *Birdie* with all the words rewritten so they're about the witches' prophecies or about murdering Duncan or whatever."

My mom laughs. "That sounds dreadful. I'm so sorry your very first Allerdale show turned out to be such a disaster. But I know you'll be flexible and make the best of it."

"I think it's kind of clever, actually," I say. "Uncle Harrison will probably like it."

"Probably, but we all know he has questionable taste at best. I swear, some of the stuff he produces at that festival of his. Why would anyone put that much effort into something that's essentially a bunch of jokes?"

Because it makes people happy, I want to say, but her tone stings so much that I can't squeeze the words out. This past week, the Allerdale company has finally accepted me as one of their own, even though I'm not performing. *They* seem to think writing a show is kind of a big deal. It hurts to remember that to my family, my hard work is just a bunch of jokes.

Fortunately, my mom doesn't even pause for a response. "Speaking of terrible shows, what ever happened with that awful side project, *Señor Magellan's Flying Circus*? I haven't heard anything about it in weeks."

I don't bother to correct her. "It . . . got canceled," I say.

"The playwright couldn't get it together, huh? That's what happens when you put someone untrained in charge of a show. Marcus should really know better by now. But having that over with must be a relief for you, right? Now you can give all your attention to *Bye Bye Banquo,* or whatever they're calling it."

"Yeah, I guess," I say.

"We'll see you on Friday before the show, right? I made us a nice early dinner reservation at that lovely bistro we went to last month. Zoe's invited, too, of course. I've been telling absolutely everyone about your hot new girlfriend."

"Mom," I moan.

"What? It's exciting. Everyone's thrilled for you. I'm so proud of you for opening yourself up to the possibility of dating girls, Brookie. Your life is going to be so much richer for it. I always hoped that if I had a daughter, she would want to date women. Men are so difficult to understand."

I should tell her Zoe and I broke up, that I'm not really sure I want to date any more girls. But in her eyes, the rest of my summer here has been a failure, so if I've failed at wanting Zoe, I've failed at *everything.* I decide not to say anything for now. Dinner on Friday won't really happen once I convince my parents not to come, and when Allerdale's over, I can pretend Zoe and I have drifted apart naturally.

"I'm really glad you like her," I say.

"I can't wait to see both of you. Oh, sweetie, I've got to go. Christa's calling on the other line. But I'll see you Friday."

"Sure," I say. "I love you, Mom."

The second I hear the click of the line disconnecting, the crushing complexity of my life rushes over me like a tidal wave, and I'm not sure I'm going to be able to walk to the theater and go about my day. My beautiful show, the one thing that was actually going well for me, feels small and silly and tainted after hearing my mom belittle it. I squat down right there in the middle of the Ramsey lawn, put my hands over my face, and try to pull myself together.

"Brooklyn?"

When I look up, Russell's standing right next to me, looking concerned. I stand up and try to paste on a smile. "Oh, hi."

"Are you okay?"

I'm about to say I'm fine, but there's really no point in pretending; I've obviously been crying. "Not really," I say.

"What's up?"

"I . . . kind of got dumped last night."

A horrified expression comes over his face, and he actually takes a step back, like my angst might be contagious. But then he recovers and pulls me into a hug. "Oh no. Brooklyn, I'm so sorry. I had no idea you were dating someone. You never mentioned him."

I ignore the pronoun. "It wasn't, like, a long-term relationship or anything."

"Even so, that totally sucks. Take care of yourself today, okay? I'll cover for you if you need to take some time out of rehearsal."

"Thank you," I say.

"Do you want to talk about what happened?"

"Not really, but thanks."

Russell guides me toward Legrand, one arm still tight around my shoulders, and we're there all too soon. He holds the door for me, but I hover outside. "You go ahead," I say. "I'll catch up with you."

"Why, what's—" Russell's eyes widen. "Wait a second. You were dating a guy from the *cast*, weren't you?"

"No," I say, and I hope he can't tell from my face how close he is to the truth. "It's not that. I just need a minute."

"Okay. I'll wait for you inside."

I hide around the corner of the building and try to prepare myself for seeing Zoe, but the passing minutes only give me more time to imagine horrible new scenarios. What if she confronts me in front of everyone and accuses me of using her? What if Livvy hears and tells Jessa, and all my friends turn on me again? What if Russell finds out what happened and decides he doesn't like me anymore?

I tell myself none of that is going to happen. Zoe's upset,

but she's not vindictive. All I have to do is avoid her until she cools down, and that should be easy if she's onstage and I'm in the audience. Maybe in a few days, she'll see how wrong she was to yell at me for being honest about my feelings, and then she'll apologize, and we can go back to being civil. Maybe we can even go back to being friends.

I spot her the second I walk into the theater, stretching onstage with the other two girls playing the witch doubles. I search her face for any sign that she regrets the things she said to me last night, but when she catches my eye, all I see is cold, hard anger. My chest tightens and aches, and I look away as Stage Manager Lauren whistles for our attention.

"We're going to start at the top of the show and work our way through with the orchestra," she says. "If you have any problems and you need to stop, stick your hand in the air and one of us will call 'hold' and help you work it out, okay?"

I wish I could stick my hand in the air right now and pause the entire world until I feel ready to deal with it again.

The actors know their lines and their lyrics, and the orchestra knows their music, so the stumble-through ends up being mostly about the awkward transitions when the doubles have to switch places with the Shakespearean actors to perform their songs. Nobody needs the lyricists for that, so I sit quietly next to Russell, reviewing every moment of Zoe's and my relationship and trying to figure out what I should've done differently. Every time she comes onstage, I scrutinize her words and gestures for some hidden meaning, something that might make me feel better about what happened between us.

But all her movements are choreographed, and all the words she's singing are ones I wrote for her. There's nothing to decipher.

I'm concentrating so hard that I nearly have a heart attack when Alex, the *Macbeth* director, sits down behind me and puts a hand on my shoulder. "I've been thinking about act two, and I think we might be missing a song," he whispers.

Russell jumps in right away. "Did we skip one?"

"No, but I feel like we need to give more weight to the moment when Macbeth learns that Lady M is dead." I flinch at the word "Macbeth"—it's bad luck to say it inside a theater, and the last thing I need is more bad luck. I remind myself that the rule doesn't apply when you're rehearsing the production.

"You mean the 'tomorrow, and tomorrow, and tomorrow' speech?" Russell asks.

"Exactly. The monologue is so short, it doesn't seem like enough to really let the moment *land,* you know? I think maybe we should put a song there."

"I'm not sure there's an appropriate song from *Birdie* that we haven't used," Russell says. "Did you have one in mind that you'd like us to rewrite?"

"I could write something original," I say. I have no idea I'm about to say it until it's out of my mouth, but it immediately feels right. I need a place to put some of these excess emotions that are spilling over my edges like coffee from an overfull cup.

"Sure," Alex says. "Take a crack at it. Nothing too over-the-top, okay? Just something honest and quiet that'll get the audience right *here,* you know?" He thumps his fist against his chest.

"Totally," I say.

I start to get up, and Russell touches my arm. "Do you want help?"

I don't want to hurt him, but I also need to do this alone. "Um, I know we've written all the other ones together," I start. "But do you think it would be okay if—"

"It's totally fine," he says. "Take all the time you need. I'll handle stuff in here, under one condition."

"What's that?"

"No writing an emo song about how love is a lie and everyone disappoints you," he says, and I surprise myself by smiling.

I find an empty rehearsal room and lock the door, and the moment I let my fake-happy facade drop, I start to feel much better and much worse at the same time. I sit down on the bench and try to focus on Macbeth. How did he feel when Lady M died? Grief-stricken, for sure. Guilty, probably, that he hadn't wanted the same things she'd wanted and hadn't been able to make her happy. I bet he wished she had been satisfied with what she'd had instead of reaching for bigger, more dangerous things.

Or maybe I'm projecting. I try to remind myself that this show isn't about Zoe and me, but *everything* is about Zoe and me right now. Maybe I should give in and let my song be about all of us.

I work all day, and by six, I've got a decent first draft. I head back to the theater to catch Alex and Russell before they break for dinner, and I find them in the audience, chatting with the *Birdie* director about the logistics of the banquet scene. "Can I play something for you guys?" I ask.

"You're done?" Alex says. "Dude, that's impressive."

"Don't say that till you hear it," I tell him, and they all laugh like I'm kidding, but I'm not joking at all. I've never performed a completely original song for anyone before, and I'm even more nervous than I usually am when I sing other people's work. I sit down at the piano in the orchestra pit, shake out my hands, and try not to care how my voice sounds— the notes and the words are what matter, not the way I execute them. I tell myself this is just like the night Russell and I wrote *A Midsummer Night's Dreamgirls*. Maybe I can't imbue other people's music with new life the way the rest of the apprentices can. But I can create something out of nothing, and that's even better.

My eyes scan the auditorium for Zoe, and I find her on the other side of the room, changing her shoes and getting ready to go to dinner with some of the other actors. There are so many things I want to say to her, and I'm not brave enough to say any of them face to face. But if she hears my song, maybe she'll at least know how upset I am that I couldn't be everything she wanted me to be. I better play it now, before she leaves.

"Brooklyn?" Alex says. "Are you ready?"

I send the universe an image of my lyrics working magic on Zoe, softening her and healing the huge rift between us. And then I start to play, singing the words loudly enough that she can hear my imperfect voice all the way across the room.

I know that I have failed you, though I promise
    you I tried.
I should've had tomorrow and tomorrow by your side.
I thought you'd always be my braver half, my champion
    and my friend,
and my love, my sweet love,
I'm not ready for the end.

I wish we could go backward to the way things
    were before.
I should've stilled your quick, ambitious hands before
    they dripped with gore.
The crowd loved Duncan, I loved you. How will we ever
    mend?
Oh my love, my sweet love,
I'm not ready for the end.

Forgive me, please; I loved you in the best way I
    knew how.
I know it wasn't good enough; it doesn't help you now.
I thought that we were happy, but you had to have the
    throne,
and once you did, it drove you mad, and now I am
    alone. . . .

Life's but a walking shadow now that your brief
    candle's out.
It seems bizarre that I'm still here, still stumbling about.

When your mind consumes you from within, there's no
way to defend,
and my love, my sweet love,
I'm not ready for the end,
no, I'm not ready for the end.

When I finish, Russell and Alex applaud, and I force myself to look up at them instead of at Zoe. "I really love it," Russell gushes. "You did an awesome job." It's possible he's saying that only because he knows what a terrible day I'm having, but his smile looks sincere.

"Yeah, it's a really good start, Brooklyn," Alex says. "Maybe a tad maudlin, but we can fix that. Can you teach it to the pianist and Macbeth tomorrow, after we iron out some of the kinks?"

"Sure," I say.

"Excellent. Really good work."

But I can't even hear the praise, because I'm watching Zoe walk up the aisle and out the far door, chatting with her friends like I haven't bared my soul to her. My music used to impress her so much, but now, when it matters most, she didn't even bother to listen. It's not like I expected her to rush up onstage and tell me she was wrong about everything, but I didn't expect her to ignore me completely, either.

She doesn't look back as the door closes heavily behind her, and I feel something slam shut inside me, too.

25

I expect that the pain of seeing Zoe at rehearsal every day will lessen as time passes, but it doesn't, not even a little. Now that she's unattainable, everything about her fascinates me again—her boisterous laugh, the inflections of her speech, the way she sings and does her eye makeup and acts like other people's personal space is nothing more than a friendly suggestion. Little by little, her stuff disappears from our room, and it depresses me to imagine her dresses in someone else's closet and her towel hanging on the back of someone else's door. I only meant to cool things off with her, not end them completely, and the way she's carved me out of her life is heartbreaking. A few days ago, I was the first person she saw when she opened her eyes in the morning and the last one she talked to before she went to sleep. Now I don't even know where she's living.

The stupid, ironic thing is that the moment I've stopped

being able to enjoy it, everything else at Allerdale is finally going well for me. I feel like an important part of the company, I have plenty of people to hang out with, and the show is coming together beautifully. By the time Thursday night rolls around and it's time to tell my parents they shouldn't bother to come upstate because I'm "too sick to perform," part of me regrets that they won't see what I've created. If only they had different ideas about what constitutes important work, they might actually be proud of me.

I call home during the intermission of our dress rehearsal, and as the phone rings, I prepare to make my voice sound hoarse and phlegmy. But when my mom picks up, she doesn't let me get a word out before she starts talking. "Brookie! I'm so glad you called. I have the *best* news! We ran into Kristen Viorst at a benefit earlier this week, and I convinced her to come up to Allerdale with us to see you perform tomorrow!"

I can tell she expects this name to mean something to me, but it doesn't. "Who?" I croak.

"She's on the admissions committee at Juilliard! Of course this won't be an official audition, but it's a perfect opportunity for her to get a sense of you as a performer before you—"

"No," I say, so panicked that I forget about my fake sore throat. "Mom, you can't bring her here."

"Sweetheart, I know it's scary, but you're going to be wonderful. And it's time to start thinking about your future if you want to—"

"You *have* to call it off," I say. "I'm serious. If you bring her here for nothing, it's going to be really embarrassing for all of us."

"What do you mean? It wouldn't be for nothing."

If I tell Mom I'm sick, I can shut this Juilliard thing down and keep my role in *Bye Bye Banquo* a secret. But even if I do, I'll be safe for only a few more weeks; once my mom sinks her teeth into an idea, she never lets go. Kristen Viorst will probably show up at our next Family Night to watch me perform, and I'll have to come up with a whole new set of excuses and lies. The idea of jumping through any more hoops for a career I don't even want is suddenly too exhausting to bear. It's time to tell the truth, once and for all.

"Listen," I say. "This show is really important to me, and I want you and Dad to come. But the role I have isn't the kind of thing Juilliard would be interested in."

"Brookie, she knows you're just part of the ensemble, and she's still—"

"That's not it," I say. "I'll explain everything when you get here, okay? I don't want to have this conversation over the phone. Can you trust me on this?"

She must hear the desperation in my voice, because she stops arguing. "Okay," she says. "I won't bring her. Are you all right? You're worrying me."

"I'm fine," I say, but I don't feel fine. I feel like I'm on a roller coaster that has started its ascent toward the first dizzying drop, way before I'm ready. Now that I'm strapped in, the only way out is through.

Time always speeds up when you want it to move more slowly, and before I know it, Friday has flown by and it's time to walk into town and meet my parents for dinner. Before I leave, I do a few affirmations in front of the mirror: *The Allerdale company respects me for what I've created, and Mom and Dad will, too. Even if I tell them I don't want to sing anymore, I'll still be part of the family.* But talking into the mirror isn't the same without Zoe, and I abandon the cause long before I start believing what I'm saying. Tonight is about being honest, and sugarcoating the truth for myself won't make things any easier.

I get to the bistro early so I'll have some time to compose myself, but Mom is already there when I arrive. She looks so happy to see me that I wish I could freeze this moment and seal it in a glass jar, so I could take it out and stare at it in the future when nothing is the same between us anymore. I love her fiercely, and I know she loves me back, but sometimes love isn't enough to mask disappointment.

Mom springs to her feet, throws her arms around me, and rocks me back and forth. "It's so good to see you," she says. "It feels like it's been forever, doesn't it?"

"It does," I say. "I'm glad you're here."

"Of course we're here! We wouldn't miss our girl's first performance in Legrand for anything."

"Where's Dad?" I ask.

"He'll be here in a few minutes—he's parking the car. Sit down, sit down."

I do, and Mom settles in across from me and pours me water from the carafe on the table. "Is Zoe on her way?" she asks.

I've been so focused on the other conversation I need to have with my parents that I completely forgot that they thought Zoe was joining us tonight. I consider telling my mom my "girlfriend" is busy—at least I could save face in one small way—but it'll hardly make a difference in light of the huge bomb I'm about to drop on her. I might as well come clean about everything.

"Zoe's not coming," I say. "We broke up."

My mom looks stricken. "Oh no! When did that happen?"

Five days, eighteen hours, and six minutes ago, reports my brain, but my mouth says, "Earlier this week."

"I'm so sorry, sweetheart. Was it because of her boyfriend? I know they have an open relationship, but men can be so possessive."

"No, it had nothing to do with him. I just . . . couldn't do it anymore."

The sympathy on my mom's face morphs into exasperation, and my stomach turns over; I've been here all of two minutes, and things are already starting to go sour. "Oh, Brookie, *no,*" she says. "I know dating women is new for you, but Zoe's such a remarkable girl, and you can't let someone like that slip away just because you're nervous!"

"It's not because I was nervous," I say. "And it's not because she's a girl, either. I'm not saying I'll never like a girl. But I wasn't into her the way I thought. I really tried, but it didn't work out." That explanation still doesn't feel like enough, so I add, "I'm sorry."

Mom puts on the patient voice she uses when she's explaining a vocal exercise to a small child. "Things don't always come easily at first when you're dating someone new. You have to give it a chance. Relationships take time and work. You had to work with Jason, didn't you? And Zoe's such a better investment. She has all her priorities in order, and she's absurdly talented, and she would fit in so well with our family—"

"But none of that matters if I'm not attracted to her," I say. "I know it's not the only part of being in a relationship, but it has to be *a* part, right?"

"It's only been a few weeks! That's not nearly enough time to figure out what you want. If you stick it out for the rest of the summer, I think—"

"*Stop,*" I say. "Please just stop, okay? It's already done. And I love you, but you don't get any say in this."

My mom blinks a couple of times, like it has never occurred to her that some things aren't her business. I can tell there's a lot more she wants to say, but she manages to swallow down the words. "Fine," she says. "We won't talk about it right now. Let's talk about why—"

Behind me, the door swings open, and I hear my dad's voice say, "Hey, Brookie." I jump up to hug him, grateful for the momentary reprieve, and that's when I realize he's not alone. My entire family is here, grinning at me from the doorway of the bistro. Uncle Harrison in his pink madras shorts. Desi with Twyla in his arms, and Jermaine, holding Sutton by the hand. Marisol, beaming and exhausted, with a tiny new baby strapped to her chest. Christa, toting the second twin in one of those car seats with a handle. A third woman, who looks like an older version of Christa, stands a few steps behind everyone with a giant diaper bag.

"Oh my God," I say. "What are you guys *doing* here?"

"What do you think, silly?" Marisol says. "We're here to see your Allerdale debut!"

"We're so proud of you," says my dad as he wraps me in his arms. I inhale his familiar wintergreen smell, and all of a sudden, I'm dangerously close to tears. My whole family came all this way to celebrate with me as I finally emerge from my chrysalis and open my shiny new wings on the Legrand stage. And instead, they're about to find out I haven't transformed into a talented, confident performer at all—and worse yet, that I never will. I can't believe I have to disappoint everyone at once.

I make the rounds and hug them all, and Christa introduces me to her mom, who's here to watch the kids while she and Marisol come to the show. The baby in the car seat wakes up and starts flailing its tiny arms and legs, and I lean over and stare into two big blue eyes. "This one's Jasmine," Christa says. "Do you want to hold her?"

"Can I?"

She looks at me like I'm nuts. "Of course. You're her family."

She unclips the car seat straps and hands the baby over, and I settle Jasmine into the crook of my arm so her head is supported. She's wearing a onesie with FUTURE TONY WINNER printed across the front, and I send the universe an image of her growing up wildly talented and living up to my family's every expectation. "Say hi to your Auntie Brooklyn," Christa croons to her tiny daughter, and Owen lets out a cry and kicks his legs, like he's annoyed by all the attention his sister is getting. Marisol starts bouncing up and down, which seems to soothe him. I wish I could be calmed that easily.

The waiter pulls a bunch of tables together for us, and everyone talks over each other and moves chairs around and passes bags and children back and forth as they attempt to settle in. The second we're all sitting, Twyla knocks over a carafe of water, and Sutton loudly demands noodles with no sauce over and over as Desi tries to mop her off with paper napkins. Being with my family is as chaotic and wonderful as always, and this time when everyone starts reminiscing about Allerdale, I'm able to chime in with experiences of my own. I've danced in the cage at Pandemonium. I know how it feels to be super-sleep-deprived during third rotation. I've taken a class with Marcus and tried all the coffee shops and ice cream places. One last time, I let myself pretend I've achieved the kind of camaraderie with everyone that I pictured during our last Family Night.

But then Marisol grabs my hand and says, "So, how much of this show do we have to sit through before we get to see your gorgeous face onstage?"

Everyone looks at me expectantly, and I spend one crazy minute wondering if there's still a way I can keep my role in this show a secret. But that's insane; my name's on the front of the program, and my family will notice when I don't appear onstage. My confession will sting like ripping off a Band-Aid, but the quicker I do it, the sooner it'll be over.

"Listen," I say. "I'm so happy you guys are here, but . . . you should know that I'm not actually performing tonight."

"What?" My mom's voice comes out higher than usual, skirting the edge of hysteria. "Why not? Is something wrong?"

"Are you sick, Brookie?" asks Uncle Harrison.

"No, nothing's wrong," I say. "Here, look."

I pull a program out of my bag and slide it across the table, and everyone leans in to look at the glossy booklet. "BYE BYE BANQUO" proclaims the cover page in thick black letters. There's a dagger in the *O,* and it's dripping blood into a puddle below. Inside the puddle, it says, "Directed by Alex Kaufman and Rico Fernandez. Book by William Shakespeare. Lyrics by Russell Savitsky and Brooklyn Shepard."

"Wait, I don't get it," Marisol says. "Didn't the songs already have lyrics?"

I tell them all about the twenty-four-hour play festival, how well *A Midsummer Night's Dreamgirls* went over with the company, how Bob decided to use our structure for the new show after the fire. I watch my family's faces as I explain how integral Russell and I were in creating *Bye Bye Banquo,* hoping someone will look impressed, but they all still seem confused.

"So, these songs are like the funny ones you write with Harrison?" Christa asks.

The parodies Uncle Harrison and I write are always ridiculous—a melodramatic rant about the New York City subway system to the tune of "Memory" from *Cats,* or a tribute to a particularly weird street performer set to the tune of "Angel of Music."

"I mean, kind of," I say. "But this is way more professional, and most of the songs aren't funny. Russell and I really tried to embody the spirit of both *Birdie* and *Macbeth.*"

My mom's mouth is set in a hard line. "I can't *believe* they pulled you out of the ensemble to write parodies," she says. "That's completely unfair to you! You came here to get performance training, not to do them favors. Your director should give you some individual voice lessons to make up for what you missed. I'm going to talk to him and—"

I cut her off. "They didn't pull me out. I was never actually in the show. I'm so sorry I lied to you, but I wasn't cast in anything except that horrible side project."

"What?" my mom yelps. "What have you been *doing* all this time?"

"Working with the scenic and lighting crews, mostly."

Everyone starts talking at once, a wash of incredulity and sympathy, and Marisol starts rubbing my back. "I'm so sorry," she says. "I know you had really high hopes for your first summer at Allerdale."

My mom looks panicked. "Why didn't you *say* something? You've wasted months of good training time, and your Juilliard audition is coming up! I could've called Marcus! Or I could've—"

"I didn't tell you because I was embarrassed," I say. "And I don't think calling Marcus would've made a difference. He already did you a favor by letting me in, right?" I wait for her to deny it, but she doesn't. At least now I know for sure.

"Don't worry too much about it, poodle," Desi says. "All I got to do the first year I was here was hold a spear and shout, 'Halt!' Everyone has to pay their dues, right? And now you've gotten it over with."

Jermaine nods. "They're definitely going to remember how much you helped them out when you come back next year. And then it'll be your turn to be onstage, and someone else will be telling you what to sing."

I'm grateful to them for trying to build me back up; it's obvious how much they care about me. But feeling supported and adored isn't the same as feeling known, and it's time to let my family really *see* me. I sit up a little straighter in my chair and hope against hope that my next confession doesn't bring everything I love crashing down around me.

"Here's the thing," I say. "Allerdale's really great, and I totally get why you guys love it so much. But I don't want to come back here next year, and I don't want to audition for Juilliard, or anywhere else. I don't want to perform at all anymore." It's hard to bite back the *I'm sorry* that springs to my lips, but I manage to keep it in. I shouldn't have to apologize for what I want.

Jermaine reaches out and squeezes my shoulder. "Don't give up on your dream because of one bad experience, Brookie. If you want it enough, I know you can—"

"That's what I'm trying to tell you, though," I say. "This isn't my dream. I want to love performing like you guys do, but I don't. And I think maybe it's time to stop trying to force things and do something that actually makes me happy."

"But you've wanted this forever," my mom says. "Everyone has doubts when the going gets tough, but you have to make an effort to push forward anyway. I know you feel comfortable writing parodies and playing the piano, but you can't just give up and hide behind that. The only way to improve and become the best you can be is to step out of your comfort zone."

"I don't want to write songs because it's easy or comfortable," I say. "It's actually really hard. I want to do it because I love it."

"Sweetheart, writing parody lyrics isn't the same thing as writing songs. You can't make a career out of—"

"But it's not just that," I say. "I write original stuff, too.

There's one in the show tonight, actually. Look." I flip the program open to the list of musical numbers and point to my song, "Tomorrow and Tomorrow." "I wrote that. It's not from *Birdie*. And . . . I think it's actually pretty good."

Everyone goes silent and stares at the program like they're trying to make sense of a foreign alphabet. Finally, Uncle Harrison says, "You wrote the music, too?"

"Yeah," I say. "I never knew I could do that, but apparently I can. Our music director helped with the orchestration, but I'm learning."

"Brookie, that's awesome," he says. "I can't wait to hear it."

I smile at him—at least someone's on my side, even if it's the black sheep of the family. "Thanks," I say. "Listen, I know the rest of you must be so disappointed in me right now. But I hope you'll still come to the show and try to keep an open mind, and—"

"Wait, what?" Marisol says. "Why would we be disappointed in you?"

"Because I didn't live up to what you wanted me to be. You guys must think I'm a total failure."

"How are you a failure? You can write *songs*. That's *so cool*."

"We're just really surprised," my mom says. "You can see how this is kind of coming out of nowhere, right? You've been begging to audition for Allerdale since you were in second grade."

"Why didn't you tell us you didn't want to go anymore?" asks my dad. "We wouldn't have forced you."

"I did want to," I say. "I thought I did. You guys are always talking about this place and how perfect it is, and I thought if I could come here, it would . . . *fix* me, you know? Like, maybe it would finally make me love performing, and then I'd feel like I was really part of the family."

My mom looks so tired and sad all of a sudden. "Brookie, of course you're part of the family. You know we're proud of you no matter what, right?"

I think of the way she told Uncle Harrison not to fill my head with trash, how she said *Bye Bye Banquo* sounded dreadful and ridiculous, how she's spent my whole life reminding me that playing the piano takes time away from the things that "really matter."

"No," I say. "I honestly did not know that. That's not how you guys act at all."

"Sutton and Twyla and the babies are part of the family, and we don't assume they're going to be performers," Christa says.

"But you *do* assume that, even if you don't mean to. Jasmine's four weeks old, and you've got her in a FUTURE TONY WINNER onesie. What if she wants to be, like, a librarian? What if Sutton wants to be a doctor?"

Sutton looks up from her crayons. "I don't want to be a doctor. I want to be a dancer like Daddy and Papa. And then I want to be a firefighter. And then I want to be an astronaut. And then I want to be the president."

"You can be whatever you want," Desi tells her. "You're a superstar."

"I'm *not* a superstar. I'm *Chinese*."

"We thought the onesie was funny," Marisol says. "It doesn't mean anything."

"You see what I'm saying, though, right? Like, I know you guys love me no matter what, but that's not enough if you don't respect me." I turn to my mom. "You're always so disdainful of people who 'aren't like us,' like Jason and Uncle Harrison's girlfriend and stuff. And no offense, but sometimes it seems like you don't even respect Uncle Harrison because he doesn't perform and you don't like the shows he produces. You've always made fun of him, and it sucked seeing that all the time and knowing you'd probably feel the same way about me if you knew I didn't want to perform, either."

Mom and Uncle Harrison look at each other for a long moment, and I get ready to back my uncle up when he starts baring his soul and spouting long-held grievances. But instead, they both burst out laughing. "Harrison's my *little brother,*" Mom says. "Of course I don't respect him. It has nothing to do with his career."

Uncle Harrison leans across the table and looks at me very seriously. "It's time you knew the truth," he says. "Your mother's a huge elitist."

"I am not! Just because I don't like *The Real Housewives of New York: The Musical,* it doesn't make me a snob!"

"Oh, please. Your nose is so high in the air, I'm surprised you can walk straight."

My mom turns back to me. "Brookie, we never meant to make you feel excluded. We're a family full of loudmouths, and we spout our opinions all over the place, but that has nothing to do with how we feel about you. I had no idea you were taking the things we said so personally. Next time I offend you, tell me to shut up, like everyone else does."

"So . . . you don't wish I were more like Zoe?" I ask. "Or Skye?"

"Oh God, *Skye*," Christa says. "If I had a nickel for every time I wanted to slap that disingenuous little suck-up . . ."

"You fit into this family better than anyone else," my mom says. "You'll still be ours even if you become a financial analyst. Okay?"

My dad takes my hand. "You're the love of our lives, kid."

I'm suddenly filled with so much relief, I'm afraid I might cry or explode or melt into a big Brooklyn-shaped puddle on the floor. But then the waiter arrives with our food, and my whole family starts talking at once again, stealing fries off each other's plates and asking for the ketchup and the salt. Marisol plunks Owen into my arms so she can cut up her steak, and Desi explains to a wailing Sutton that the "sauce" on her macaroni is only butter, like they have at home. Everything's exactly the same as it's always been; I belong to these people, and even now that they know who I really am, they still want me.

"It's okay if you don't like *Bye Bye Banquo*," I tell my mom as I stroke my nephew's downy head. "I'm glad you're here to see it anyway."

"Honestly, I think it sounds kind of brilliant," says Uncle Harrison. "I can't wait."

"You're such a philistine," says my mother.

They both snort-laugh, and this time, so do I.

26

When I get to Legrand an hour later, the house isn't open yet, but audience members are already congregating on the lawn and in the lobby. I walk around to the side door and slip into the empty auditorium, hoping for a few minutes alone to collect my thoughts. An assistant stage manager is setting props, and a couple of orchestra members are warming up in the pit, but otherwise the theater is serene and empty. I sit down in an aisle seat, close my eyes, and breathe in the smells of sawdust and paint as I try to pull myself together.

Things with my family went way better than expected, but I'm totally wrung out from our conversation, and on top of that I'm nervous about the show. In half an hour, an audience of real, live theatergoers—ones who are used to Allerdale-quality productions—is going to see my work for the first time. Bob Sussman has been praising *Bye Bye Banquo* all week, but he's genuinely delighted by *everything,* and the rest of these fifteen hundred people will probably have much higher standards. It's possible I'm about to discover I'm not actually cut out for writing musicals, immediately after telling my entire family I want to make it my life's work.

"Hey," Russell's voice says very close to me, and I nearly jump out of my skin.

"Oh my God, you have got to stop sneaking up on me like that." I look up at my friend, who's wearing a suit jacket and a green tie printed with tiny whales. His curls don't look as wild as usual—he must've gelled them into place—and I have a weird urge to mess them up.

"You look really nice," I say.

"Thanks. So do you." He pulls a bunch of flowers wrapped in paper out from behind his back. "Happy opening night, Brooklyn."

I stand up, too surprised to speak, and he thrusts the flowers into my arms. They're gorgeous, giant pink peonies with something small and blue filling the spaces in between. They look really expensive.

"Russell, they're beautiful," I say. "You didn't have to do that. I didn't get you anything."

"That's okay," he says. "I just wanted to tell you that, um, it was . . . it was so much fun working on this show with you. You're a really amazing lyricist. And composer. And an amazing person, in general." He keeps shifting his weight from side to side and tugging on his cuffs.

"Aw, thank you. You're amazing, too." I put the flowers down so I can hug him. He holds on to me a little longer than I expected, but it makes me feel calmer to be held so tightly.

I close my eyes and lean my cheek against his crisp white shirt. "Thank you for everything," I say. "Working with you has been the very best part of my summer."

"Me too," he says. He pulls back a little bit, and I'm about to ask whether his parents are here to see the show, when my friend cups my face in his hand, leans in, and *puts his lips on my lips.*

I stumble back a few steps. "What are you *doing*?"

Russell stares at me in horror, like he's just realized he's naked in a room full of people. His hand still hovers in the air where it was resting on my cheek. "Wow, I'm so sorry," he says. "I thought . . . Did you get back together with your boyfriend?"

"My . . . what?"

"The guy who . . . You said someone broke up with you earlier in the week?"

"It wasn't a guy," I say, because I'm too shocked to keep my filter in place. "It was Zoe. I was dating Zoe."

"*What?* Didn't you say she had a boyfriend?"

"She did. She does. It's complicated."

Russell blinks a bunch of times. "So, wait. You're *gay*?"

"No," I say. "I thought for a while that I might like— I mean, I *tried* to— No. I'm not gay. But I, um, I thought *you* . . ."

I didn't think his eyes could get any wider, but they do. "Are you serious? I've had a crush on you *the entire summer.*"

"But . . . I thought you and Olivier . . ."

"*Olivier?* He's, like, fifty! That's disgusting!"

"But you always seemed so happy whenever you were with him, and you said that thing about how you wanted to staple yourself to his side and how you'd die to get inside his studio. You complimented his hair. You have a *picture* of him in your *phone*."

"The other person in that picture is my sister," Russell says. "He spoke at her school, and she went and got his book signed for me."

"Oh." I feel unbelievably stupid now; it's not like Russell ever *said* he had a crush on his boss. "Sorry. It's just . . . you're always talking about how great he is."

"He *is* great. That's why I want him to give me a *job.* My career has a crush on Olivier. The rest of me likes *you.* I thought you knew that."

"No," I say. "I had no idea." But now that I'm looking back on my interactions with Russell, I can't believe I didn't figure this out sooner. He wasn't even subtle about how much he liked me. I was just too preoccupied with Zoe to notice.

Russell runs his fingers through his gelled hair, and the left half sticks straight up. "I mean, you never pulled away when I put my arm around you, and you, like, cuddled with me on my *bed,* and I guess I thought—"

"Everyone here touches each other like that," I say. "Tons of gay guys like to snuggle with girls. I thought you were one of those."

"Oh. I . . . Wow." Russell looks around the empty theater, like he's trying to find a solution scrawled on the wall. "So you don't . . . I mean, you wouldn't even consider . . ." He makes a vague gesture at himself.

I look at him—really look hard at that face that's become so familiar and comforting to me—and I try to figure out if I could have the sort of feelings for Russell that I thought I had for Zoe. But it's not something you can pinpoint like that. Attraction's not like a Breathalyzer test—blow into a tube, and you know if it's in your system. It's more like an unpredictable pet. Sometimes it plays dead at your feet when you expect it to jump up and lick your face. Sometimes it wakes you up in the middle of the night when all you want is to be left alone.

"I don't know," I say. "I like you so much, Russell. But I've never really thought about you like that, and I need to take a break from dating right now, anyway. I need some time to get over all the stuff with Zoe."

"What exactly happened with you guys?"

I shrug. I don't know how to talk about any of it yet, so I go for the simplest possible explanation. "We tried to be together. It didn't work out."

"Because you don't like girls."

"Well, yeah. I mean, I don't know. I didn't like *her* the way I thought."

"So you dumped her? I thought you said she broke up with you."

It's so obvious, but somehow, I haven't thought about it that way until right this minute. I've been waiting for Zoe to tell me she was wrong for yelling at me, that she was sorry for the way things turned out between us. But I'm the one who ended things. Of course she's not going to apologize to the person who rejected her and made her feel worthless. If I ever want her to speak to me again, it's my responsibility to make things right. Playing a subtextual song about Macbeth in her vicinity doesn't count. It's not even a good start.

"Yeah," I say. "I guess I did."

"I get that you need some time," Russell says. "But maybe someday, when you're feeling better, we could give this a shot?"

He looks so adorable and hopeful. And who am I to say things wouldn't work between us? Russell's the perfect creative partner for me; maybe he'd be the perfect partner in other ways. Maybe I could like him. Maybe I deserve the opportunity to find out. But I'm not ready to do that right now.

"Can we just see what happens?" I say. "We're both going to be in the city this year. Maybe we could . . . keep hanging out and see how we feel?"

His face falls. "You're not even going to let me take you on a date?"

"Not yet," I say. "But . . . not never. Okay?"

For a second I'm afraid he's going to storm out of the theater and never speak to me again, that I've managed to ruin things with the one real friend I have left at Allerdale. But then, slowly, he starts to nod.

"Okay," he says. "I'll pencil you in for 'not never.'"

—

Half an hour later, I'm sitting next to Russell and Alex and Rico in the sixth row of Legrand, almost exactly where I sat during our first company meeting, and the houselights are going down on the opening performance of *Bye Bye Banquo*. As the curtain rises and the first witch says, "When shall we three meet again, in thunder, lightning, or in rain," Russell reaches down and takes my hand. Yesterday I would've laced my fingers through his without even thinking about it, but now that I know how he feels about me, everything is different. I give his hand a quick squeeze, then pull away and loop my arm through the crook of his elbow instead. Even though touching him is awkward now, I'm really glad he's here next to me. I need something to hold on to.

There are no songs in the first few scenes, and I can feel the audience settling into the rhythm of Shakespeare's familiar text. But when the orchestra starts playing in the middle of scene three and witch doubles come out to replace the original witches, everyone seems to wake up a little, and programs start rustling all around me. Somewhere in this theater, I know Uncle Harrison is smiling.

Banquo and Macbeth approach the witches, who start singing to the tune of *Bye Bye Birdie*'s title song:

We brew potions, newt's eye and toe of frog,
and your future rises from the fog!
Thane of Glamis, draw near and hear us sing!
You'll be Cawdor, then you shall be king!
We know we're just a bunch
of crones upon a heath,
but gaze into our eyes.
We're psychics underneath. . . .
Hail to Banquo; no, you shall never reign,
but your sons will rule this whole domain.

When the song ends, nobody applauds at first, and I'm pretty sure my heart stops beating entirely. But then someone in the back starts clapping, and when everyone else joins in, it actually sounds pretty enthusiastic. "They don't hate it," Russell whispers into my ear. We smile at each other in the dark.

I feel almost removed from my body as I watch our creation unfold before us. The ensemble sings our version of "The Telephone Hour," spreading the rumor around the kingdom that Macbeth has become thane of Cawdor. Lady Macbeth convinces her husband to murder Duncan, then does it herself when he's unable to follow through. When Macbeth is crowned king, Lady M sings my favorite song in the show, our parody of "How Lovely to Be a Woman." Her double is Julianna, the woman who was supposed to play Rosie in *Birdie*, and somehow she manages to seem scary-ambitious and darkly comic all at once as she sings our lyrics:

> *How lovely to be a monarch, and rule o'er all the*
>   *land,*
> *how lovely to mete out judgment and wear a crown so*
>   *grand.*
> *How lovely to have men slaughtered if they show too*
>   *much vim,*
> *and order a flashy banquet whene'er I have a whim!*
> *How wonderful to know*
> *that I can overthrow*
> *the highest in the land*
> *with this hand*
> *and one good murderous blow!*
> *How lovely to be a monarch, a castle for my home,*
> *to order the men around, though I've no Y chromosome!*

How lovely to bask in my regency. . . .
Life's lovely when you're a monarch, like me!

The audience doesn't seem to know quite what to make of the song at first, but the mood in the room shifts as the verses unfold, and soon they decide collectively that it's okay to laugh. It's one thing to have a few directors and cast members giggle at something you've written, but it's entirely different to know a whole room full of people thinks what you've created is funny. I close my eyes and soak in the uproarious applause when the song is over, and for the first time, I feel like everything is going to be okay.

Things get more serious after Macbeth and Lady M have Banquo murdered and his ghost shows up at their dinner party that night. Macbeth's double appears to hover on the brink of insanity while he sings our reprise of the title song:

Lord, it's Banquo! Foul scorpions fill my mind.
You're before me, though the rest seem blind.
Do you mock me? Will you expose my lies?
Must you stare so, with your cold dead eyes?
Oh, why did I assume your death would set me free?
I'm feeling such remorse. I should've let you be. . . .
Bye bye, Banquo, good friend, our time is done.
Fleance flew, though, so you still have won.

Macbeth revisits the witches, and they sing a song full of prophecies, warning him to beware Macduff and that he'll be safe until Birnam Wood comes to Dunsinane Castle. Duncan's son Malcolm raises an army and heads toward Scotland to challenge Macbeth. Lady M goes mad and kills herself, and Macbeth's double does such a gorgeous job with my original song that someone actually yells "Bravo!" when it's over. Finally, Macbeth rides into battle with his army and dies at the hand of Macduff.

The show closes with the royal soldiers grouped around Malcolm and Macduff, who holds Macbeth's severed head aloft. Malcolm delivers his final soliloquy, and then the soldiers sing a cappella, their voices ringing eerily through the auditorium:

We love you, Malcolm, oh yes we do.
We love you, Malcolm, our sovereign true.
Let's build our kingdom anew.
Oh, Malcolm, we love you. . . .

Our sound designer puts a creepy reverb effect on the stage mics, so their voices linger for several moments after the lights go down. And then the curtain falls, and it's over.

The audience is perfectly silent until the last traces of sound fade away, and then they go crazy. When the curtain rises again, everyone around me leaps to their feet, and we stand with them. The cast take their bows, and I whoop and cheer and smile so hard, my face hurts. This, right here, is the feeling I've been chasing all summer. This is what the rest of my family feels when they perform, and I've finally found my own way in.

The conductor climbs out of the pit and heads up the center

aisle until he reaches our row, and I barely register what's happening until he grabs my hand and tugs me toward the stage. My feet move forward without any input from my brain, and Russell, Alex, and Rico file out of the row behind me and follow me down the aisle, up a tiny flight of stairs, and onto the stage. Then the lights are in my eyes, blindingly bright, and the cast parts to make room for the five of us in the center of the line. We bow, and we smile, and we bow again, exactly like I dreamed about in the weeks leading up to the festival.

As the wave of applause and cheers sweeps over us, I scan the audience for my family. It takes a minute to find them, but right before the curtain comes down again, I spot my mom's orange dress. My parents and Desi and Jermaine and Christa and Marisol and Uncle Harrison are all on their feet, beaming at me from the dark as they give me my very first professional standing ovation.

Out of habit, I close my eyes as the curtain drops, and I try to call up an image to send the universe. But nothing comes. For this one perfect moment, there's not a single thing I would change.

—

After I've hugged my family in the lobby, shaken hands with Russell's incredibly tall parents, and promised Stage Manager Lauren I'll come to the cast party in Dewald, I slip out the side door of Legrand and into the cool night air. The audience is pouring out of the lobby and onto the front lawn, and I kind of want to lurk around the side of the building and listen to what they're saying about our show. But there will be more nights for that. Right now I have a job to do.

Main Street is mostly dark, but Kayla's Cakes is still open, and I get in line with the crowd waiting for post-show pastries and coffee. The barista looks confused when I order a single doughnut hole—"You know you can get a dozen of these for five dollars, right?"—but she takes my change and hands me a tiny pink bag.

On my way back to campus, I text Zoe.

Meet me outside Dewald? Really need to talk to you.

For ten minutes, my phone is quiet, and I start to think she's not going to respond. It's totally within her rights to ignore me if she wants. But when I round the corner and the dorm comes into view, there she is, waiting for me under the floodlights. She's wearing that same black dress she wore to our failed romantic picnic, and a small stab of jealousy goes through me as I wonder who she's trying to impress tonight. The little flyaway wisps of hair around her face are still wet from the dressing room sink, and she looks so beautiful, I can barely stand it. It seems impossible that she's so close to me and I'm not allowed to put my arms around her.

When she sees me, her face hardens. She looks right into my eyes, but it doesn't seem like she wants to; it's like she's trying to prove to herself that she can.

"Hey," I say. "You sounded great tonight."

Zoe doesn't smile. "Thanks. What did you want to talk to me about?" Her voice isn't cold, exactly, but it's businesslike, as if she wants this interaction to be over as quickly as possible. It's the kind of voice I might use if I were trying to cover up how much I was hurting.

I hold out the little pink bag. "Here."

"What's that?"

"It's for you. Just take it, okay?"

She accepts the bag and angles it toward the floodlights so she can see what's inside. Her eyebrows scrunch together in that adorable way I've seen a million times, but now I'm not allowed to reach out and smooth the little crease between them. "Is this . . . a doughnut hole?"

"It's the opposite of a doughnut," I say, though the whole gimmick seems cheesy and ridiculous now that I have to explain it out loud. "I know it's silly, but it's supposed to symbolize that even though I don't think we should date, I do really, really want to be your friend. And I know you're not ready for that yet, and maybe you never will be, and I understand if you're not. I know how much I hurt you, and I'm so, so sorry, and I hope you know that I never meant things to turn out this way. But you don't have to, like, hide from me, okay? If you come back to the room, I won't bother you. I won't even talk to you, if you don't want me to. I just don't want things to feel so broken between us. And I'm sorry it took me so long to say all of this. I should've told you how I felt much sooner. And . . . that's all, I guess."

A tiny, irrational part of me hopes Zoe will throw herself into my arms and tell me she forgives me, that she wants to be friends, too. But of course that doesn't happen. Zoe doesn't say anything at all as she reaches into the little pink bag and pulls out the doughnut hole. For a few seconds, she holds it in her cupped palm and stares at it, like she thinks it might explode. And then she stuffs the whole thing into her mouth at once, cinnamon and sugar dusting the corners of her lips. As she wipes her mouth with the back of her hand, I let a smile bloom across my face.

I can't totally tell, because she's chewing, but I think I see Zoe give me the ghost of a smile back. And when she turns around and walks into the party, she holds the door open for me.

Acknowledgments

Thank you, thank you, thank you to the following people:

My editor, Wendy Loggia, master of building a structurally sound story. Thank you for always challenging me to think bigger ... and to express those big ideas in fewer words.

Holly Root, agent extraordinaire, who laughed the first time I said "Bye Bye Banquo" and assured me other people would find it funny, too. Thanks for staying on my case to write this book. I'm so lucky to have you on my team.

Everyone at Delacorte Press who works tirelessly to make my books beautiful. Special thanks to Krista Vitola; my cover designer, Angela Carlino; and my copy editor, Bara MacNeill.

My brilliant beta readers: Lindsay Ribar, Michelle Schusterman, Kayla Olson, Corey Ann Haydu, Jennifer Malone, and Claire Legrand. I have no idea how anyone manages to write books without your help. Thank you for your honesty, kindness, patience, and perspective. I would be lost without you.

Jenna Scherer, who taught me about voice class; Sean Kelso, who filled in the gaps in my technical theater knowledge; and Elizabeth Otto and Mark McCauley, who explained how to fight electrical fires.

Williamstown Theater Festival, where I spent the most exhausting summer of my life working as a "lighting design assistant" (read: manual laborer) in 2004. As I hauled equipment up endless flights of stairs with my wimpy spaghetti arms, I told myself these experiences would be useful to me someday. And now, twelve years and two professions later, they finally have been.

The Hangar Theater in Ithaca, New York, where I had nearly all the best moments of my lighting design career. Marianna Caldwell, Evelyn Gaynor, and Rachel Handshaw, whom I met on the Hangar stage and who continue to be the best friends a girl could ask for. Pesha Rudnick, the director who told me it was my responsibility as an artist to show my audience how I see the world—I still think about that every time I write. And Kevin Moriarty, our artistic director and the man who coined the phrase "warriors for art." Thank you for your boundless enthusiasm and support, and thank you for telling me it was okay to quit theater and seek artistic fulfillment elsewhere.

Elizabeth Little, who somehow survived being my roommate during my lighting design years. I'm so sorry about the performances I made you sit through.

My wonderful community of YA writers, who cheerlead and commiserate like champions. Thank you for being my people.

My mom, Susan Cherry, and my sister, Erica Kemmerling, who have always supported me no matter what I chose to do. Knowing you're there for me makes everything seem possible.